Chandelle fingered the fabric she'd been quilting.

How had this compartment become intimately small and completely separated from the rest of the train . . . from the rest of the world? Matt's hand reached under the table and covered hers. She could not smother the sound or the delight rushing through her like a storm over the mountains.

"You've taught me," he murmured, his breath as teasing as his fingertips on hers, "not to jump to conclusions about you. How about another lesson? I thought I might teach you something now."

She said, "I think—"

"You think too much." His laugh was hushed and as rough as his skin. "But *I am* thinking now. I'm thinking how soft you are, how sweet each puff of your breath is against my face, and how you look as if you need to be kissed."

The Coming Home Quilt

JOANNA HAMPTON

JOVE BOOKS, NEW YORK

If you purchased this book without a cover, you should be aware that this book is stolen property. It was reported as "unsold and destroyed" to the publisher and neither the author nor the publisher has received any payment for this "stripped book."

A QUILTING ROMANCE is a trademark of Penguin Putnam Inc.

THE COMING HOME QUILT

A Jove Book / published by arrangement with
the author

PRINTING HISTORY
Jove edition / August 1999

All rights reserved.
Copyright © 1999 by JoAnn Ferguson.
This book may not be reproduced in whole or part,
by mimeograph or any other means, without permission.
For information address: The Berkley Publishing Group,
a division of Penguin Putnam Inc.,
375 Hudson Street, New York, New York 10014.

The Penguin Putnam Inc. World Wide Web site address is
http://www.penguinputnam.com

ISBN: 0-515-12552-0

A JOVE BOOK®
Jove Books are published by The Berkley Publishing Group,
a division of Penguin Putnam Inc.,
375 Hudson Street, New York, New York 10014.
JOVE and the "J" design
are trademarks belonging to Penguin Putnam Inc.

PRINTED IN THE UNITED STATES OF AMERICA

10 9 8 7 6 5 4 3 2 1

For Gini,
who shared her joy of quilting with me,
and
for Bill,
who's the best to come home to

This book would have been much more difficult to write without the help of George S. Deeming, the curator of the Railroad Museum of Pennsylvania, and his staff. Your help on everything from fixing my van door to allowing me to sit in a late nineteenth-century train car I appreciate deeply. Through your enthusiasm for train travel and your wonderful archives, you transported me back to a time when traveling on the train was the height of glorious living. I hope I have shared that delight with readers.

1

"I HEAR THAT YOU'LL do anything for money."

Matt Winchester raised the hat that had been covering his eyes while he had been napping in his chair and lowered his feet that had been propped on his battered desk. A whistle formed behind his lips, but he kept it silent as he regarded the woman standing on the other side of the desk. Sometimes, a man could be fooled by a sugary Southern drawl, but this woman looked as good as she sounded. If he had not known better, he would have thought that a page of *Godey's Lady's Book* had come to life in front of him.

Golden curls refused to remain contained behind a prim bonnet topped with flowers that were the same dusty rose as her cheeks. Her gown, which was a deeper shade of rose, clung with a minimum of flounces and kilting to her contours. And very nice contours they were, he had to admit as he leaned his chin on his palm and smiled. The kind of contours that made a man think of something other than napping on a hot afternoon here in Asheville, North Carolina.

With her satin gown and the scent of sweet jasmine, she was as out of place in his office as a saddle on a sheep. Elegance did not go with his gouged desk and the pair of chairs that each lacked a slat along the back. She belonged in a pleasant parlor with flowers and tranquil paintings on the wall instead of this place where the only decoration was a feed-store calendar from 1883. Last year's calendar, and it was June of this year. One of these days, he needed to replace it.

So what was a lady doing here? Not that he was complaining, because he enjoyed such a fine sight. That cameo pinned at the base of her ruffled collar led his eyes right to the line of buttons that followed the curves of her breasts before accenting her slender waist.

"Mr. Winchester!"

He raised his gaze to her face, which was taking on a tint closer to her gown. Soft lips and a pert nose, but those eyes . . . They were as cold as steel and only a slightly deeper blue.

Trouble! The voice in his head, the one he always listened to when he wanted to keep himself in his skin, shouted a warning. He did not need it. Lovely blondes with inviting curves usually led to trouble, even if they did not have eyes staring at him like a preacher's facing down a sinner.

"Are you Mr. Winchester?"

She was persistent, he had to give her that.

"Yes, I'm Matt Winchester." He motioned toward the chair in front of his desk. "Sit down, Miss—"

"McBride. Chandelle McBride."

He wrinkled his nose. With that fancy name and her fancy clothes, she could be either a harlot or a daughter of Asheville's close-knit society. Either way could spell trouble. He would be a gentleman, hear her out, and send her on her way.

He ignored the laugh from that irritating voice in his head as he thought the word *gentleman*. He still remembered the rules. He just did not use them, unless they came in handy. In the past few years, he had discovered how seldom that was necessary.

"Sit down, Miss McBride."

For a moment, he thought she would refuse, but, with an

enticing rustle of satin, she sat primly on the very edge of the chair. Her hand went to her side, and she winced.

He bit his lip to hide his smile. So the fine lady was an image she had donned for this call, because the tight lacing of her corset bothered her. Then she could be neither whore nor debutante. This was getting more interesting.

"Thank you, Mr. Winchester," she said, a touch of breathlessness in her voice.

Blast! He hoped she would not swoon, but he liked the wispy huskiness of her voice. It was a sound that a man could wrap around him and take with him into his dreams. Was he insane? He had better get this over with before she turned any paler.

"What can I do for you, Miss McBride?"

"Is it true?"

"Is what true?"

"That you will do anything for money?" Those cool eyes regarded him without compromise.

"What I will do depends directly on how much money you have, Miss McBride." He opened a drawer in his desk and pulled out the only things in it, two almost clean glasses and a bottle of whiskey. Pouring a glass for himself, he glanced toward her.

"No, thank you," she said as primly as if he had offered her tea. Good! She was not insulted by a man having a drink. "Mr. Winchester, I need you to help me find something that was stolen."

"I've done that before."

"And were you successful in your search?"

He resisted smiling. Who was this woman? She looked as decorous as a schoolmistress but discussed business like a horse trader. "Miss McBride, I am always successful in doing what I set out to do."

"That sounds like bragging."

"Bragging is only when one exaggerates the truth. I'm simply stating the facts."

She smiled, but her expression was as cool as her eyes. Not her customary expression, he guessed, for it seemed strained on her face. This woman was becoming more intriguing all the time.

Trouble! reminded the little voice. He heeded it and sat back in his chair. That she was powerfully pretty was not enough to set aside common sense.

"Then, Mr. Winchester," she said with all the emotion of an undertaker, "I would like you to help me find a quilt."

"A quilt?" He leaned forward again. This was all about a quilt? And he had thought it would be interesting! He might as well have stayed asleep.

"It's very important that I find this quilt without delay."

"What's so important about it? Is it lined with gold?" He chuckled.

She did not laugh, leaving him feeling absurd. "It might as well be, Mr. Winchester. It possesses a great deal of sentimental value for my grandmother. It's her coming home quilt."

"Her what?"

He wondered if Miss McBride had heard him. The words poured from her so quickly that he suspected she had practiced them before coming to his office.

"Mr. Winchester, the quilt has been missing for around twenty years. During the War of Northern Aggression, my grandmother and mother had their home taken as a command post by a Yankee captain. They offered him hospitality, but he was not grateful with that alone. He stole my grandmother's coming home quilt when he left."

"Her coming home quilt?"

"I have written letters, but it took me months to discover where the Yankee captain lives in the North. I have his address and have written there several times. I have received no response. I don't have much more time to wait. My grandmother is quite frail, and she needs her coming home quilt."

"Why? What is a coming home quilt?"

Again she seemed not to hear him. "Mr. Winchester, I would like to hire you to accompany me to get it back. I'm not sure, in light of the lack of a response, that the Yankee captain would receive me."

"So you want me to tag along in case you have to persuade the Yankee captain to return this coming home quilt to you?" He tipped back his glass, then realized he had finished his whiskey. When? This woman was too beguiling for his own good. "Is the quilt valuable enough to cause all this trouble?"

"It is to my grandmother. It has no use to me. I'm making my own coming home quilt. I must get her coming home quilt for her without delay. Will you help me, Mr. Winchester?"

Standing, he asked, "How can you expect me to give you an answer when you haven't told me what in perdition a coming home quilt is?"

She came to her feet, and he was pleased to see, when she tilted her head, that she was close to his own height. She was no more than a hand's breadth shorter than he was. Few women were so tall.

He forgot her height when she said in that irritatingly proper voice, "Mr. Winchester, there is no need for that sharp tone."

"If you don't like my habits, Miss McBride..." He motioned toward the door.

"I don't like your habits, sir, but that has no bearing on this discussion of business between us." Before he could retort to her surprising answer, she went on, "A coming home quilt is the most precious tradition in the McBride family. Every woman in the family starts her coming home quilt by the time she is eight years old. From that time until she is betrothed to be married, when she works to make her wedding dress, she adds to the quilt, stitching in material that suggests special times and memories."

"And she prepares it for her dowry chest?"

"No, not exactly."

She was, he decided, worse than irritating. He could not recall the last time someone else had controlled a conversation with him. She was doling out information to him as if he were a child incapable of understanding it. He did not need the little voice to remind him again that she was trouble.

"And what does she make this quilt for exactly?"

She clasped her hands in front of her. "In our family, after a woman is married, she begins to add more to the quilt for the rest of her days. By the time she is an old woman, the quilt is large enough."

"For what?"

"For her to be buried in it. That's why it's her coming home quilt. She's coming home to heaven."

Matt grimaced and shook his head. "That's a gruesome tradition."

"I told you that I have no interest in your habits, Mr. Winchester. I would appreciate you having the same lack of interest in my family's."

"I will from this point forward, because this doesn't sound like anything you need me for."

"Mr. Winchester—"

It was time he took control of this conversation. "Miss McBride, you do not need my assistance. I suggest you contact the authorities to assist you in whatever place your Yankee captain has gone to."

"Not *my* Yankee captain!"

He arched a brow, and her lips clamped closed. He had not heard that much emotion from her before. A sore spot with her, something he should remember. *Don't be crazy! You don't need to remember anything about any of this after she walks out of here.*

"Mr. Winchester," she said, once again serene, "I know nothing about how to approach the Philadelphia police with my concerns."

"Philadelphia?"

When she arched her brows in an easy imitation of his condescending expression, he scowled. When was he going to stop acting as if he had just perched on a porcupine every time Philadelphia was mentioned? The city was seldom spoken about down here in North Carolina. Any connection it might once have had with the South had been severed during the War Between the States. That had been the reason why he had settled here in Asheville. High in the Blue Ridge Mountains, he was far enough from his past to keep it out of his present and let it have no influence on his future.

"Do you have a problem with Philadelphia, Mr. Winchester?" She eyed him up and down and gave him that cool smile. "Or does Philadelphia have a problem with you?"

"You're right on both counts." He was not going to let her get him hot under the collar again, especially when just standing there she was causing a pleasing heat to spread all through him. "Good day, Miss McBride, and good luck in your search."

"You won't reconsider?" Her taut smile fell away, and he guessed he was seeing the real Chandelle McBride for the first time. A delicate, although not fragile woman, who seldom had to wear the frigid armor she had donned today to come here. Yet he noticed no tears filled her eyes. She might be facing a setback with his refusal to help her with her silly quest, but she was not defeated.

"No. Sorry." He added the last before he could halt the word from slipping out. Why was he sorry? That was a stupid way to feel when he should be asking her to close the door after her on the way out, so he could get back to his nap.

She stared at him for a long moment, so long that he heard his breath puff out. He had not realized he was holding it. She was unsettling him far too much. The sooner she left, the better it would be. Lovely, curvaceous blondes were bad enough, but a lovely, curvaceous blonde who could match him in a battle of words was dangerous to the life he had built for himself here.

When a smile curved her expressive lips again, he wondered how he had betrayed himself. It appeared that she could guess what he was thinking. This discussion had gone in the wrong direction from the start, and it was definitely time to put an end to it.

"Very well, Mr. Winchester," she said as she held out her hand. "I want to thank you for listening to me and for your advice. I shall decide what I will do when I call on Captain Friedlander."

Matt's hand froze a finger's length from hers. He stared at her in astonishment. "Friedlander, did you say? A Captain Friedlander from Philadelphia?"

"Yes. Do you know him?"

"The Friedlander family is very well-known in Philadelphia."

Her smile drooped. "So I've heard. That's why I had thought it might be advisable to have someone of your ilk, Mr. Winchester, accompanying me when I present myself at Captain Friedlander's house."

"Wise of you."

"Pardon me?"

"It's wise of you to take such precautions when you are dealing with one of the most powerful families on the east coast."

"Most powerful?" The pink in her cheeks became a wan gray.

"So I've heard." He sat back against his desk and smiled. "All right, Miss McBride. You've convinced me. I'll do it."

"Help me?"

"You're going to need help, and I could use the money, so why not?"

"But you said—"

"Do you want me to help you get back your grandmother's coming home quilt or not?"

She flinched, then nodded. "Of course, I want you to help me get it back. I thought . . . That is . . ." She held out her hand again. "It's a deal, Mr. Winchester."

"Just like that? No question of how much?"

"How much?"

He smiled. Good, now he had the conversation in his control. "You should have asked that before you told me how much you needed to retrieve this quilt. You're in a very poor bargaining position, Miss McBride."

"You're right, but at least one of us needs to be honest

if we are to have any chance of getting Grandma's coming home quilt back."

"And at least one of us, I suspect, will be." He paused, but she waited with a patience that he had not expected. What was wrong with him? Usually he could guess exactly how someone would react to his outrageous comments. He had not guessed right once with Miss McBride. That was going to make things difficult, but, if he worked this right, losing control of a few conversations would be worth the final reward he would be getting. Folding his arms over the front of his black frock coat, he said, "I shall charge you my usual rate plus expenses."

Miss McBride glanced at the wall where a sheet of paper announced, *One day, one dollar. Two days, two dollars. Same rate by the week, the month, the year.* Taking a deep breath, she nodded. "All right. I will pay you your usual rate, starting tomorrow."

He took her hand in his and smiled as he shook it. "You just bought me and my time." He raised her hand to his lips. The soft aroma of jasmine threatened to intoxicate him as he brushed her soft skin with his mouth. Releasing her fingers slowly, he drawled, "I'm all yours, Miss McBride. Do with me as you wish."

A flush climbed her cheeks. Her eyes grew wide, and she pressed her hand to her bosom. A mistake, but he would not tell her, for the motion gave him the excuse to admire her curves again. His fingers itched to sweep around her and pull her toward him. How much would she blush if he really kissed her, deep and hard until that cold exterior melted like high slopes snow? His face would sting as much as if he had rubbed that snow into it when she slapped him, he suspected. Maybe, before this little trip up to Philadelphia was over, he would find out whether she would slap him or draw him closer.

This time when he laughed and she did not join in, he kept laughing. This job and this woman might be trouble, but trouble with a bit of fun—and a bit of revenge—was worth it.

∞

CHANDELLE MCBRIDE CLIMBED INTO the buggy with its peeling seats and stained dash. She reached for the reins that needed cleaning. Everything had been neglected since Grandma had taken to her bed, and all the work in the house on the mountainside had fallen to Chandelle.

She had known it would be degrading to come here to Matt Winchester's office, but what other choice had she had? No one else in Asheville wanted to help. They acted as if they intended to forget the Yankees had ever stuck a single toe on North Carolina soil, and she could understand that all too well. Few had suffered as her family had, for their house had been turned into a command post for the Yankees and her father had gone off to fight in the war and never came home. If her mother had not been weakened by the lack of food, she might have survived Chandelle's birth.

But the war was over, and Chandelle needed to get Grandma's coming home quilt before it was too late. If the situation was not so desperate and Grandma so frail, she would not have come here today.

She had to believe that Matt Winchester would do what he must to help her and keep his unblemished record of successes, although he sounded as slick as an unabashed carpetbagger. As she steered the buggy onto the road leading out of the valley cupping Asheville and into the mountains, she squared her shoulders against the shiver climbing her back. She did not trust him, although a few questions about Asheville had garnered her his name and a suggestion that he truly was not bragging. She had heard that he was good at finding missing things and people, even when they did not want to be found. Some suggested he had been a Pinkerton agent, who had left to strike out in his own business. Others whispered that he had not left of his own volition, that he had skirted the law too many times and been asked to resign.

But he was the only one who had agreed to help her find Grandma's coming home quilt.

Her fingers tightened on the reins as the buggy climbed a steep hill. If all went well, she would not need Mr. Winchester's questionable skills to help her bring the quilt back to Asheville. Certainly Captain Esau Friedlander would not be able to deny her request, because she could describe every piece of material in the quilt. Grandma had spoken of it so often that Chandelle knew the exact shape of the fabric that had been in Grandma's gown the first night she put her hair up and which paisley was from a vest belonging to her first husband who had died fighting in Texas during the war with Mexico. Pockets and buttons had been included in the quilt, so each piece was unique and memorable.

She hoped Captain Friedlander still had it. Another shiver coursed along her spine at the thought. She did not want to tell Grandmother that the quilt had been thrown away. Right now, the only thing that was keeping Grandma alive was the sheer will to see her quilt again.

Even working with Matt Winchester was worth it if it meant Chandelle could bring the coming home quilt back to Grandma.

She drew in the horse in front of the cottage built close to the mountainside. On the other side of the twisting road, the creek whispered its song so softly she had not been able to hear it until the buggy wheels stopped. When a young boy ran out to take the reins, she smiled.

"Thad, when did you get here?" Chandelle asked as she stepped out of the buggy.

"A few minutes ago." He gave her a grin, revealing his new teeth were coming in fast. Putting his finger to his lips, he added, "Be quiet when you go in."

She ruffled his hair, which was as brown and unruly as the horse's mane. Giving him a smile, she turned toward the house. If Thad was here, Marnie must be, too. She knew she could depend on her neighbor to look after Grandma until Chandelle brought the coming home quilt home.

Going into the cozy kitchen, she smiled at gray-haired

Marnie Peterson. She was sitting in the rocking chair, which Grandma insisted no kitchen would be complete without.

"She's asleep." Marnie did not rise from the rocking chair or slow in knitting. McBride women had their tradition of making coming home quilts, but Marnie's family spent hours knitting stockings. Every child in the church at the base of the mountain must have received at least one pair of Marnie's brightly striped stockings in the past year.

"She needs to sleep." Setting her bonnet on the peg by the door, Chandelle went to the bucket by the pump. She ladled out some cool water and drank deeply. Summer was already coming to the valley, although the nights up here on the mountainside were cold enough to keep the water chilled. "Did she eat anything?"

"Not much. Some of the potato soup."

"That's something, at least."

"How did it go with Mr. Winchester?"

"Better than I had hoped." Staying honest would be the best thing she could do, because she knew how easy it would be to get seduced into lying as easily as Mr. Winchester did. Seduced . . . A heated quiver ran along her back, and she ran one finger against the hand he had kissed. She should know better than to be captivated by a rogue's brash kiss, but the caress of his mustache against her skin had sent delight swirling through her.

"So he'll help you?"

"For his usual price. He—" A knock sounded on the kitchen door. "Who could that be?"

Marnie came to her feet. "Go and change before you peek in to look at your grandmother."

"She's sleeping. I shouldn't go in."

"But you will." Marnie gave her a shove toward the stairs inside the parlor. "Go. I'll see who's at the door."

With a grateful smile, she nodded. "Thank you."

"You've been doing too much, and now you'll be leaving tomorrow to go to Philadelphia. You should rest." Marnie picked up an embroidered bag leaning against the cold stove. "Sit with your grandmother and quilt for a while. It will do you good."

The knock came again, much more impatiently.

Chandelle took the bag, and a sense of serenity swept over her like a gentle breeze washing winter down the mountainside. Working on her coming home quilt always eased her tension. Holding the bag helped today. Her grandmother had once held her coming home quilt in the same way. She had to believe Grandma would have it again before she died.

Gathering up her skirt to climb the stairs, she paused as she heard, "Miss McBride?"

She turned, sure she had not heard correctly. She stared at the back door. What was Mr. Winchester doing here? She had not guessed that he would follow her from his dusty office up here to the mountain.

In the moment that he tipped his hat to Marnie, the sun glinted with blue fire off his ebony hair. His face was so bronzed that she knew he seldom spent time in that disgusting office. Scuffed boots and well-worn denims spoke of a man who rode often and hard. But not even his funereal black frock coat and neatly trimmed mustache could add an aura of respectability to him.

When his grin widened, she knew he had noted how she was appraising him. He had stared at her even more boldly in his office, but that gave her no excuse for poor manners.

"What are you doing here?" she asked.

"I thought you and I should talk." He gave Marnie a scintillating smile. "Alone."

Marnie flushed like a young girl and giggled. Chandelle stared. She had never heard Marnie giggle, for she usually was as solemn as a sermon.

"Is something wrong, Mr. Winchester?" Chandelle asked. "You haven't changed your mind, have you?"

He leaned one elbow on the open door and stuck his other hand in his pocket. "I wasn't planning on it. Were you hoping that I had?"

"As I told you," she said, walking to the door as Marnie eased out of the kitchen, "at least one of us has to be honest. I was quite honest when we spoke."

"So be as honest now."

"About what?"

His mud-brown eyes crinkled around the edges as he grinned. "Why are you going through all this? Why don't you simply make another quilt to match the one your grandmother described and give it to her?"

Chandelle pulled back. This man had the morals of a polecat. No, he was worse, because he should know better. "I wouldn't think of doing such a thing!"

"All right. It was only a suggestion. Let me know when you're ready to leave for Philadelphia."

"Tomorrow on the first train to Statesville."

"Tomorrow?"

"I told you I was in a hurry."

"And honest." He slapped the door and pushed himself away from it. "Just remember that I gave you this alternative."

"I will."

Looking back, he added, "And remember that I'm not going to be a hero, because heroes have a bad habit of getting themselves killed. So don't expect me to be your hero."

"I don't, Mr. Winchester." She raised her chin and looked him in the eyes. "I knew I was hiring you, not a hero."

"When things get complicated, you'll probably be glad you did."

"*When* things get complicated?" she gasped. "Don't you mean *if*?"

His smile grew taut. "Trust me, Miss McBride. I mean when."

2

CHANDELLE RAPPED LIGHTLY ON her grandmother's bedroom door. All night while she had tried to find sleep, she had practiced what she would tell Grandma before she left with the dawn. Knowing that she should have mentioned something about going to Philadelphia last night added to her anxiety.

The words were not set in her mind when she opened the door and tiptoed in. Was Grandma still asleep? Leaving without telling her grandmother good-bye was unthinkable, but she must not be late getting to the train station.

Grandma's bed was simple, the one made by her late husband as a wedding gift almost fifty years ago. Covered by one of her most fanciful quilts, an explosion of flowers found on their mountainside, it looked as if no one was sleeping there. Only when Chandelle crept closer could she see Grandma's gray hair wisping across the pillow. Elitta McBride's skin retained its porcelain beauty, but now seemed almost translucent as if she were fading away right in front of Chandelle's eyes.

Her grandmother opened one eye and frowned. "Child, you shouldn't be skulking up on a soul like that."

"I . . ." No excuse would do, so she said, "I'm sorry, Grandma."

Her grandmother smiled and motioned for her to come closer. When she pushed herself up against the mound of pillows, she looked, in the first twilight of morning, as fragile as a child's doll. An illusion, Chandelle knew so well. Nothing was amiss with Grandma's mind, and her will was undaunted.

"You appear to be all set to start a journey, child."

She touched the beribboned front of her long deep-pink pelisse. The ruffles at the throat and the bow on her bustle matched her emerald gown with its box pleats. Her flowered bonnet was the same one she had worn to Mr. Winchester's office yesterday, for it was the only hat she owned.

"I came to tell you that I'm taking the train today, Grandma."

"The train? In that outfit?" Grandma shook her head. "Child, you shall be covered with cinders in no time."

"The trains are better now, I hear, since they began to burn coal. No cinders to burn the passengers."

Grandma sniffed. "*I hear* that they still are dirty, horrible things. You should wear your black dress, Chandelle, instead of keeping it for my funeral."

"Grandma! Don't say that."

"I am old enough to say what I wish." Her grandmother's face became a new pattern of wrinkles. "So you are going on the train. Where? To Spartanburg to see your cousins there?"

"No."

"Then you must be going either toward Louisville or Statesville."

"Toward Statesville." She swallowed harshly, then added, "And north."

"Why?"

"I hope to find your coming home quilt."

Grandma's eyes sparkled as they had before she became ill. "You know where it is?"

"Philadelphia."

She pressed her vein-lined hand to the thick lace on her nightgown's bodice. "You are going so far?"

"On the train, if all goes well, we should be there in two or three days."

"We?"

Chandelle's smile became brittle. Grandma would be outraged to think that Chandelle was traveling with a man and no chaperon, even though Mr. Winchester was now her employee. Fragments of memory rushed through her head. In each of them, Grandma was telling her how she should always do the proper thing, for that was how a lady was judged. No matter if Grandma had given a neighbor or one of her many relatives or even the sheriff a tongue-lashing that nearly skinned them alive, she expected Chandelle to remain demure and gracious at all times.

"Your papa was a man of education and some money," Grandma had repeated often when Chandelle was a child. "You mustn't shame his memory."

Chandelle shook those thoughts out of her head. Lying to her grandmother was something she knew better than to do. Grandma had a way of ferreting out the truth.

Patting the coverlet, she said, "My fellow travelers, Grandma."

"A lady should not travel alone."

"I have made arrangements to travel with others." Again that was not a lie, but it was not the exact truth either.

"Be careful amid all those strangers." She shuddered. "Especially in the North."

Chandelle smiled. Grandma would still gladly fight the War of Northern Aggression by herself, especially if Captain Esau Friedlander was commanding the Union troops in this area again. Half-tempted to soothe her grandmother's fears by telling her about Matt Winchester and his reputation for finding what he went after, she bit back the words. Matt Winchester's reputation would upset Grandma more than it would cheer her.

"I shall send you a telegram as soon as I reach Philadelphia," she hurried to say. "I hope it will be followed quickly by one to let you know I have the quilt and am on my way home."

"You are a dear child." She patted Chandelle's hand. "I shall ask the good Lord to let me stay here until you return with it."

"I hope it will take no more than a week."

"A week should be something He can give me." The pious expression fell away from her face as it took on the crafty smile of a tent preacher. "When you go down to Asheville, stay far away from the courthouse."

"Why?" She gripped the headboard. "Has the sheriff called again? Are we supposed to appear in court?"

Grandma's smile broadened, shocking her. "Even the sheriff won't throw a dying woman off her farm simply because we're a bit behind paying the bank."

"Two years." How she wished her bag held enough money to pay off the stack of loans against this land! Then Grandma would not, despite her brave smile, have worried herself this close to death.

"We've been on this mountain since our family came here almost a hundred years ago. We're not leaving now."

"Then why don't you want me to go near the courthouse?"

"Today's the day your fifth cousin Pike's trial starts, and I don't want you dragged in there as a witness."

Chandelle was not surprised. Grandma might have had to take to her bed, but she continued to find out about everything that happened down in the valley. Chandelle had not heard the exact day when the government was bringing Pike to trial for making moonshine on the other side of the mountain. Or had she? She had been so caught up in trying to retrieve Grandma's coming home quilt that she had let everything else pass her by.

"It wouldn't do them any good," she replied. "You know that you've never allowed me to visit Pike's still."

"For this very reason. Your grandpapa knew enough to help the government turn a blind eye on his whiskey."

"By making sure the mayor drank himself blind with some of Grandpapa's best every time he fired up his still."

Grandma nodded. "Your grandpapa was a smart man. You need to be as smart when you're among those Yankees. Maybe you shouldn't go. If—"

"Nonsense." She bent and kissed her grandmother's cool cheek. "I shall be fine. I'm a McBride, after all."

She had thought that Grandma would chuckle with the pride she had sought to instill in Chandelle. Instead, for the first time in Chandelle's memory, Grandma lowered her eyes.

"Grandma?" She could not imagine what would upset Grandma so. "What's wrong?"

"Nothing, child. Just disturbed by you taking off like this. You're so young."

"I'm quite grown. Didn't I hear you tell Marnie last week that I was woman-high, and you wondered if I'd ever realize that and get myself a husband?"

"I reckon having you grown makes you going off like this even worse." She took Chandelle's hand. "You are pretty, and there are some men who think pretty women are waiting for them to play court on them. Not nice men, child."

"I understand, Grandma." She kissed her grandmother's cheek again. If she stayed here and kept talking, she would miss her train that was scheduled to leave exactly at six a.m. She did not want to cut this time short, for it might be the last chance she had to speak with her grandmother. *No!* She would not think that. Grandma would not die until she and she alone was ready. "I'll remember what you've taught me."

"See that you do!"

She grinned. The scold in that no-nonsense voice was more like Grandma.

"There is money for you on the dresser, child." A smile rushed across her face and vanished. "I know you are paying highly for a detective to help you bring my coming home quilt here for me."

"Who told you? I mean . . . Why do you think that?"

Grandma pointed at her head. "My ears still work, even if my heart is getting weaker. I heard that man out in the kitchen last night. I can't say I approve, Chandelle."

"I thought it would be wise to hire someone . . . just in case."

"Maybe you are right. Take the money."

"I cannot take your money."

" 'Tis not mine. I saved it for your wedding, but stubborn child that you are, you have not been interested in any of the fine beaux who have come to call on you."

Chandelle went to the other side of the room, careful not to let her face reveal her thoughts, because it would be reflected in the glass over the dresser. She had no interest in any of the men who had climbed up the mountain on some weak pretense or the other. Some had been distant cousins from the hollows along the mountains around Asheville. Others were boys she had known for years, and, while she had matured, they seemed to have stayed boys. One or two had been strangers. None of them had intrigued her.

As much as Matt Winchester did.

She froze in mid-step. Where had that thought come from? Yes, he was intriguing, but so was a bear hibernating in its cave. She knew better than to trust either of them.

Picking up the coins and bills, she gasped, "Grandma, there has to be eighty dollars here!"

Her grandmother chuckled. "Count it again, Chandelle. You never have been able to do any ciphering when you're nervous."

She had to smile at her own silly mistake. Grandma was right. Rushing things might be Chandelle's greatest fault, and making mistakes with numbers was the usual result. "It's over one hundred dollars!"

"One hundred and three dollars and twenty-seven cents to be exact. I expect you to use that and be back in licketysplit time with my coming home quilt. I don't intend to die without it, and I'm getting tired of bothering the good Lord for another day on this earth." She folded her arms over her chest, and Chandelle wondered if even death could triumph over her grandmother's powerful determination.

"I will do the best I can."

"I'm sure you will. And remember the most important lesson I've taught you, Chandelle."

"Think before I speak?"

Grandma's eyes twinkled again. "And speak before you act, but act when you must."

"I shall try to remember, Grandma." She squeezed her grandmother's hand and, grabbing her bag with her coming home quilt in it, rushed out of the house before she could change her mind.

In spite of her grandmother's insight into the rest of the world, Grandma had not guessed how Chandelle dreaded this journey so far from her familiar mountain. Or maybe Grandma knew, but knew as well that a single word would persuade Chandelle to change her mind and stay.

She could not stay. She had to get her grandmother's coming home quilt with all possible speed.

"Wagon's all set, Chandelle," called Thad as she walked to where he held the reins. "Can I drive?"

"Once we get down the hill." She took a deep breath of the aroma of the trees that were still damp with the night's dew. With luck, she would be home enjoying these precious scents in, as Grandma had ordered, lickety-split time.

He stubbed his bare toe in the dirt. "Gee, I wanted to drive."

"I need you to be certain my trunk doesn't slide all over the wagon."

His face brightened. Clambering onto the single seat, he asked, "Is it true? Are you going all the way to Phila—Phila—?"

"Philadelphia." She chuckled as she sat beside him and gathered up the reins. Grimacing, she tugged at her coat. Maybe putting a bow on the back of it as she had seen in the magazine had been a mistake, for it bunched uncomfortably beneath her. "Yes, it's true. I'm going to Philadelphia, up north in Pennsylvania."

"Watch out for the chaps up there. I hear they're a strange lot."

"I suspect they say much the same thing about us."

"I reckon so, but watch out just the same." He leaned toward her, his grin as mischievous as a squirrel taunting a cat from a high branch. "If one of them makes trouble, you can always use the razzle-dazzle-one-two-three."

Chandelle smiled. "Thad, you know your mother doesn't like you using that kind of language."

"All the boys say razzle-dazzle."

"Don't let your mother hear you."

"I know better than that."

"I'm sure you do."

"But don't forget the razzle-dazzle-one-two-three. You might need it."

"I won't forget." She slapped the reins on the horse and steered the wagon out of the dooryard and down the mountain toward Asheville and the train station on Depot Street.

She did remember the trick Thad had taught her last summer on a balmy evening while Grandma had been sitting on the front porch rocking and cutting fresh green beans from the garden. The razzle-dazzle-1-2-3 consisted of a quick motion that knocked an opponent off his feet. Grandma and Marnie had chided her for indulging the boy and acting like a hoyden, but Thad had been thrilled that she was willing to try.

She knew the trick, but she hoped she would have no need for it. If she did, she was sure she would be in every bit of the trouble Matt Winchester had hinted about. And that was far more than she wanted to think about.

∽

MATT BLEW A WHISTLE as he stepped out of the carriage he had hired to bring him to the depot in style and picked up his bag. It was as black as his coat, but showed every mile he had traveled since he had come south.

Here he was.

Even an hour ago, when the first tendrils of sunlight had invaded his room, he had not been sure if he would bother to come here to meet Miss Chandelle McBride. He was still wondering if he was about to make the biggest mistake of his life. He grinned as he paid the coachman, offering him a generous tip. This could not be the biggest mistake of his life. He had already made that years ago. Now he might be able to make things a bit more even.

Hearing the locomotive's puff that made it sound like a giant, winded beast, he stepped from the mud by the tracks onto the platform. Men, both black and white, loitered under the wooden awning where a porter was collecting the passengers' luggage on a waist-high cart he pushed ahead of him. No one was hurrying because the engineer was out of the locomotive, talking to someone through a window at the depot. Odors of sweat and steam and anticipation swept over him on the hot breath from the train.

He nodded to the men, but scanned the platform. His smile broadened when he saw Chandelle McBride in earnest conversation with another porter. Among the dreary black coats of the men boarding the train and the dusty ones worn by the men remaining behind, she was a bright flower of pink and green. He was not surprised when one man walked past her, tipping his hat, and nearly collided with another man who was staring at her.

She glanced at the two men and quickly away before they noted her motion. Smart woman! It was probably because she was aware of the dangers faced by a woman traveling alone that Chandelle had hired him.

And, as he was planning to collect a dollar for today as well as one for yesterday, he should get to work. The first thing he should do was make it clear to the other men, gentlemen and scoundrels alike, that she was not alone here.

In a few steps, he crossed the platform. "Good day, Miss McBride." He put his fingers to the brim of his hat, smiling.

She faced him with a scowl he had not expected. "You're late. If the train had not been delayed, you would have missed our departure." She eyed him up and down. "I trust this tardiness is not a sign of the quality of the rest of your work, Mr. Winchester."

She nagged worse than a wife. Avoiding any scolds like this was why he had resisted any temptation to get married. And he had to admit it had been easy because, other than for a brief, bittersweet moment when all his youthful delusions had been stripped away, he had never given a thought to the idea of taking on the complications and obligations of a wife. This chiding told him he had made the right decision about marriage. Now if he had been so wise about staying home today . . .

The locomotive's horn blew. He winced, wondering who was in the locomotive. Finishing that bottle of bourbon last night had seemed like a good idea at the time. Now his head ached as if the train had rolled over it a few times. He did not watch as several men jumped to assist one of the trainmen in some task near the front of the train.

"You're lucky I'm here at all," he grumbled.

That got her attention. Her eyes widened with dismay. "You weren't going to join me after you agreed to?"

Matt noticed the porter eavesdropping avidly. Pressing two bits into the man's hand, he motioned with his head for the man to leave them alone. The porter tipped his cap and wandered toward the baggage car to talk with some of the other men.

"I considered it." He gave her a grin he knew was going to get her riled. "But, lucky for you, I'm here."

"Barely in time to board the train." Her voice remained taut but did not rise. "Do you have your bags?"

He simply stared at her. Already, somehow, and he had no idea how, she had taken control of the situation again. She had wrested it away from him before he realized what was going on. Maybe he should have stayed home in bed with some ice on his throbbing skull.

"Mr. Winchester, do you have any bags to go into the baggage car?" She looked at him as if he had lost most of his mind and the rest had ceased to function.

If she was not so pretty and he was not so all-fired-up curious about what had changed in Philadelphia, he would call off this deal right now. But he was curious, and she was so pretty. He had gotten accustomed to the perfectly attired ladies who were squired about Asheville on the arms of their perfectly attired gents. Chandelle was wearing a dress that, if he was right, was more out-of-date than the calendar in his office, and he doubted if she would be quiet and complaisant and smile adoringly at her escort.

"Mr. Winchester!"

Now she was irked. He gave her a lazy wink, then wished he had not. Another pulse of the dregs of that bottle bounced through his head.

He must have winced because she asked, "Are you ill?"

"Not yet." Matt held up his bag. "And I'm all set to travel. Where are your bags?"

She pointed to the embroidered bag on her arm and at a trunk waiting by the porter's cart. It had already been marked with a brass tag which matched the one she held in her hand. As she put the tag in her bag, so she could have it to collect her trunk at the other end of their journey, she said, "It was about to be loaded aboard when you intruded."

"I'm quite impressed."

"Impressed? What do you mean?"

"That you could get everything you're going to need during the trip in that small bag on your arm." When her eyes widened and she glanced anxiously at the trunk, he asked, "You did pack whatever gewgaws and private linens you will need for our journey in that bag, didn't you?"

"Mr. Winchester, your questions are inappropriate and—"

"As I'm working for you during this trip, Miss McBride," he returned with all the cool composure she had in her voice, "it behooves me to advise you whenever I deem it appropriate. 'Tis your choice to heed my advice or not."

Her gaze slid away. "Forgive me. You're right."

He doubted if he would hear that from her often, but crowing over regaining control of the conversation would make the situation worse. He suspected it would get worse without any help from him. Glancing at the men crowding the narrow platform, he wondered how many of them were boarding the train.

"This small bag," she said, "holds the quilt I'm working on."

He frowned. "I thought you said you weren't going to make a quilt to replace your grandmother's quilt."

"This is *my* quilt."

"Your quilt?" He grimaced. "Are you telling me that you're continuing this macabre tradition?"

"I see nothing macabre about it."

"Then you haven't looked at it very closely." Before she could hurl the angry words that glittered in her eyes, he asked, "So all your clothes and such are in the trunk?"

"Yes."

"And how do you intend to get anything out of it while we're on the train?" He pointed to the maroon baggage car closer to the front of the train. "This train doesn't have one of those newfangled portable platforms that lets you walk from car to car. Once your trunk goes in the baggage car, you won't see it again until we reach Philadelphia."

"The baggage car has some seating."

"For gentlemen." He smiled. "I doubt if they would welcome you as an intrusion when they wish to drink, smoke, and play cards."

"But my clothes are packed."

"So unpack them and put what you need in my bag. There's room in it for whatever you need for the next two days."

"You want me to unpack my private things here?"

He started to answer, but the engineer climbed into the cab and blew that blasted whistle again. Twice. His head was going to explode like the boiler of a runaway train. Pain whetted his voice. "Where in perdition else?"

"Mr. Winchester, please watch your tongue around me."

He bent and undid the latch on her trunk. Looking up at her, he smiled. "I know you mean watch what I say, but you should as well. I could interpret that to mean you have suspicions of other ways my tongue might unsettle you."

Color burned on her face as she knelt and gathered some clothes to shove into his battered bag. A vagrant sense of decency, which he had thought he had squelched long ago, made him look away, stepping between her and the curious stares from the others on the platform. Tipping the trunk's top closed with his foot, he latched it.

"All set?"

"Yes." Her voice was no more than a whisper, but the single word hissed like the steam coming off the locomotive.

He picked up his bag and motioned for the porter to load her trunk into the baggage car. "Then let's go."

"Mr. Winchester?"

"Yes?" He reached for the metal rail by the steps leading up into the closest passenger car.

"If you do that again, I shall terminate your employment."

"Do what?" He figured he should know, because the crackle of anger in her eyes warned that she would prefer to terminate *him,* instead of his job.

"Embarrass me."

"I'll do my best."

She started to nod, then asked, "Do your best to embarrass me or not to?"

With a laugh, he took her hand to help her up the steps. This trip might be worth the trouble, after all. "We'll just have to see how it goes."

3

THE TRAIN WAS CROWDED. Chandelle held the bag with her quilting close to her as she walked along the cramped aisle that was made even more crowded by the spittoons by each seat. Most of the travelers were men, but she saw some women surrounded by their children. She wondered how far they were traveling and if any of them was on a quest as important as hers.

The maroon car was not one of the fancy Pullman palace cars, which were as elegant as a fine country estate. It was not even a Pullman parlor car, which was reputed to be even nicer than Grandma's sofa set. This coach with its gold-colored trim could boast no more than double seats along each side of the car and a carpet runner of maroon and white that matched the upholstery. The roof was high, so high that Matt's tall hat did not brush the kerosene lanterns hanging from it.

She should have guessed the train would be like this when the man who had sold her the long strip of tickets that would allow her to ride from Asheville to Philadelphia had told her that the mail train was already full. This mixed train would take nearly twice as long to reach Statesville, but she did not want to wait until tomorrow to begin their trip.

Matt paused by a pair of seats. He flipped one so that the seats faced each other and stored his bag on a brass rack near the windows in the roof of the car. The brass glittered in the sunshine splashing through the windows and glowing on the oak trim. When he held out his hand for her bag, she shook her head.

"I would rather keep it with me," she said as she sat in the seat that allowed her to look forward.

"As you wish, boss."

She was amazed when, instead of sitting beside her, he dropped into the seat across from her. Amazed and relieved, because the plush seats would have seemed too small with him right beside her. When he settled one boot on his opposite knee, she did not acknowledge his easy grin. The motion gave her very little room for her own knees if she wanted to keep from brushing his. And that blasted bow . . . She should have removed her pelisse before she sat, but she had not wanted to hold up the others in the aisle. Everyone seemed to be in such a hurry.

"Is your seat uncomfortable, Miss McBride?" Matt asked, warning her that he missed nothing. That skill would be useful when they got to Philadelphia, but his intuition was disconcerting now. "I would be glad to switch seats with you, if you wish."

"The seat is fine, thank you."

"Then why are you shifting like a chap trying to find a comfortable spot on a hot ember?"

She smiled. "You've got a colorful manner of expressing yourself."

"No more than you Southerners." He chuckled. "I should warn you. I tend to pick up everyone's bad habits everywhere I go."

"I'm sure you do."

Laughing loud enough to make heads turn as people selected seats around the car, he said, "I suspect that is a warning that I shall learn no bad habits from you, because you have none."

"You are wrong. I have more than my share."

"Thanks for that warning." He relaxed against the seat. "Maybe I'll learn some new bad habits from you then."

"I hope not." Opening her bag, she drew out her ticket. "Will the conductor be by to collect this before we leave?"

"He or the trainman will take it when they get around to it. Sometimes before the train starts, sometimes after." Matt's smile vanished as he reached over and plucked from her fingers the ticket that was as long as her forearm. The white ticket with its brown lettering announcing in intricate style that it was for the Western North Carolina Railroad. "This is only one ticket. Where's the other one?"

"Other one?"

"*Your* ticket, Miss McBride."

Before he could slip the ticket under his coat, she snatched it from him. "This is my ticket."

"Then where is mine?"

She frowned. "Didn't you buy one?"

"Why should I?" He smiled, but his eyes remained focused on the ticket she held. "Our agreement was my usual rate plus expenses, if you will recall."

"Plus expenses?" Her voice sounded faint even in her own ears. "Mr. Winchester—"

"I prefer Matt."

"*Mr. Winchester,* if I agreed to that, it was a mistaken thing. I can't afford to pay you a dollar a day plus whatever you deem your expenses to be." Her nose wrinkled. "Although I would guess, by the strong odor of that bourbon you have been drinking, that your tastes are not expensive." When he started to reply, she held up her hand. "You do need a ticket, and we need to reach a new understanding of this arrangement before we reach Philadelphia." She withdrew enough money from her bag to pay for another ticket and slapped it into his hand.

Looking at it, he grinned. "Are you buying me a Pullman seat, boss?"

"Of course not!"

"Then you might want to recount this."

She took the money and, trying to calm herself, handed

him the amount he needed for a ticket in this coach. She could not afford to make such a mistake. Her money would be stretched too thin as it was.

"Thanks," he said. "And you could say thanks, too."

"Me?"

"I could have pocketed the extra." He arched an ebony brow at her and grinned, his mustache twitching to a roguish angle.

"You should hurry," she replied, wanting to put an end to this humiliating conversation.

"I should, shouldn't I?"

Chandelle watched while he stood, pocketed the cash, flipped the coins she had given him into the air, and caught them handily as he strolled along the aisle as if he had no cares. What a peculiar man he was!

She had been certain her imagination had created a memory of him that was not accurate, but she had been wrong. He was too good-looking for his own good. Or hers. Had he seen her flinch when he crossed the platform, his frock coat billowing after him with the dark wings of an avenging demon? Every motion he made suggested he was daring anyone to challenge his plans. And woe be to the one who did. She had already learned that, for he had not hesitated to open her trunk to reveal her most personal possessions to anyone who cared to peer in.

Glancing out the open window, she watched him cross the platform to the ticket window. He turned and, winking boldly at her, waved. She clenched her hands on her bag. If she did not suspect that she might need his assistance in Philadelphia, she would bid him good day and send him on his way. But she might need him.

Chandelle ignored how her hands shook as she opened her bag again and drew out the small frame that held the section of her coming home quilt she was working on. The strips of wood were not much bigger than an embroidery frame, but thicker, so they could hold the layers of fabric. Setting it across her lap, she frowned. Blast that bow at the back of her pelisse!

Pulling her scissors from the bottom of her bag, she drew

off her coat. She spread it across the seat. With a couple of quick snips, she released the bow.

The train whistle blew long and hard as if it wanted the sound to reach Grandma up on the mountain. Folding her coat, she sat again. She stuffed the ribbon into her bag as Matt ran up the steps as the door was being closed.

He dropped heavily into the seat across from her and closed his eyes. "Whew, I could use something cold to drink. I wonder if this train has hawkers to bring drinks around."

"I reckon you've had enough to drink already."

"Last night maybe." He winced as the train shifted into motion with a screech of gears. "My head feels ready to explode."

Chandelle drew a small canister from her bag as she glanced out the window. The depot was sliding out of view. She was on her way. She was really on her way. And with the most unlikely traveling companion, one she could not have imagined even two days ago. "Here. This might help."

He opened one eye and looked at the small container that had ribbons and flowers painted on the side. Shutting it again, he muttered, "No thanks."

"It might help."

"I need something stronger than lemonade."

"Then try this." She undid the top.

Matt peered at her through half-open eyes. "Tea isn't any good either. I need—"

"Something stronger." She glanced nervously over her shoulder as the conductor stepped out of the small compartment at the other end of the car. "Do you want it or not?"

"If it will make you be quiet for a moment." He took it and sniffed the top. His eyes widened. Taking a deep drink, he choked.

"You weren't supposed to drink it!" she gasped.

He scowled at her as the train wheels began to turn beneath them. Trying to speak, he choked and then coughed. He wiped his mustache with the back of his hand.

"Don't you have a handkerchief?" she asked as she took the canister, closed it, and put it in her bag. "Your manners belong in a sty, although I'm not sure the pigs would have you."

He gave a scratchy laugh and leaned toward her. "Do you have any idea how very provocative you are?" His finger under her chin kept her from turning away. "As prim as a fashion plate in some lady's magazine, but carrying around whiskey like a moonshiner. Don't tell me it's purely for medicinal purposes."

"Actually it is for medicinal purposes. You were supposed to rub it on your aching forehead, not swallow it." She drew back from his intense gaze. "And it's not exactly moonshine, although it comes from a still. We use it as liniment."

"I drank liniment?"

She nodded. "Grandma puts it on her knees sometimes after church to give her strength for going up the mountain. I carry it for her."

"You're a good granddaughter to do all this for her."

"She's all I have."

"There was another woman in the kitchen yesterday." His voice was regaining its strength with every word.

"Marnie is my grandmother's friend."

"So the two of you live alone on the side of the mountain?"

"Yes, it's been just Grandma McBride and me for as long as I can remember."

"Her name is McBride, too?"

"I know what you're thinking."

"Is that so?" He grinned. "So you are—"

"You don't have to say it." She should never have hired this crude man. "My parents planned to wed, but my father was called away by the war. He never came back. I've lived with my grandmother since I was born." She looked down at her quilt. Why was she telling him this? She usually remembered Grandma's admonition to think before she spoke. "Do you want some of the liniment for your head?"

"Does it work better than it tastes?"

She drew out the canister again and undid the top. "Hold up your hands."

"Why?"

"I'll pour some on them, and you can rub it where the pain is."

She thought he would ask another question, but he offered his hands, palms up. She let a few drops fall on his fingers. "Rub it in."

He raised his hands to his temples. Rubbing, he groaned. "I think that's making it worse."

"Of course it is!" She frowned. "You aren't supposed to rub as if you're currying a horse's coat." Putting her fingers to her own temples, she touched them gently. "Like this."

"Like how?"

"Like this!" How obtuse was this man?

He grasped her hands and pulled them up against the sides of his head. "Show me."

She tried to pull her hands away as he brushed them against his wind-roughened skin. "I think you've seen enough."

"Have I?" He chuckled. As he released her hands, his fingers coursed along them to her wrists, grazing her bare skin.

She could not move as his finger lingered just over her pulse. Warmth oozed out from it with the same sensation Cousin Pike bragged his whiskey caused to seep right through the stomach. This must be like that. Hot and dangerous if she enjoyed it too much.

Chandelle picked up the needle that was stuck into the fabric she was quilting and hoped he would pull his hat over his face and take a nap. Grandma had laughed when Chandelle had asked for a piece of the old tablecloth before it was ripped up into rags. Even though there were a few stains on the section she had cut out, it reminded her of all the meals she and Grandma had enjoyed together, and the stain in this section was from her first attempt to copy Grandma's recipe for ketchup.

The unbleached linen wavered in front of her eyes. She

could not imagine her life without Grandma in it. It was impossible to think of a day when Grandma would not be there to tease her, to sing as they worked together to finish that day's chores, and to teach her.

"You seem to have a lot of your quilt done," Matt said with a chuckle. "Planning on needing it soon?"

"What a horrible thing to say! I plan to live a long life."

His smile remained, but his eyes took on the intensity she had seen in his office yesterday afternoon. "I only wanted to remind you that playing a hero isn't something I do."

"You've made that clear."

He flicked his fingers against the quilt. "I'm glad that's clear, because while you may have your coming home quilt all set, I'm planning to have a lot more experiences that I don't need a quilt to remember."

"I don't intend to be using it for a very long time. I only have this small section done." She drew more of the quilt out of the bag and let it spill across her lap. She outlined a section from the white of her baptism gown to where she was working on the strip from the tablecloth. "This part here."

Matt frowned. "Then what's the rest of the quilt?"

"It's one of Grandma's old quilts." She ran her fingers across the tiny stitches. "I'm using it for the backing for my coming home quilt."

"A continuation?"

"Exactly." She smiled.

He folded the material carefully. "I think I'm beginning to see how this tradition came about. Odd that your family should develop a custom of preparing for death like the ancient Egyptians with their pyramids."

Chandelle regarded him with amazement. She had not guessed that he was so well educated. If he had had the luxury of such a good education, why was he doing such work?

He continued, keeping her from asking, "Most fascinating, although I still think it's more than a bit grotesque."

"You aren't the first one to say so." She began to sew

the curling diamond pattern that she had decided, when she was eight and beginning her quilt, that she would use to sew together this special quilt.

"But why your grandmother's quilt? What about one from your mother? Wouldn't that be more fitting?"

Chandelle's fingers halted in mid-stitch. "My mother died when I was born. She didn't have time to make many quilts."

"Oh."

When he added nothing else, curiosity brought her gaze up. His eyes held it, refusing to let her look away. When his fingers brushed hers, whatever she had been about to say was gone before the words could leave her throat. Staring at him, she wondered if those gold flecks had glittered in his eyes before.

"You sound," he said softly, as the conversations throughout the train flowed around them, "as if the grief is fresh."

"I don't speak of it often."

"Why?"

"There's no need. Everyone knows everyone else on the mountain."

"And everyone else's business?"

"Yes."

"So they all know that you're on your way to Philadelphia to get your grandmother's quilt?"

A throat cleared before an impatient voice asked, "Tickets?"

Chandelle jerked her hand from beneath Matt's and groped for her ticket. Hearing a yelp, she looked across the seat. Matt had his finger in his mouth. Taking it out, he shook it, but she saw the drop of blood.

The assistant conductor chuckled as he took their tickets and continued on his way down the aisle toward the fretwork that hid the stove that would heat the car when the weather turned cold.

"I'm sorry," she said. "I didn't realize the needle would jab you."

"No?"

"No!" How much more exasperating could this man become? She hoped she would not have an answer to that question during the trip to Philadelphia and back. "If— We're slowing down." She peered out the window, but saw only trees edging the tracks.

"These mountains are pretty steep." He pulled his hat forward over his eyes. "Don't let every change in speed worry you, Chandelle."

Instead of retorting to his impertinent use of her name, she looked out the window. She had wanted to watch how the train flowed out of Asheville, following the bends in the river before climbing into the mountains, but Matt's questions had kept her busy.

They were going slower. Much slower.

With a clank, the train came to a standstill. The trainman rushed along the aisle, not pausing to answer the questions fired at him. Conversation buzzed, growing louder in the car.

Chandelle glanced at Matt. If he was not asleep, he was doing a good imitation of it. His arms were folded loosely across his chest, and he was slouched in the seat. Shaking her head, she picked up her needle. He had told her he was no hero, ready to leap to battle at the first sign of trouble. This proved his assertion.

"And proof that I'm wasting my money paying this man," she murmured to herself as she tried to concentrate on her work.

It was impossible as the train remained motionless. The voices at the front of the car rose, one man's especially irritated. She looked at Matt through her lowered lashes, but he was as motionless as the train's wheels.

The assistant conductor came through the car. His expression was grim. "We'll be here awhile. Scree is across the track ahead. It should be cleared in an hour or two." He took a step toward the rear door. "Even with the windows open and the shutters drawn down, it can get hot in here when we're not moving, so you might want to wait outside. Don't go far."

He rushed out with several men following, asking more questions.

Chandelle sighed. This was not a most auspicious beginning for her quest to get Grandma's coming home quilt. And, she realized, as she pressed her hand to her suddenly pounding heart, every moment that passed waiting here might be the very one that delayed her too long from returning to Asheville in time.

"Do you want an escort outside, miss?" The deep voice was not Matt's.

Looking up, she saw a man tipping his dark hat to her. He wore a smile on his angular face, and his blue eyes seemed genuinely solicitous.

"How kind of you to ask," she replied.

"I travel this way often on business, and I'm sorry to have to tell you that these delays are not unusual along the steeper sections of the rail." He bowed his head. "Arnold Eagan, at your service, miss."

"Thank you, Mr. Eagan, I—"

"Miss McBride already has an escort," Matt said, tilting back his hat with a cool smile that suggested he had heard every word.

"Of course, of course," Mr. Eagan hurried to say. He tipped his hat to her again and scurried away along the aisle.

Chandelle folded her quilt and put it in the bag. "That was rude, even for you."

"Doing my job, boss."

Hooking the top of her bag closed, she asked, "How? By insulting that pleasant man?"

"Chandelle—"

"You should not call me that."

"Give me one good reason why not." He caught her hands in his. "*After* I say what I have to say. This is not your mountain, Chandelle. You don't know everyone on this train, and they don't all know you, although, from what I've observed already, several of the men here would be glad to get to know you much better."

Fire streamed up her face at his insinuations, but it was

not as hot and not as delightful as the warmth surging from his fingers across hers. She wanted to look away from his abruptly somber face. She could not.

When his hand rose toward her cheek, she held her breath. His touch was as light as a spring zephyr amid the pine trees. Closing her eyes, she savored his fingers' sandpaper texture. They lost their gentleness when he cupped her chin. Opening her eyes, with a gasp, she stared as his eyes became ebony slits.

"Didn't your grandmother ever teach you to be careful around strangers?" he demanded in a hushed, biting voice.

"Of course." She tried to pull away, but his fingers tightened on her. "Let me go!"

"When you promise me that you'll stop being so accursedly naïve. I can't keep an eye on you every day and every night of this trip." A rakish grin deepened the threat in his eyes. "The days I might manage, but I doubt if you'd agree to every night."

She pushed herself to her feet. "May I remind you, Mr. Winchester, that I'm not the one with a reputation for doing anything for money?"

"Talk so nicely to the men on this train, and you might get that reputation." He stood and motioned with his head toward the door. "Might as well get some fresh air. It's getting kind of stuffy in here."

She was not sure if that was another veiled insult, so she ignored his words. Drawing on her pelisse, although the day was too warm for it, she reached for her bag.

"Leave it," Matt said.

"I'd rather not."

He shrugged. "Carry it, if you wish. It's not as if anyone else is interested in your shroud." He started along the aisle toward the door.

Chandelle considered sitting back in her seat, but the heat was already building in the car. Staying here and sweating would gain her nothing, although she hated the idea of following Matt's orders like a well-trained dog.

Walking to the door, she was aware of the glances in her direction from the men still aboard. Too aware of them,

THE COMING HOME QUILT 41

and, for that, she blamed Matt. He was putting appalling ideas in her head. No one, except for Matt himself, had been anything but polite since Thad dropped her off at the depot.

Matt waited by the door. Again he had assumed a nonchalant pose, one shoulder against the door, his hands in the pockets of his denim trousers. Only his gaze, which swept the car, not missing a glance in her direction, warned that he was thinking of anything other than getting out of the car. He offered his arm as she reached him. His smile grew taut when someone a few seats away muttered. She did not catch the words, but she guessed he did because he hurried her down the steps.

"Wait here," he said as loose cinders crunched beneath her shoes.

"What—?"

He was climbing into the railcar before she had a chance to finish her question. Blast him! She had hired him, not the other way around. She should be giving orders, not him.

Turning, she forgot Matt Winchester and his outrageous ways. She stared at Asheville cradled in the valley below. All her life, she had looked out over the growing city from her perch on her mountain, but this view in the early morning sunlight was different because she was higher up and looking west across the valley. The shadows clung to the bottom of the eastern side of the valley, because the sun had not climbed high enough to beat them back within the mountains.

Until she had learned that Captain Friedlander and, she hoped, Grandma's quilt were in distant Pennsylvania, she had never given any thought to leaving this ring of mountains that had always been home. Why should she leave when everything and everyone she loved was here?

"I'll be back as soon as I can, Grandma," she whispered as she tried to pick out the exact spot on the mountain where their home was. "Hold on."

"To what?"

Chandelle took a steadying breath before she faced Matt. "I was talking to myself."

"Not a good sign." He grinned as if neither of them had spoken a cross word. "I've always heard that is a symptom of an unstable mind."

"I'm sure you have." Holding her bag close, she frowned when she saw he carried his own battered valise. "Are you leaving?"

He shook his head. "We haven't gotten your grandmother's quilt yet." He pointed with the bag to another car farther along the train. "I thought it might be wise to choose another car for the rest of our trip into Statesville. One with a few more women and families riding in it so you don't catch the attention of every traveling salesman with too much time on his hands and a single thought in his head."

"You are overreacting."

"Maybe."

She had not guessed he would agree. Swallowing her astonishment, she said, "I don't see how it would do any harm to sit in a different car."

"You're welcome," he said as he led the way along the tracks to another car.

"Excuse me?"

"You're welcome for me watching out for your best interests, Chandelle."

She paused. "May I remind you, Mr. Winchester—"

"C'mon, Chandelle, it won't ruin you to call me Matt. It's a long trip, after all."

"May I remind you," she repeated, not willing to acquiesce when she had a point to make, "that I hired you to help me retrieve my grandmother's quilt, nothing else?"

"Everything else is part of the Matt Winchester service." His teasing smile returned.

She could not, in spite of all her efforts, stop herself from smiling. When he wore that expression, she dared to believe he was not simply a rogue. There must be something good about him other than his overpowering touch.

As the back of his hand brushed her cheek lightly, she did not close her eyes. Instead, she watched as his eyes began to glow as hot as the train's boiler. She tried to dampen the quivers cascading along her.

"Is *this* part of the Matt Winchester service?" she whispered.

"Not usually." His palm curved along her cheek. "Chandelle, listen to what I said. You need to be careful on this trip north and even more careful when we get to Philadelphia."

"Why should there be a problem in Philadelphia?"

He shrugged as he had on the train, but she was not fooled by his attempt to appear indifferent. He was tense, balancing lightly on his feet as if he expected someone to surge from among the trees and ambush them. "There might not be any problems, Chandelle, but I don't want you to think this will be easy."

"I don't think that."

"Good." He paused as the whistle blew from the locomotive and the call of "All aboard" came. "That's our signal. Let's find a place to enjoy the rest of the trip to Statesville. I could use a nap, and I can't sleep if I have to worry about you every moment."

Chandelle walked with him to where several children were running to leap aboard the train. As she set her foot on the first step to follow them, Matt put his hand on her arm and laughed.

"What is it now?" she asked, unable to curb her irritation at his endlessly bizarre actions.

"Hold still." He bent behind her.

She yelped when he pinched her bottom. Whirling, she raised her hand. He caught her wrist easily before she could give him the slap he deserved. Grinning, he held up his other hand. Two short threads were pressed between his fingers.

"I didn't think," he murmured, "that you wanted these tiny tails hanging off your coat."

Her face scorched with a blush. "Thank you," she whispered.

He tossed the threads away and slowly lowered her hand to her side. His mercurial smile vanished as he took a step toward her, backing her up against the steps. Although she knew there were dozens of people in the cars, they might have been alone on the mountainside when his gaze held hers.

He bent toward her. Heaven help her, he was going to kiss her! Right here in public! She dampened her own lips as his edged ever nearer to hers. She must tell him to stop this immediately. She must remind him that he was her employee and that he should treat her with the respect due to her. She must . . . She must be crazy to want him to kiss her, to discover if his expressive mouth was as hot as the fire in his eyes or as cold as his words.

"You must remember one thing," he said in a husky whisper.

"What is that?" Her voice was breathless.

"No matter what you think now, Chandelle, you aren't wasting your money paying me."

Her eyes widened. "You heard . . . I thought you were asleep . . . I assumed—"

"Don't assume anything with me." He winked at her, tapped the brim of her bonnet, and, picking up his bag, walked up the steps. Turning, he held out his hand to her. "C'mon, Chandelle, the fun's just beginning. You don't want to miss a moment of it, do you?"

The engineer blew the whistle again wildly, the sound careening across the mountain.

Gathering up her skirts, Chandelle hurried to climb up into the car. She was glad for the excuse not to answer, because she was not certain what she would have said. However, she *was* certain of one thing. She would not label whatever was going to happen in the days ahead on this journey with Matt Winchester fun.

4

MATT FOUGHT THE YAWN tickling his throat. He had forgotten how lulling a train ride on a sunny day could be. The sun warmed the car, adding to the music of the endless repetition of the wheels turning on the tracks, the drone of conversation throughout the car, the faint sound of a mother singing a lullaby to a baby. Each sound continuing on and on without cessation, urging him to surrender himself to sleep.

As Chandelle had on the seat beside him in the crowded car.

He smiled at her, knowing that she was truly asleep and would not snarl some comment that was guaranteed to lead to another contest of words. With her hand between her cheek and the shutters pulled down over the open window, she was threatening to crease the brim of her bonnet. He did not consider loosening the ribbons, because she would be outraged at what she would see as an overly intimate motion.

He should be grateful that she used propriety to build a wall between them. He wasn't, even though he knew how badly it would have messed up things if he had given in to the temptation to kiss her as they were reboarding the train.

Keeping this simple was what he needed to do. It was sure to get complicated enough once they were in Philadelphia.

Pulling his hat forward over his eyes, he tried to fall asleep, too. It was a waste of time, he realized within a few minutes. Thoughts of the past and what might be awaiting them in Philadelphia bounced through his skull, leaving a twang in their wake that reminded him of the tolling of doom.

But not for him. He was determined that the tables would finally be turned. No longer did he have to prove to anyone that he could get along without his family's finances and their interference. He had proven that, as well as showing that he did not need to fall back on their assistance to make himself a life. For too many years, he had listened to his father extol the pleasures awaiting his son when Matt assumed responsibility of the family business.

"You shall be able to build on what I have created from what my father first built for me." How many times had he listened to his father say those exact words? So many times that he could still recall them with ease almost a decade later.

Of all the decisions he had made in his life, leaving Philadelphia without looking back had been the one he regretted least. He would not be returning now if not for that unfinished business between him and the family of the man Chandelle called Captain Friedlander. It was about time he put the finishing touches on it.

The train's whistle blew, jolting Matt awake. When had he fallen asleep? He grimaced. His mouth tasted as if something small and furry had died in it. Just the thought of the Friedlander family left this bad flavor in his mouth. Something cool to drink would wash it away.

Beside him, Chandelle murmured something. She must still be asleep. He wondered if she had gotten more sleep than he had last night. Guilt pinched him. Her grandmother was ill. Maybe she had been up all night tending to her.

He could not resist taking a moment to admire her smooth cheek and her softly parted lips. In her sleep, the gentleness that she fought to conceal gave her a waiflike innocence. He wondered if this was the true Chandelle McBride. Or was this a part of herself that she despised as a weakness, as he tried to ignore his own sympathetic side? Turning the other cheek only left a man with two sore jaws.

The train slowed to a stop, and Matt glanced out the window. Seeing a double door thrown wide at one end of the station, he smiled. This must be a choke-'em-off station, a place where food was available for those fleet enough to grab some and get on the train before it left. When his stomach growled, he chuckled. Even the most horrible slop would be better than being hungry. Too bad Chandelle had not gotten them seats in a Pullman car. Then they could eat aboard the train with all the amenities he had not enjoyed in a very long time.

Chandelle's eyes opened. Confusion lined her forehead as she blinked.

"Nice nap?" he asked.

She glanced at him. Her eyes widened, then narrowed as the wariness returned to her expression. "Not the most comfortable place I've ever slept."

"I won't ask you to list everywhere you've slept." When she opened her mouth to retort, he added, "You should be careful not to nod off unless you have your things secured. A light-fingered chap would be able to relieve you of your valuables in no time."

"I have you to guard me, right?"

"Not when I'm all cuddled up asleep here with you."

"You were what?" All color flashed out of her face, leaving it as pale as the aftermath of a bolt of lightning.

He laughed. "Don't worry, Chandelle. Half the train was put to sleep by sunshine and boredom." Coming to his feet, he said, "We can argue about this inside."

"Inside what?"

He pointed out the window. "Time for dinner."

"Already?" She rubbed her eyes and stood. "Ouch!"

"Did you hurt yourself?"

"I'm not accustomed to sitting all day. My muscles are protesting."

"Stretch."

"Excuse me?"

He chuckled. "It wouldn't be the least bit unladylike to stretch out your arms a little. Like this." He spread out his fingers as if to touch the windows on either side of the train. Resting his hand on the seat, he smiled. "Your turn."

She started to stretch, then winced. Her hand went to her side, pressing against it. "Maybe that isn't such a good idea, after all."

"Maybe you should get rid of the corset."

"Matt!"

He grinned. That was the first time she had used his name. "I'm only saying what you're thinking."

Her eyes shifted away, warning him that he was right. He let his hand slide from the seat and around her waist. With a gasp, she tried to move aside. She could not, caught between the seats.

"Chandelle, let me give you a word of advice," he said quietly. No need, he realized, for a quick scan of the car told him that the others had rushed to the eating house. "A man doesn't fancy the hard edge of a corset when he puts his arm around a woman."

"But you men do seem to like the shape a corset gives a woman."

He almost chuckled again. She would never surrender to his opinions without a debate, even when her expression warned that she agreed with him. He could agree with her as well. "True, but some women don't need help to attain that shape. I suspect you're one of them." His fingers splayed across her side.

"Then you suspect wrong." She pushed his hand from her waist. Her eyes widened as his fingers brushed her hip. "Will you behave like a gentleman?"

"I was trying to." He stepped out into the aisle to let her precede him out of the train. "You were the one shoving my hand where it shouldn't go."

Her shoulders stiffened, and she picked up her quilting bag. He grinned as she marched, rigid as a soldier on parade, out of the car. Her taut pose added a delightful sway to her hips.

He forced his hands to unclench. Son of a gun! Somehow, she made a man's thoughts linger on ways to get his face slapped. He should have followed his first inclination when she walked into his office and sent her about her business without him. He could have come up with some other excuse to pay Philadelphia a visit. Not that it would have mattered, for he had not been able to get the thought of Chandelle out of his head.

"Ain't you getting dinner, mister?"

Matt turned and smiled at a trainman, who was regarding him with astonishment. "On my way."

"Only a short stop, mister. Fifteen minutes. No more." The assistant conductor pulled out a pocket watch that was the same silver as his buttons and looked at it. "We weren't supposed to stop before we reached Statesville, but folks have got to eat."

"And eat fast."

"We're behind already what with that rock slide."

"I'll swallow it whole."

The assistant conductor grinned and continued along the car.

Matt climbed out. Looking along the crowded platform, he saw Chandelle easily. She might have been one of the last off the train, but she was about to enter the door of the eating house. Here was an advantage he had not considered when he had decided to let her pay him to help her find her grandmother's quilt.

He caught up with her as she stepped inside. She was better than a Colt pistol for clearing a path through the crowded room. The men jumped aside, tipping their hats as if she was preceded by a royal page announcing her. In her wake, Matt wore a superior smile, but it did not matter. Their eyes were focused on Chandelle.

Matt edged a step closer to her when he noted that she was the only woman without children in the choke-'em-off station. Even the women putting food on the counters had children running about their skirts. If these men thought she was traveling without an escort, they might think she was the kind of woman who would travel alone. Not a lady at all, and one who could be approached boldly.

"Don't run me over," Chandelle chided under her breath as she paused in front of the counter.

"Just doing what you're paying me to do. Keeping trouble away so you can find your grandmother's quilt."

"What—?" She glanced around the room. "Do you expect trouble?"

"Naw." He smiled when she frowned at him. He doubted if she believed him, and she shouldn't. This room was as full as a circus tent and about as primitive. With surprise punching him right in his empty stomach, he realized that he had no idea which station this was.

"If you are trying to take advantage of this situation to make me uncomfortable, you need not." Her voice was no more than a whisper. "I already am."

"Good. That's how you should be. These chaps will most likely behave themselves toward you, but there's no telling what they could do when they're all fired up on thinking what they'd like to do."

"Maybe we should go back to the train."

"Nonsense. I'm hungry. You're hungry. Let's eat." He slipped her arm through his. When her breast brushed his arm, an inadvertent motion as she moved to let one of the workers pass, longing rushed through him with the power of a locomotive.

She looked up at him, her eyes glowing silver-blue in the light from overhead. She said something. He could not comprehend the words as he was mesmerized by her inviting mouth.

He tore his gaze away. These were the wrong thoughts when he was working for her. He should not be tempted by lips that could send words slicing through him or by curves that offered a one-way ticket to disaster.

"Fifty cents for dinner?" Chandelle asked. "That is highway robbery."

He wondered how she could speak of something so prosaic, but he heard her voice quiver. Two could play this game of pretending that nothing had happened. With a grin, as he took a plate and handed it to her, being careful his fingers did not come into contact with hers, he said, "Actually it's train robbery. We're not on the road."

"But fifty cents for this?" She motioned toward the fried chicken that had what looked suspiciously like pinfeathers poking out of it, the platters of fried okra, and what he guessed was supposed to be fried cornmeal. It had broken into chunks on the plate, looking as appetizing as a worn shoe. Everything was greasy and certain to stick to his ribs one way or the other.

"You get iced tea, too," he replied when he saw her grimace at the odor of lard.

"For that price, it should be delivered on a silver tray by a butler."

An elbow in Matt's spine was an impatient reminder to get what they wanted and let others do the same. Piling some food on a plate, he grabbed a cup of coffee. It smelled as strong as kerosene. Just what he needed to keep him from falling asleep again. He was not sure if he dreaded having more pleasant dreams of Chandelle or nightmares about what might be waiting to keep her from getting her grandmother's quilt in Philadelphia.

Chandelle stepped back as Matt brushed past her. She was not going to let him touch her again, not even inadvertently. Maybe it had not been inadvertently before. She could not guess with him, but she knew what she had felt, she knew it was wrong. This man had admitted that he would do anything for money. She hoped he knew that she *would not*.

She reached for a glass of the iced tea, then scowled as she yanked her hand back. The glass was covered with dirt. Grandma would be outraged to see her in such a place. She selected another glass. Putting some of the fried okra on a plate, she made room for the others. She smiled wryly as the men rushed forward to fill their plates as if they had not eaten in a year. Maybe they were as starved as she would have to be to eat that grease-laden chicken.

The men clumped near the counter, eating with the eagerness of pigs in a sty. She looked about for a fork but saw none. When she saw the men eating with their fingers, she sighed. Maybe she should have spent the extra for Pullman service. No, that would have been impossible. She barely could have paid for a single ticket to travel in that luxury. Two tickets would have cost her more than she had for the full trip.

"You'd better eat up. Only a few more minutes before we've got to leave." Matt's smile bolted when he glanced at her untouched plate. "Aren't you going to eat?"

"No." She set the plate on the counter. "I think I'll wait until we get to Statesville to find something decent to eat."

"I doubt if you'll find anything different there."

"A restaurant—"

"Any there may already be closed by the time we arrive." He picked up her plate and handed it to her. "There's a bench over by the wall, so we can sit while we enjoy this repast."

"I've been sitting all day, and I doubt I could ever describe this as enjoyable." She smiled. "Sorry. I know it's not your fault. I should have packed some food."

He grinned and led her across the room that seemed empty compared to the area by the food counter. A bench edged the room, but only a few people sat on it. The men remained clustered next to the counter as if hoping better food would be served.

Chandelle sat beside Matt and sipped on her iced tea. It was strong enough to wash away the flavor of the overcooked food. Knowing that she needed to eat, she picked up another piece of okra. Her elbow struck someone, and she discovered they had been followed to the bench that was becoming as crowded as the area by the counter.

"Here." Matt put a piece of chicken on her plate.

"I don't think eating that would be a good idea."

"I don't think you passing out from starvation would be a good idea either." He jumped to his feet as a gray-haired lady approached. "Please sit here," he said, doffing his hat.

The woman gave him a grateful smile as she took his place on the bench. "You are very kind, sir." Looking at Chandelle, she added, "You are lucky, ma'am, to have such a gracious husband."

"He's not—"

Matt interrupted with a grin, "I'm not good at taking compliments." He put his hand on Chandelle's shoulder. "But thanks."

She wanted to denounce him, but she could not without embarrassing the older lady, who was chatting with him as if they had known each other all their lives. Coming to her feet, she nodded when the lady thanked them again for letting her sit on the bench. She did not dare to open her mouth to reply, because she was afraid the truth would explode out.

When Matt set his plate next to hers on the counter, he said, "Don't get your back up simply because I let her assume we're man and wife."

"I don't like lies."

"I never spoke less than the truth to her." His easy smile was irritating as he hurried her toward the door and the train that would be leaving any minute. "And her voice carried far enough so that any of those men who might be interested in you will believe you are being escorted by your husband on this trip."

"Why can you be nice to that lady, but it's wrong when another man wishes to be pleasant to me?"

"She's old enough to be my grandmother." He propped his chin on his palm as his elbow rested on the counter beside where a woman was collecting money for the food. "You are the right age to put the wrong ideas in a man's head."

Instead of answering, Chandelle handed a dollar to the woman and sighed. Thank goodness Grandma had given her this money. Chandelle's own money would be gone long before they reached Philadelphia if she continued to have to pay this exorbitant rate for food. If all went well, they would get to Pennsylvania in another day and a half. She hoped getting the quilt would be quick, so she could return it to Grandma before next week was over.

The bell clanged on the train.

Matt grasped her arm and rushed her across the platform. A man tried to elbow past them, but a growl from Matt reminded him of his manners. If only she could remind Matt of *his* manners so readily!

"Be careful," she said as they reached the train. "My bag is open. I don't want to lose anything."

He started to answer, but the whistle blew. He grasped her at the waist and tossed her onto the steps. Grabbing the railing, he jumped up beside her as the train wheels began to turn. The man behind them yelled.

Matt turned and held out his hand to him, swinging the man onto the narrow step. He bumped into Chandelle. With a gasp, she gripped the railing before she could fall between the cars.

"Thanks, pal," the man said, pushing past both of them and going into the car.

"Sure." Matt frowned. "Are you all right, Chandelle?"

"Y-y-yes." With a shiver, she stared down at the tracks.

"You don't sound all right." He put his arm around her shoulders and opened the door to the car. "You didn't lose anything out of your bag, did you?"

Horror cramped through her. She opened her bag wider to peer into it, but paused as Matt led her to an empty seat. He sat beside her, oddly saying nothing, as she drew out her coin purse and her quilt. Looking within, she saw everything else was still there.

"Was anything lost?" he asked.

"No." She smiled as she folded her quilt carefully to store it in the bag. "Next time you decide to play the hero, warn me."

"Hero?"

"You saved that man from having to wait for the next train. I'm sure he considers you a hero." She laughed. "I thought you said you weren't going to be a hero on this trip."

"*Your* hero." He put his hand out to halt her as she was closing her bag. "Before you put that away, don't forget you agreed to pay me a dollar a day."

"I shall pay you when we return to Asheville with Grandma's quilt."

Smiling cooly, he shook his head. "A dollar a day, Chandelle. That's what we agreed to."

"But—" Blast this man! He thought only of himself.

"Why should I trust you to pay me," he asked lowly as he put his finger under her chin, "when you don't trust me?"

She wanted to give him an answer that would shock him so utterly that it would curl his hair, but a jolt raced through her instead. Something flickered in his eyes. Was he riveted, too, by this amazing tumult that was unsettling and fascinating at the same time? Heavens above, she did not even like this man! He was arrogant and barely polite and treated her as if she should be honored that he was charging her so dearly to help her retrieve her grandmother's coming home quilt. Yet, when he touched her, even this chastely, something within her wanted to believe he was as beguiling as the eager sparkle in his eyes.

She turned away. A mistake, for his finger swept along her jaw, a caress that scored her with pleasure. He was right about her not trusting him, but only half-right. When he touched her, she could not trust him or herself.

"All right," she said, so low she could barely hear her own voice above the clatter of the wheels on the track, "I shall pay you your dollar at the end of each day." She pulled her coin purse out of her bag. Counting out the coins, she pressed them into his hand. "Here you are."

"That's only a dollar." He smiled. "You owe me two bucks, Chandelle."

"Two?"

"You hired me yesterday. A dollar for yesterday and a dollar for today."

She shook her head. On this, she was not going to budge. She must save money for the cost of rooms when they arrived in addition to the telegram she had promised to send Grandma.

"One dollar for today," she said quietly. "I will not pay for yesterday. You didn't do anything to help me yesterday." She frowned. "To be honest, you haven't done much today either."

He put his hand on the seat in front of them. As he leaned toward her, she pressed against the sharp slats covering the window. He would not do anything outrageous, would he? They were surrounded by people who would keep him from releasing the wrath she could see in his eyes.

"So you think I've done nothing for you today?" He gripped her chin. "Chandelle, what would have happened to you if you were traveling alone on this train?"

"I would have been fine."

"A fact that every bored rogue would have been eager to prove. Only harlots, seeking new customers, travel alone on the train."

Heat surged up her face. "You shouldn't say such things. You shouldn't even think them."

"I have to. It's my job. To get you and that absurd quilt back to Asheville safely." A smile fought to soften his lips beneath his mustache, but his eyes remained hard. "And I take my work very seriously."

Chandelle pulled away again. She would not let him intimidate her with his threats of what could happen if she did not heed his every word. She had hired him. He should listen to her, not debate each thing she said.

"I take my task very seriously," she replied, not lowering her eyes. "Finding Grandma's coming home quilt and bringing it to her is more important than arguing about everything."

"I agree."

His quick answer astonished her. "About arguing?"

"What kind of beast do you think I am?"

"One who will do anything for money."

"That's honesty, Chandelle." He laughed and relaxed against the seat as if they were discussing something no more inflammatory than the weather. "Finally, honesty."

"I have been quite honest about my anxiety about this."

"True, and I shall be as honest and say that, no matter how much you might think to the contrary, I understand the importance of your errand to Philadelphia."

"Do you?"

"I envy you."

Chandelle forced her mouth, which had dropped open, to close. She had not guessed he could say anything that would amaze her more, but she had been wrong. "Why?"

"You and your grandmother have something very special. You should treasure that."

"I do." She was glad he kept his voice low, because this conversation seemed too private to share. "And I shall for as long as I can."

"You love your grandmother very much."

"Yes."

"Yet, when she's nearing the end of her time, you leave her."

"I must find her coming home quilt for her before it's too late." How many times had she repeated those words? For weeks before she had gone to hire Matt. For weeks, she had been told she was silly. The quilt must be gone by now. Why would a Yankee captain hold on to the very thing that proved he was a thief? It was no grand war trophy, just a simple quilt that meant everything to her grandmother.

She put her hand over her bag, seeking the comfort of her quilt. Knowing it was close, that she could work on it to escape the cares of the day, had never failed to strengthen her.

"You could have sent someone else," Matt said, drawing her gaze to him.

"Someone else might not recognize it, even if Captain Friedlander handed it right over."

"Which you don't expect to happen."

She was glad he had not made that a question. Dealing with false hopes might betray them into complacency. "If he had intended to do that, don't you think he would have had the decency to respond to my letters?"

"Decency is not a word I've heard used to describe that family."

Her eyes widened as his shoulders tensed. They had stiffened exactly like this in his office when she mentioned Captain Friedlander's name. Dismay poked a hard finger at her, churning up more despair in her stomach. "Matt, what do you know about the Friedlander family?"

"Enough so that I can tell you this won't be a cakewalk. If you think otherwise..." He stared at the front of the train, pausing so long that she would have guessed he had fallen asleep if his eyes had been closed.

She tried to think of something to say that would convince him to continue. This blank expression could not hide his reaction. A shiver cut through her. It had been the mention of the Friedlander name that seemed to have convinced him to help her. But why? Too many explanations burst through her mind, each more appalling than the previous one. She dismissed them all, save for one that refused to be dislodged.

Matt Winchester was unquestionably a Yankee. His way of speaking, his motions, even the way he looked at those around them were very different from the people she knew in Asheville. Yet he was living far in the South. Could it be because he was ashamed to go home to face those who knew he had deserted during the war? She quickly figured the age he should have been about then. He should have been, she realized, little more than a young adolescent, but even boys were tapped to fight as the war was brought to a close. Maybe he had been under Captain Friedlander's command. That would account for the hatred that dripped into his voice and the rigid line of his shoulders each time the captain's name was spoken.

She almost asked him if her thoughts were close to the truth. No, she must not. It did not matter why Matt despised Captain Friedlander. What mattered was that he was willing to help her find Grandma's coming home quilt.

But if he deserted before, how do you know he won't leave you in the lurch if things get complicated?

She had no answer and hoped, by the time she faced Captain Friedlander in Philadelphia, that she would not regret having none.

5

CHANDELLE SMILED AS THE baby blew bubbles of bright orange. Wiping his face and making sure he was still propped securely between the rolled blankets on the train's seat, she offered him another bite of food. She pulled back the spoon when he sneezed.

"Bless you," she said with a smile as she wiped his face with a cloth. Putting the spoon to his lips, she handed his older sister a cracker at the same time.

"How long will it take you to eat this cracker, Patsy?" she asked the little girl.

"Last one took almost ten miles." Patsy's pixie grin broadened, bouncing her curls around her full cheeks. "Bet I can make this one last twenty miles."

"You'll have to take teeny nibbles."

"I can do that!" She sat on her heels and held the cracker to her lips, barely moistening it. "See?"

"Why don't you try for making it last only a few miles and see if you can take a thirty-mile nap?"

"Thirty miles?"

"It won't take long for such a short nap. Just a little longer than it took you to eat the other cracker."

"All right. I'll try."

Chandelle gave her a smile and turned to the baby, who seemed more interested in playing with the bowl of mashed carrots than eating them. Holding the spoon up, she managed to get it into the baby's mouth. He turned to watch everyone on the dimly lit train, as if trying to decide who was the most interesting.

Mrs. Riley and her five children had come aboard the train in Statesville, which had departed right on time at shortly after one a.m. All of the youngsters had been cranky and half-asleep, and Chandelle had offered to help settle them down for the night. As the train rumbled through the night toward Salisbury, she was glad of the excuse to put a few seats between her and Matt.

He had said very little since they got on the other train after supper. When they pulled into Statesville and they faced several hours of waiting for this connecting train, he had found her a good seat on a chair at one side of the station and gone to speak with the men smoking out on the platform. Only the sound of the station's clock and the telegraph had kept her company.

She was not, she reminded herself, paying for his companionship. However, after all his protestations about how dangerous it was for a woman to travel alone, she had not guessed he would leave her in the station like that. She had been relieved when Mrs. Riley arrived.

Looking toward the ladies' bathroom by the rear door of the train, Chandelle saw no sign of the children's mother. Mrs. Riley had taken her three older children in there to wash their faces and get them ready to sleep. Chandelle had been half-tempted to tell the short, dark-haired woman she was wasting her time because they would be arriving in Salisbury within an hour and would have several hours to wait before the mail express to North Danville, Virginia, departed. As soon as Mrs. Riley got the children settled down, they would need to get off the train.

Again Chandelle wished she could have afforded Pullman tickets. Then they could have remained in the same car for the whole trip, even when they switched from one train line to the next. That comfort was part of Pullman service.

"Just a few more bites, darling," she whispered to the baby. Speaking more loudly was sure to garner her more of the venomous glances that had followed Mrs. Riley and her children when they came into the car. Several of the men had gotten up and stamped off to search for another car where there was no chance of having a nap interrupted by a tired baby's crying.

"You do that well." Matt rested his arms on the back of her seat.

Although she wanted to ask where he had been and why he was here talking to her as if their last conversation had not happened, she said, "When you grow up with a mountain filled with cousins, you learn to share in taking care of the younger ones. Careful there," she added as the little girl slid off the seat. Watching when she walked unsteadily down the aisle to where her mother was convincing the other three children to lie down on the seats and try to sleep, Chandelle laughed. "Grandma is our family's matriarch, so holidays are always busy at our house. Once, when we got together after harvests—"

"You don't do that anymore?"

She spooned the carrots out of the bowl and held them out to the baby. "You've been around Asheville for a while, haven't you?"

"Two or three years."

"Then you should know there hasn't been much reason to celebrate any harvests the last few years."

"Yes, I'd heard that harvests have been lean." He sat beside her. "Some kind of bug in the corn."

She nodded. "Even if the corn had been fit to sell, there hasn't really been any place to sell it lately. It's taken a long time for us to recover from the War of Northern Aggression."

"That's a term you shouldn't use up north." He grinned as she offered another bite to the baby.

"What term?"

"War of Northern Aggression. They might take it the wrong way."

"Oh, I never considered that." She searched her mind, which seemed to be turning even more slowly than the train's wheels had up the mountains around Asheville. "War Between the States is what you call it, right?"

"I call it many things which I wouldn't repeat in your hearing." He stretched his arm along the seat as he smiled at the baby. "All that killing and dying and nothing much has changed."

Dampening her lips, she asked, "Would you have fought in the war?" She should ask him outright if he had deserted from Captain Friedlander's command, but she could not. He might leave her at the next stop, and she had seen enough to know he was right. A lady did not travel alone on the train.

He grinned. "I'm not planning to mess up my life by being a hero, remember?"

"How can I forget when you remind me of that endlessly?" She did not want to believe that her imagination had been so close to the truth, that Matt Winchester was truly a renegade from the army. If she asked him if he had once served with Captain Friedlander and then deserted, what would his reaction be? Anger? Very possibly. Honesty? That was always possible, too, although she was unsure how straightforward he had been with her up until now.

"If you don't forget anything while we're in Philadelphia, Chandelle," he answered so evenly that if his words brought any past guilt to his mind, he was hiding it well, "remember to be careful what you say and who you say it to."

"Think before you speak. Grandma says that to me a lot."

"Do you listen?"

"Sometimes." She shoved the spoon into his hand. "Give the baby the rest of the carrots while I help Mrs. Riley settle the other children."

"Me?" He looked at the spoon, baffled.

"You can feed a baby, can't you?"

"I haven't in a long time."

"Dip the spoon into the carrots, get a little on the spoon, and feed it slowly to the baby."

"And if he doesn't want to eat it?"

She stood, and he set himself on his feet to let her out into the aisle. As she edged past him, taking care that even her dress did not touch him, she said, "Tell him about the food at the next eating station. He'll be glad to eat these carrots instead."

When he sat again, Matt's dubious expression looked almost as boyish as the baby's, despite the dark beard woven unevenly across his face. She had not expected him to look like this, and that the result would be so undeniably charming. Her fingers were ruffling his hair before she could halt them. With a gasp, she pulled her fingers back. Not quickly enough, for he caught her wrist and gazed up at her.

"Pardon me," she whispered, glancing to where Mrs. Riley was tucking a crocheted blanket around her six-year-old twins. "I should—"

"Do that more often." His words were hushed, but their intensity was unmistakable. "Just as I should do this."

He pressed her wrist to his lips. Grasping the seat, she struggled to keep her knees from buckling as her blood became liquid flame. Slowly, his gaze locked with hers, he bent to tease the arc of her palm. She closed her eyes as the heat from his mouth became fiery shivers that cascaded along her.

The baby gave a cry of complaint.

"He's hungry," Chandelle murmured.

"That makes two of us."

This time, she did not have to ask what his peculiar words meant. The emotions blazing in his eyes and the tantalizing tilt of his lips made them so very clear. She should be outraged that he would regard her with such blatant desire and then speak of it candidly. She should be, but how could she when her thoughts were reeling in the same direction?

Chandelle hoped the sway of the train would be blamed for her uneven steps as she walked to the back. She did not want anyone, especially Matt, to guess how unsteady her knees were. Taking a deep breath, she tried to slow her trembling hands as she reached Mrs. Riley, who looked ready to collapse with fatigue.

"Let me help," she said, not daring to raise her voice above a whisper.

"What about the baby?" Mrs. Riley asked. She straightened, but the top of her head came only to Chandelle's shoulder.

"Mr. Winchester is feeding him. I thought you might need help here."

"Thank you, but they are almost asleep. At long last. This has been a taxing journey for all of us. Before this, I had never been more than a day's ride from my home." She sat across the aisle and sighed as she folded her hands in her lap. "I shall be more delighted to see my husband's parents than I have ever been."

"Is that where you are bound?"

She nodded. "My husband arranged this trip when the bank took everything we . . ." Rubbing her eyes, she said, "Forgive me, Miss McBride, for wearying you with troubles that are my own."

"I understand all too well. The bank has been threatening to foreclose on my grandmother's home for months now."

"But they haven't?"

"My grandmother has little time left. Even the bank has enough of a heart to let her spend her last days in her home."

Mrs. Riley sighed. "I wish our bank had—"

A curse erupted through the car. Chandelle whirled as the sleeping passengers grumbled. She pressed her hand over her mouth to silence her laugh as she rushed to Matt. It bubbled out as he wiped futilely at the orange spots speckling his shirt and coat. The baby's sneeze had covered him with carrots. More bright dots made a crazy design across his face.

"Oh, dear!" gasped Mrs. Riley. "Miss McBride, you should not have asked Mr. Winchester to help. If his coat is ruined, I shall never forgive myself."

Matt pulled out his handkerchief and cleaned his face. "Don't worry, Mrs. Riley. My expenses are all covered on this trip." He flashed Chandelle a grin.

She refused to let it taunt her into saying something she probably would not regret much. Instead, she bent to tend to the baby. Once Mrs. Riley was out of earshot, she would let Matt know that expenses did not include laundering his clothes if he was not smart enough to get the spoon out of the way when the baby was about to sneeze.

The third most important thing they must get clear between them before they reached Philadelphia would be not to feed a sneezing baby. The second would be a clarification of what expenses she would pay for him.

And the first, the most critical thing they had to talk about, was making sure there was no chance, not even the slightest one, that he could kiss her again . . . no matter how much she wished he would.

∞

CHANDELLE STEPPED OUT OF the Salisbury station. The hour was dawn, and the rain hid the landscape in a foam of fog. Clouds clung close to the ground as if they did not want the train to find its way out of North Carolina and north into Virginia. The town surrounding the station had vanished. The downpour was held at bay by the wooden awning over the platform in front of the Pullman car. Passengers climbing aboard would remain dry. Those who were riding in the coaches behind the glorious green car were being forced to scurry through the rain.

Drawing the collar of her coat higher, she took a deep breath before she stepped out into the rain. The day was not cold, but the idea of riding for hours in a soaked dress was daunting. She hoped her hat would not be ruined, because she could not call on Captain Friedlander with a bonnet topped by drooping flowers.

"Whoa!" called Matt as she was about to duck into the rain. "Where are you going?"

Turning, she saw him coming out of the station. Except for the stains on his shirt, he looked better than he had when they met at the train station at sunrise yesterday. His hair and face glistened with drops of water, but his clothes were dry. He must have shaved during the two hours they had waited for this connection.

She glanced down at her own wrinkled dress. Grandma had been correct. Chandelle should have worn her black dress instead of being so shortsighted to choose this gown. Oil spotted her sleeves. Her single attempt to brush the spots away had left smudges she feared would never come clean. Shutting the window was impossible, because the car would be as comfortable as the inside of an oven. It was too late to worry about this now, but she wished she could look as fresh and cheery as Matt.

As he walked toward her with easy grace, she could not help comparing him to the other men on the platform. His commanding presence drew the eyes of those around him, men as well as women. Watching the men appraise him as if he were a threat, she noted how the men accompanied by a woman stepped between their companion and him. It was no use, for the women smiled in his direction. Some boldly, some shyly.

He seemed unaware of the attention. At first, she thought he was simply pretending, but when he continued toward her without looking around or pausing, she wondered if it could be possible that he was oblivious to the admiration. He seemed to note everything else around them.

His grin when he paused next to her gave no sign of being anything but teasing. Either he did not notice the glances in his direction, or he did not care.

"Where are you going?" he asked again.

"Our car is back there." She looked along the train that, in the rain, seemed a mile long.

"Our car is right here." He pointed to a green car by the awning.

She frowned. He had admitted that he had not slept much

the night before they left Asheville. Had two nights with little sleep unhinged his brain? Maybe that explained his unaffected demeanor. "That's the Pullman buffet car. Our tickets are for the coach."

"Not any longer." He pulled out a strip of blue tickets that were not as fancily engraved as the ones she had purchased in Asheville. The word Pullman on the reverse caught her eye. The front listed their names and the name of the car in a handwritten scrawl. "From here to Philadelphia, we're going to travel in style." He hooked her arm with his. "C'mon. If we don't get on board right away, they'll leave without us."

"I don't understand." Maybe it was her brain that was lost in a lethargic morass from too little sleep. His words made no sense. Her ticket had been for the coach cars all the way north. The money she had given him for his fare would have bought the same tickets.

"It's simple. I showed them our tickets and paid the extra for seats in the buffet car."

"Our tickets?" She opened her bag to look inside. Her tickets should have been right on top of her quilt. "My tickets are gone!"

Matt took her bag and closed it. "I told you that someone could come along and steal your valuables while you were asleep." He grinned as he drew her arm within his again. "Lucky for you, the thief was me."

"You took my tickets out of my bag?" She could not imagine how many more ways he could reveal his contemptible habits.

"I couldn't purchase you a Pullman ticket if I didn't have them, could I?"

The bell clanging on the locomotive warned Chandelle she had no time to argue. Acquiescing without protest seemed unbearable, but lingering on the platform where the wind was beginning to puff rain toward them was silly.

As Matt handed her up onto the steep steps of the car, Chandelle smiled at the porter who held the door open for them. The poor man was trying to look welcoming even as the rain struck him.

She forgot the porter and the rain and even her vexation with Matt when she stepped into the car. It was as if she had entered the parlor of an elegant house. The arched ceiling was decorated with gilt, and the headliners over the seats had been engraved in a glorious vine pattern. At the rear, a wall with an aisle-wide door revealed a hint of the buffet tables and the kitchen beyond.

Instead of the narrow horsehair seats they had had in the coach car, pairs of overstuffed chairs in the same green as the outside of the car were arranged on either side of the aisle. Each of the more than twenty chairs was offset from its partner, so the feeling of being in a private house was not marred. Fringe and tufting added an aura of grandeur to each seat. Even the ever-present spittoons were shining brightly.

The conductor approached them, tipping his hat with its gold emblem above the brim. No assistant trainman would do for this car where only the supervisor of the whole train should ride.

"Good morning, ma'am, sir," the conductor said. "If you will follow me, I'll show you your seats. I trust you would enjoy some coffee at this early hour."

"Yes, yes," Chandelle managed to say. "Thank you."

Matt chuckled as they followed the conductor about halfway to the back of the car. "Good thing there are no flies in here, Chandelle. Maybe you'd better close your mouth just in case."

She ignored him. Yes, she was impressed by this incredible train car, but she would not let him irritate her further. As she sat in a chair which was even more comfortable than her favorite one at home, she leaned her head back and shut her eyes. She was not sure she could fight off the silvery web of sleep that closed over her, refusing to release her.

"Just what I need."

At Matt's voice, she was about to tell him to leave her alone. She flinched when something draped over her, and his strong, steady hands swept down her sides. How dare he touch her like this in public! And why was she vibrating like a pin dropped onto a stone? She must become as indifferent to his touch as he had been to the looks on the platform.

Opening her eyes, she discovered he had placed a blanket over her and tucked her in gently as Mrs. Riley had her children. She had let her absurd delight with his impertinent touch lure her into believing the worst—and the best—of him.

Chandelle waited until he took a tray with a fragrant pot of coffee from the conductor and set it on a small table that was hooked to the wall. Then she said, "Thank you."

"I thought you were asleep," he answered as he rested his elbow on her chair.

"I'm tempted."

"But you can't sleep until you scold me for helping myself to your tickets."

He guessed her thoughts too easily when she could not perceive his at all. "When did you take them?"

"When you were feeding Mrs. Riley's youngest." He looked down at his shirt, which was still discolored with specks of carrots. "Before you turned the job over to me."

"Which you handled pretty well, other than one mistake." She settled her cheek against the chair, because her head seemed to weigh too much to lift it away. "You shall be a pretty sight when we arrive in Philadelphia." She was not able to stifle her yawn.

He laughed as he poured a cup of coffee. When he offered it to her, she shook her head. She doubted if even the strongest coffee could keep her awake now.

With a smile, he took a sip. "Me with my orange-spotted shirt, and you with dark circles under your eyes from not sleeping. Why don't you try to get some sleep? It'll take us a little over four hours to get to North Danville and our next connection."

Drawing the blanket over her quilt bag, she said, "I should watch out for thieves."

"That's my job."

"Even when you're the thief?" She yawned again. "Tell me one thing."

"How I paid for the Pullman car tickets?" He chuckled. "My last job was pretty profitable."

"I won't ask what it was."

"Smart of you." He brushed a strand of hair under her bonnet. Smiling, he murmured, "You wouldn't want to know."

"But why did you buy me a ticket to sit here in the Pullman car, too?"

He laughed quietly, but the sound swirled through her as wondrous as the first spring breeze. "I thought you, who seem to consider propriety of the utmost importance, would realize that me traveling here while my employer rides in coach would be unheard of. Now, when you pay me my dollar for my day's work, you can rest assured that I have done something for you today."

"Thank you." It took all her flagging energy to speak those two words.

"My pleasure," he murmured.

She closed her eyes, but the glow within his remained like a dazzling star against the darkness of her lids. She should not trust its warmth. He had readily confessed taking her tickets from her bag without asking. What else might he have taken? She should check before sleep gave him another opportunity to search through her quilt bag.

Opening her eyes was almost impossible, but she did. Her breath caught when she saw he had not moved. He still leaned over the side of her chair, so close that a single motion would bring her face directly under his. All she needed to do was move forward. Staring at his lips, she was swept by the memory of them against her palm, dangerous and daring her to defy the dictates of society.

He bent toward her, and she could not move. She did not want to move. She longed to discover the incredible delight of his mouth on hers. Not even exhaustion could force her eyes to close as she watched him come closer. Would his kiss on her lips be as amazing as when he kissed her hand, or would it be as acerbic as his wit? She yearned to find out.

He tipped back her bonnet, and his lips brushed her forehead. "Sleep well, Chandelle. I'll wake you before we reach North Danville."

"But . . ."

"But what?"

She blinked once, then a second time. Before she could devise some way to explain without saying that she had hoped he would kiss her, her eyes shut, taking her into sleep and a dream of what must never come true.

6

THIS MUST BE THE most decadent luxury. Chandelle ran her fingers along the china set on the table in front of her. If the floor below had not been vibrating with the motion of the wheels along the tracks, she could have believed that she sat in some fashionable house in Charleston or even New York. The porters in pristine white coats moved silently between the four tables that were built against the walls, making sure that no glass was allowed to get empty and that every stomach was filled. The menu offered soups and meats and vegetables and pie before fruit was served with cheese and a pot of tea.

"May I join you?" asked a chirpy voice.

On the opposite side of the table, Matt came to his feet as Chandelle glanced over her shoulder to see a bright-eyed girl who looked too young to be traveling alone. She fought to hide her irritation. Why did Matt offer every other woman respect when he treated her with the informality and insolence of an older brother? No, he did not treat her like a brother would, for her reactions to his bold touch were not sisterly. She had been glad, when she woke before they changed locomotives in North Danville to continue north, that he had not been privy to her dreams.

Forcing a smile, Chandelle said, "Of course, you are welcome to join us. I am Chandelle McBride, and this is Matt Winchester."

The young redhead nodded her thanks to the porter, who rushed forward to put a place setting in front of her. Sitting, she replied, "I am Olive Southey. Please do not think me overly bold to approach you like this."

"Trains are a sociable community," Matt said as he slid onto the bench seat again. "Are you traveling alone, Miss Southey?"

"Unfortunately, yes. Two other girls were scheduled to travel to Washington with me, but both took ill. It was decided I must go ahead by myself, so that the telephone company would not be in dire straits."

"Telephone company?" he asked with a smile.

He had tried to start a conversation with Chandelle more than once since they came aboard this Pullman buffet car. She had attempted to answer, but she was accustomed to looking at whomever she spoke to, and she could not look directly at Matt without the images from her dream oozing forth to taunt her. Dreams were uncontrollable, she had reminded herself over and over. They had nothing to do with reality, and most certainly, they had no bearing on her real desires. Yet, if all that were so, why was she unable to shake off the memory of that dream of Matt pulling her into his arms and kissing her with all the fire in his eyes?

Miss Southey dimpled. "Mr. Winchester, I'm on my way to Washington to become a hello girl."

"A hello girl?" Chandelle's curiosity overcame her consternation, and she glanced at Matt.

He shrugged.

"That's what they call the girls who work the switchboard for telephones." Miss Southey raised her fingers and wiggled them in midair. "You've heard of telephones, haven't you?"

Chandelle nodded. "I read something about them in the paper a few years ago. Grandma said it would be a very long time before anything like that came up the mountain to where we live."

"I tried one once," Matt added, giving Miss Southey a generous smile that added a charming glow to her face. "It seemed to me that they're going to be pretty useless unless there are more of them."

Her dimples returned. "And that's why the telephone company is hiring us hello girls to help connect calls that people make from one phone to another. At first, the girls at the switchboard answered with 'Ahoy,' but that seems rather silly, don't you think?" She did not pause to let them answer. "So it was decided we would answer by saying, 'Hello.' Soon everyone took to calling us the hello girls. It is very serious work, don't you know. If we were to connect to the wrong telephone, it would cause such a mix-up that we might lose our positions. People want their calls to go through correctly and quickly."

"If their business is so important," Chandelle said quietly, "you would think they would go in person to handle it."

"But the telephones are so much more convenient."

She could not argue with that, because she had never used a telephone. It was just as well, because Miss Southey gave her no chance to retort. Like a zealous professor trying to teach a witless fool, the young woman launched into her supper at the same time she began a monologue outlining the reasons why anyone with a lick of sense would rush out immediately and arrange for a telephone to be installed.

Every effort Chandelle or Matt made to speak was squashed by Miss Southey's exuberance. Chandelle sighed with relief when Miss Southey excused herself at the end of the meal.

"She should be selling telephones, not connecting one call to another," Matt said, smiling as the porter cleared away the plates.

"I think that is what she is trying to do." Chandelle was able to smile. Speaking of Miss Southey was a safe subject that would not lead anywhere near her disturbing dreams.

"At least, as she is going to Washington, she will be leaving the train in only about nine more hours." He put his hands up to the side of his head. "I hope my ears can survive this."

"Hush! You don't want to hurt her feelings with such coarse words." She reached across the table and grasped his hands. Drawing them down, hastily she released them. Was she mad to touch him like this? Even the most casual contact set her heart to thumping like cartwheels on a corduroy road.

"She should become accustomed to them if she prattles like that when someone is anxious to make an important telephone call." He stood. "Shall we return to our seats so the table may be cleared? I make it a practice never to get in the way of a man doing an excellent job."

Coming to her feet, she smiled as she picked up her quilting bag. "Because you might get tapped to do that work?"

"There's always that risk." He led the way along the aisle to their seats. When she set her bag by her chair, he said, "You don't need to tote that everywhere. We're all prisoners in this car while it's moving. No one would try to steal it, because there is no escape but jumping."

Chandelle sat, being careful not to hit the spittoon by her seat, and looked out the window at the fields rushing past. "After what happened to my grandmother's coming home quilt, I want to make doubly sure mine does not disappear."

"I can't imagine anyone wanting your shroud enough to snatch it."

"Captain Friedlander took my grandmother's."

"So you were told by her."

She frowned as he sat. "What do you mean by that?"

"I mean that you know only what your grandmother has told you," he said quietly.

"She has never lied to me, and she certainly would not about something like this. What is wrong with you? I thought you said the Friedlanders were low-down skunks."

He chuckled, but with sparse humor. "I'm not sure I used those exact words, but they fit."

"So why are you suggesting that my grandmother was not honest with me?"

Again he shrugged as he had at the table. "I'm not suggesting she told you something false. I'm simply saying that truth is not always a solid thing. It's fluid, changing with time and the teller until what it was when it began is very different from what it becomes." When he rested his arm on her chair, his fingers cupped her shoulder, tilting her toward him. His voice remained low, becoming more strained on every word. "Your grandmother believes that her quilt was taken by one of the hated Yankees, a man she has led you to believe is Esau Friedlander. But what if, when you reach Philadelphia and call at the Friedlander house, they sincerely know nothing of such a quilt?"

"I don't want to think about that."

"You must."

She raised her eyes to see concern in his. It tempted her to soften and let all her anxiety spew forth. From the beginning of her search for Grandma's coming home quilt, she had feared that it had been destroyed or lost. She had tried not to let her hopes rise when she discovered an address for Captain Esau Friedlander, but that had been as impossible as keeping Matt out of her outrageous dreams.

When she did not answer, Matt stood. "You look as if you've got a lot to think about. I'll leave you to that."

"Where are you going?"

"Some of the gentlemen arranged to play cards after supper was over. They asked me to join them."

"And you're going to leave me here?"

His scowl threaded his forehead. "You can't be afraid of some boogeyman popping out at you here on the train."

"No." She glanced past him to where Miss Southey was walking toward them.

He chuckled. "Now I understand. Are your ears as tired as mine?"

"Yes."

He held out his hand. She looked from it to where Miss Southey had paused to speak with an older gentleman. Her laugh trilled along the car, bringing another flurry of words with it. Wondering if the young woman ever took a breath, she started to rise.

All thoughts of Miss Southey bounced out of her head when her leg bumped against Matt's. It was as if she had run full speed into him, for her breath exploded out and she could not draw in another. All along her body, she tingled with the power of a headlong impact.

"Are you going to sit here or join me?" Matt's voice was impatient.

That commonplace sound jolted her out of her mesmerism with these odd, unquestionably pleasurable sensations. Not looking at him, she said, "Let me get my quilting bag."

"Chandelle . . ."

"I have put up with your vexing idiosyncrasies without comment—"

"I haven't noticed you ever being without a comment."

"So," she continued tightly, "I trust you can put up with mine."

He smiled. "Does that mean, instead of snarling at each other all the time, that you want to be friends, Chandelle?"

"I would just as soon we keep this completely business between us."

"I was being polite. A gentleman, if you will."

"Then step aside, so I may stand."

He laughed shortly. "Now I understand. Being a gentleman means taking orders from you."

Chandelle refused to answer such an outrageous comment. Coming to her feet, she gathered her quilting bag into her arms.

Just in time, she realized, when Miss Southey asked, "Are you leaving?"

"Mr. Winchester is joining some friends, and I thought I would keep them company," she replied.

Edging aside so Miss Southey might pass, she held tightly to the seat on the other side of the aisle. The flounces on Miss Southey's bustle pressed against her, and she moved back farther. She bumped into Matt, but stepped forward before he could do something else to unsettle her.

The train suddenly tilted to the right as it took a corner. As she fought to keep her footing, she shrieked, "Matt!"

The cry hung in the air when she fell into the lap of the burly man on the other side of the aisle. He woke with a grunt that became a curse when she crashed into his chest. As she tried to stand, her bag struck him. His face turned a bizarre shade that mixed rage and a stomach about to revolt.

"I'm so sorry," she said over and over as she found her feet.

He glowered at her, then turned his back to her. She flinched as if he had hit her. Glancing along the car, she saw people standing to see what had happened. Her face flashed with heat.

Matt bowed smoothly and motioned for her to lead the way toward the tables at the rear of the car.

"Stop it!" she hissed under her breath. "You're making this worse."

"I doubt if anything *I* could do would make it worse."

With another apology to the man, she walked along the aisle. There was no use pretending not to see the grins or hear the whispered asides. She had made an utter fool of herself. Pausing beyond the last seat, she said, "You could have made it better by steadying me when I lost my balance."

"You gave me instructions, Chandelle. All business. Hands off."

"But not when I was falling on that poor man."

His roguish grin returned as he stepped past her. "He enjoyed it. I bet it's been a while since a pretty girl landed in his lap."

"Matt!"

Walking through the doorway to the dining section of the car, he said, "You can sit at the table on this side while I join the other gentlemen at one on the other."

Chandelle was ready to bristle at his easy orders, but knew retorting was useless when he went to join four men clustered around the table by the kitchen door. They had pulled the shades over the windows and lit the lamps overhead. Smoke from their cigars and pipes filled the small space, but the kitchen door had been left open to suck out the odor.

Setting her bag on the table, she ignored the yearning to hide her face in her hands and give in to tears. That craving was easier to resist than the temptation to bash her bag against Matt's head and knock some sense into it. But even that longing was overwhelmed by her desire to throw her arms around him as she begged him to make her dream of his kiss come true.

Had she lost her mind? She was beginning to think so, and she must find every bit of her common sense before she began the search in earnest for Grandma's coming home quilt, or her mind might not be the only thing she risked losing.

∞

MATT COLLECTED THE CARDS dealt to him and glanced over his shoulder. He would not have guessed that Chandelle would still be sitting here stitching on that blasted quilt. He did not blame her for wanting to give her ears a rest from Miss Southey, but he had not thought she would remain in the buffet section for hours like a silent wraith. Or, he thought with a grimace, like one of the Fates measuring out the length of her life in that quilt.

"Your chaperone, Winchester?" asked a short man named Adams as he toyed with his cards.

"Don't you know?" retorted Borden with a chuckle. His graying hair stretched across his head that was far balder than when Matt had first met him on another train last year. "She's his boss."

"His wife?" Adams frowned. "When did you do something so stupid as getting hitched?"

Matt smiled and tossed another dollar onto the pile in the middle of the table. "Gentlemen, gossip all you wish, but I'm here to play cards."

"And win apparently," grumbled Adams as he threw his

cards onto the table. "One thing hasn't changed. You still have the devil's own luck with cards."

Hall, who had not said more than a dozen words since Matt was introduced to him, picked up his cigar and his cards in one smooth motion. "But why is *she* here?"

"I told you," Borden said with another chuckle when he added his money onto the growing pile. "She's his boss. Isn't that right, Winchester?"

"The lady is paying me, gentlemen." Matt's gaze swept over the men at the table. "That's all I'm at liberty to say."

Borden blew a smoke ring, but his laugh broke it into pieces. "Winchester, you always manage to make the best of every situation. Although this one doesn't look too bad. Not too bad at all."

"Where are you headed?" Hall asked, glancing at Chandelle.

"Are you always so nosey?" Matt set his cards facedown on the table. "I thought this was a friendly game."

"Just trying to be friendly," Hall grumbled, but asked no more questions.

Matt picked up his cards and rearranged them. Not a bad hand to begin with, and, if the others continued to be distracted by Chandelle, this could be a profitable way to pass the rest of the journey into Washington. He did not know if any of the men would be traveling farther north, because his previous trips along this route had terminated south of Lynchburg.

The time flowed smoothly as the money collected in front of him. Every snip of Chandelle's scissors drew the men's eyes, so he guessed they were unable to ignore her.

Nor was he. That was why he had chosen this seat with his back to her. Then he did not have to risk being caught by her captivating gaze or her intriguing smile that was as innocent as a child's, yet had the come-hither warmth of a courtesan's. He could concentrate on his cards, although every face card with its patchwork of suits reminded him of that ridiculous quilt . . . and Chandelle. Keeping a light conversation going around the table, he listened intently to every opinion offered. Any unguarded word might be the very one he needed to help him complete this job and get Chandelle and her quilt to her grandmother's mountain in record time.

"Enough for me." Borden slid out of the buffet seat and stood. "Lady Luck always seems to be on the side of those who need her favor least."

"I'm not usually this lucky." Matt scooped up his winnings.

"I'd say not." Looking across the car, Borden put on his hat and tipped it toward Chandelle. "But I'd say that you are one lucky man now, Winchester." He walked into the main section of the car, Hall following like a slow shadow.

Adams said, "It looks as if it's the two of us, Winchester."

"And that's boring."

He frowned. "You've got to give me a chance to win back some of what I've lost."

"Not one against one when you are the other one. I like a bit more challenge myself."

With a curse, Adams banged his fist on the table.

"I suggest you remember that a lady's present," Matt said quietly.

Adams muttered something that Matt guessed would have turned Chandelle's ears a pretty pink. Or maybe not, because he could never guess how she would react. She had not been upset by the oaths fired at her when she fell into that man's lap, only that Matt had not kept her from embarrassing herself.

Without another word, Adams followed his companions toward the front of the car.

More slowly, Matt stood. That bench was not meant for hours of sitting, or maybe he was just getting older. It seemed as if it had been a lifetime ago when he had rejected the idea of spending his life in a chair, controlling everything around him. Then, he had vowed to choose a life of action and adventure and connections to no one. Odd that the very life he had selected often found him sitting for hours going someplace or another.

Chandelle put her quilting on the table. "Is the game over?"

"Unless I'm playing solitaire." He gathered up the playing cards that the porter had provided. Setting them in the middle of the table, he added, "By the way, in case you are wondering, I won."

"Of course you did." She rose. Opening the pack, she turned the cards over to look at the design on the back.

He said nothing as he admired her lithe hands that made every motion seem set to music. That was why, although he would not divulge the truth to her, he had been astonished when she tumbled into that chap's seat. His gaze slipped along her as she placed the cards in their box. She must have no idea how the long trip and her short nap had molded her dress even more closely to her curves, giving him a pleasant view of what his fingers longed to explore. Her skin had been a sweet banquet, although he had tasted no more than her hand during that chaste kiss, and he wished to feast more.

He turned away. Irritating woman! Why was he thinking about how lovely she looked when she was doing everything she could to make him hot under the collar? Being hot under his collar was the least of his worries when her eyes glistened like freshly minted silver dollars and her arms were folded over her breasts, drawing his eyes to that enticing roundness.

"I'm not surprised you were the winner," she continued as she took the cards to the table where she had been sewing. "I assume you choose to play with fellows whose skills are even less than yours."

"Less than mine?" He smiled coldly. "I believe I have been insulted."

"I believe you are right." She spread the cards across the table and flipped them with the skill of a cardsharper. Looking up at him, she gave him a smile as chilly as his. "I was watching, and you were lucky they did not jump on some mistakes you made."

He scowled, then realized, while he had been sitting with his back to her, she had been able to see his cards easily.

"Am I to assume by your comments that you think that *you* can play cards better than I can?"

"Yes."

There it was again. That quiet assurance nothing seemed to shake. Prim voice and prim smile and even more prim stance, all exactly as a lady should be except for that challenging fire in her eyes. He suspected that fire revealed more than her demure pose concealed. It was about time he discovered exactly what it revealed. The best way he could do that was to show her who was in charge on this trip.

Sitting across from her, he said, "Then prove it."

"I thought you said you did not find playing a two-handed game enough of a challenge."

"I did not want to take all of his money."

"Just mine?" She laughed lightly. "I guess, on the unlikely chance that you win any money from me, I shall have to consider that you were paid in advance for the work you have yet to do."

Dash it! She was trying to enrage him to the point where he lost his temper. Was this her way of paying him back for not helping her keep from falling? He forced a smile. "How about a wager?"

"On top of what we bet on the cards?" She shuffled the cards with an ease he had to admire. He wondered where she had learned to do that so well. Chandelle McBride was becoming more intriguing with every mile of this trip. "Don't risk more than you care to lose."

"You are quite confident about this."

"Yes."

A smile twisted across his lips as his eyes narrowed. "All right, Chandelle. What shall we wager?"

She plucked his carrot-stained handkerchief from his coat pocket. "You may wager this."

"My last good handkerchief? Why?"

"No reason that we need to bother with now." Chandelle dropped the handkerchief in the middle of the table and drew a handful of pennies out of her bag. She faltered as she noticed the fancy monogram on his handkerchief.

How odd that he would put his first initial on it! Did she have it upside down? No, the design suggested it was an *M,* instead of a *W* embroidered beautifully into the lawn.

Why was she letting the initial on a handkerchief intrude on the concentration she would need for this game? After two hours of watching him play cards, she suspected she could guess when he might bluff and when not. She heard her grandmother's admonition that gambling on cards was wrong, but she needed to teach Matt Winchester a lesson about respecting her.

"You know what I want," she said. "What do you wish of me?"

When he chuckled as his gaze swept over her, she knew she had been a fool to ask such a question. "If I were a gentleman, I would say I wish no more than a lock of your hair or your fond regard. However, I am not a gentleman." He leaned back in the seat and said, "If I am ahead in the winnings after an hour, I want you . . ."

She stared at him as his voice drawled off into silence. He did not speak about what he wanted if he won. She could see that in his eyes that burned through her, searing away each layer of her defenses to leave her naked before him. She should look away. She should denounce him as a mannerless cad. She should toss the cards in his face and tell him to find another employer, that she would figure out a way to get her grandmother's quilt on her own. She should, but all she could do was melt in that fierce fire.

". . . to polish my boots."

"What?" she gasped, sure she had misunderstood him.

He put his hand on her arm, giving her a gentle shake. "Chandelle, didn't you hear me?"

"Yes, I heard you. It simply took a moment for me to realize what you had said."

"Why?"

Blast him! He knew why. Didn't he? How could she accuse him of lascivious thoughts when the whole of it had been in her head? Despite his words, he was acting very much the gentleman, while her fantasies were unspeakable.

Squaring her shoulders, Chandelle smiled. He was so

certain he was going to defeat her, but she would show him that he was not the only one who could play this game of words at the same time they played cards.

"I was," she said, "hoping you would select something even more outrageous."

"Were you?"

"So I might enjoy my victory over you even more."

"I've heard it's a fool who spends his—or her—winnings before they're won."

She laughed as she handed him the cards. "You might want to keep that in mind and get rid of that gloating smile."

He did not scowl then, but as the minutes passed and she won hand after hand, he did. She did not win them all, but at the end of the hour, she had more pennies in front of her than when they had started. She pushed the pennies she had won toward him.

"What are you doing?" he asked.

"I've proven my point, and, as you should know, a lady," she said in the dignified tone she had used when she went to his office, "never plays cards for money."

"Another lesson from your grandmother?"

"A fact."

"A gentleman would not deprive a lady of her winnings, no matter how ill-gotten." He chuckled and scooped up the coins. "It's a good thing I'm no gentleman."

"It is, isn't it?" She picked up the section of the quilt she had been working on and spread it across her lap. "But you do owe me that monogrammed handkerchief of yours."

"I thought a lady did not collect debts from a gentleman."

"I said, if you will recall, that a lady doesn't gamble for *money*. And you said—"

"That I'm no gentleman." He nodded and picked up the handkerchief. Slipping it into his pocket, he said, "You're right about that and about winning my handkerchief. After all, a bet's a bet, Chandelle. Once we reach Philadelphia, I shall have it laundered and delivered to you to be stitched into your quilt.''

"How did you know that was what I planned?"

"Everything for you is connected in some way to that quilt. It was an easy guess." His voice deepened to an uneven whisper. "I'm honored to be a part of your quilt, Chandelle."

"This trip is an important event in my life." She fingered the fabric she had been quilting, being careful not to look at him. How had this compartment become intimately small and completely separated from the rest of the train . . . from the rest of the world?

His hand reached under the table and covered hers on her lap, a motion so downright intimate that she gasped. She could not smother the sound or the delight rushing through her like a storm over the mountains.

"You've taught me," he murmured, his breath as teasing as his fingertips on hers, "not to jump to conclusions about you. How about another lesson?"

"Lesson?" Surprise yanked her head up. She wanted to look away, but her gaze was caught and held by his as gently and as persuasively as his fingers closed over hers. "What sort of lesson do you want me to teach you?"

"I thought I might teach you something now."

She forced her eyes to look down at her quilt. Folding it over and over, so she could stuff it into her bag, she said, "I think that's a bad idea."

"Do you?" He stood and sat beside her. Drawing the end of the quilt out of her hands, he placed it carefully on the table. "Why? You haven't even heard it yet."

"I know that glitter in your eyes. It means trouble."

"I didn't realize that you had come to know me so well in this short time." He laughed softly as a vagrant strand of her hair sifted over his fingers. "You obviously are a quick student, or you have put a great deal of effort into your studies."

"Your peculiar ways are difficult to ignore."

"Ah, another insult." His hands curved across her cheeks, grazing her ears. She gasped at the light caress.

"And here I was about to say how lovely this rosy glow of victory is on your face."

She said, "I think—"

"You think too much." His laugh was hushed and as rough as his skin. "Sometimes not thinking is the best thing you can do."

"For you."

He tilted her face toward him. His voice became a gravelly whisper. "But I *am* thinking now. I'm thinking how soft you are, how sweet each puff of your breath is against my face, and how you look as if you need to be kissed."

"You shouldn't." Her words were as faint as his and more unsteady.

"You're probably right, but the things we shouldn't do are sometimes the most fun." His mouth lowered toward hers.

All she could see was the enticing glow from his eyes, the flame that was brighter than the lamps overhead. She put up her hand to halt him, but her fingers uncurled across his face, savoring the hard line of his jaw. She closed her eyes, but the fire still burned her. His fingertips were lightning rods, gathering all the power of the storm swirling around them and sending it surging through her.

After two heartbeats, she opened her eyes. He had been going to kiss her, hadn't he? Then why was he hesitating? In her dream, he had been audacious and kissed her eagerly. She looked up at him and saw a satisfied smile. She tensed. If this was his idea of another jest, she did not like it one bit.

He laughed quietly. "You look as if you're about to spit at me like a doused cat!" Again his voice grew deep and beguiling. "Can that mean you want me to kiss you?"

"I don't know."

"I know." His hands slipped from her face, except for a single crooked finger that tipped up her chin. "Don't close your eyes."

"What?" Could he be any more baffling?

"I know that you are a woman who likes to see what she's getting herself into."

Before she could answer his bewildering comment, he captured her lips. Again he cupped her chin, tilting it toward him. Gently, so gently that she leaned toward him to savor every bit of his kiss, he explored her lips. Each touch was a separate, excruciatingly sweet ecstasy. As her fingers slid along his shoulder and up into the silken caress of his hair, the sensations surging through her threatened to drown her in pleasure. Nothing, not even her own dreams, had been this glorious.

She gasped as his mouth left hers to sample the flavors of her cheeks and along her chin. When he kissed the tip of her nose, she laughed. The sound was muted as his mouth found hers again. Drawing her to her feet, he tugged her to him. She slipped her arms up his back, then pulled away.

"What are you wearing under your coat?" she asked.

He laughed. "You are brazen to ask that after just a kiss."

She would not have called this *just a kiss,* but she would not allow him to change the subject either. Grasping his lapel, she started to pull it aside. He clamped his hand over hers, pinning it to his chest. Too late, for she had seen a flash of silver and mother-of-pearl.

"You've got a gun!" she gasped.

He lifted her hand to his lips and kissed it lightly. "Why are you letting silly things bother you now?"

Again he gave her no chance to answer. She considered protesting, but, as his mouth slanted across hers, she knew it was futile. She wanted his lips on hers. She wanted to be in his arms, even though he vexed her as no one else did.

"The train is stopping. If someone gets on, they could see . . ." She sighed as his mouth caressed her cheek.

"We are still—" He punctuated each word with a kiss that sent sparks across her face. "We are still half an hour from our next stop."

"You know that?" She wondered how he could think of anything but this unbelievable enchantment.

He took her face between his broad hands again. "I decided to check out the schedule before I checked out your lips. But in case someone comes by..." He stretched past her to raise the globes on the lamps hanging overhead. Blowing out the flames, he drew her into his arms as sable shadows draped over them.

His lips touched hers just as a woman screamed. Releasing her, he whirled, then froze as someone shouted, "Nobody move. This is a robbery."

7

CHANDELLE KNEW BETTER THAN to gasp when Matt shoved her to her knees and under the table on the other side of the aisle. He crouched beside her. She reached to gather up her quilt. Her fingers found only air when Matt motioned for her to make herself small in the shadows.

She looked at him. His gaze was riveted on the door to the main compartment. Although his face was lost in the darkness, she could see the muscles in his jaw stiffen.

"Sit and be quiet!" came another shout. "Hand over your valuables, and no one will be hurt."

Matt muttered something.

She whispered, "What—?"

He waved her to silence. Even though she could not see his glower, its cold fire struck her like a fist.

Sitting on her heels, with her head pressed against the bottom of the table, she watched as a man appeared in the doorway. He motioned into the compartment, and she struggled to breathe. Then she realized that he had not seen them, because the porters and the cook came out of the kitchen and went silently into the main part of the car.

She could not believe this was happening. She had heard the tales, as everyone else had, of the train robbers who waylaid trains out west. But this was Virginia, a civilized area where men did not force trains to halt and then leap aboard to rob the passengers.

When she saw a pistol in the man's hand, she grasped Matt's arm. "Do something!"

"What," he asked with a serenity that eased her panic, "exactly do you expect me to do?"

She stared at him. As her eyes adjusted to the dusk, she saw his hands were lying loosely over his knees. Was he about to jump to his feet to bring down the robber or to flee? "I don't know, but we should do something. We—"

His hand clapped over her mouth as another shadow moved out of the kitchen. Clasping his arm in fright, she hoped the second bandit did not look in their direction as he herded the last of the car's crew past them.

Shaking Matt's cool palm off her mouth, she whispered, "We have to do something."

"No, we don't."

"But you have a gun."

"I told you I don't plan to be a hero on this trip."

Chandelle stared at him in shock. How could he stay here and let those thieves terrorize the rest of the passengers? She wanted to peer out and see what was happening elsewhere along the train. Cut off as each car was from the others, there was no way of knowing what the other passengers might be facing.

The horn from the front of the train gave a mournful howl. Was it a signal of some kind? A call for help? She had no idea where they might be, but she suspected these thieves would not have stopped the train near a town. Maybe they had taken control of the locomotive as well.

When Matt put his arm around her shoulders, she shivered against it. He was right. Without knowing how many bandits might be within this car and outside, they must not do something that would make things worse. But how could they do nothing? He had that gun. If he challenged the robbers, they might flee.

She winced and hid her face against his shoulder when she heard a woman's scream from the far end of the car.

Every instinct warned her to heed Matt. Every thought urged her to do something.

"I thought you said this car is full." That voice she recognized. It belonged to the first robber who had shouted.

"Yes, sir, it is." Was that the porter who had served them supper? His lush drawl belonged to the low country.

"There are two empty seats up here."

Matt whispered, "I'm getting out of here, Chandelle."

"Where are you going?" she asked, terror returning full-force to twist through her stomach.

"Hopefully not to my grave." He grinned and winked at her. "I plan to make a few hundred more memories, even if I don't have a coming home quilt to put them in." He held out his hand. "Let's go."

"Where?"

"I'm not sure yet." He slipped out from under the table before she could reply.

Clinging to the wall and holding her breath, she watched him slip past the open kitchen door. She had no idea what he had planned. *Maybe he's deserting again.* She tried to disregard that nagging thought that refused to be kicked out of her brain. She knew nothing about Matt Winchester's past, and she did not care about it right now. All she wanted was to get out of here alive.

And with her quilt bag.

She heard a low hiss. By the kitchen door, but still hidden by the shadows, Matt was signaling to her to join him. She inched toward the aisle. He hissed again, a bit louder. Wanting to tell him that she had heard him the first time, she edged closer to the end of the table. Yes, she could reach across the aisle. All she had to do was slide the quilt and the bag toward her. Gathering it in, she could skitter around the door to where Matt waited.

Peeking out, she saw one man by the door to the main section of the car. His back was to her. Good! Her fingers crept across the aisle and up on the table, stretching toward her bag. The man moved, and she froze, not daring to pull back. Would the darkness conceal her? Her lungs burned, but she did not release her breath.

She smiled as she touched the smooth satin that had been part of her baptismal gown. Closing her fingers cautiously over the fabric, she gave it a gentle tug. The quilt did not move. What was holding it in place?

Again she dared to look out from under the table. The bag was atop the quilt. Good! Her bag was there, too. Somehow, she had to get the bag and her quilt to ease toward her without drawing the attention of the large man standing in the doorway.

"Chandelle!" Matt's voice was almost drowned out by a woman's loud sobbing. "Let's go! Now!"

She should listen to him. She could not. She could not leave her things here to be stolen. Tensing her shoulders, she tightened her grip on the quilt.

A screech raced down her back, setting every nerve afire. Voices scrambled together like breakfast in a cast-iron pan erupted from the front of the car. The man in the doorway let out a holler and stepped away from the buffet compartment.

She jumped forward and grasped her bag. Dropping to her knees under the security of the table, she stuffed her quilt in it. She looked toward the kitchen door. No one was there! Where was Matt? Had he left without her?

I told you I don't plan to be a hero on this trip.

If he wanted to be a coward, let him! She had her bag and quilt, and she would—

A massive hand closed over her wrist. In horror, she looked up at the man who had been standing in the doorway. She had not guessed how huge he was, as broad as the table and even taller than Matt.

He jerked her out from under the table and to her feet. "Well, well, what do we have here?"

"Release me at once!" She tried to pull away.

His eyes between his thick hair and the kerchief tied around his lower face widened. "Feisty one, aren't you?" He pushed her up against the wall.

As he ogled her, she sucked in her bottom lip to keep from calling to Matt. He really had not left, had he? Why wasn't he coming to her rescue? She had paid him to help her. Good heavens, why wasn't he doing his job? Her hand clenched. Maybe he was. Maybe he was sneaking up on this thief even now. She tried to peer past the man's broad arm.

"Who are you looking for?" he demanded, glancing back. "The other one?"

"The other what?"

"Passenger." He caught her chin in his hand and pushed her head against the wall. Hard. "Where is he?"

She blinked as everything whirled around her. She should have listened to Matt and scurried away like a frightened rabbit. Without her quilting bag? Impossible!

The big man growled, "Where is he?"

"I don't know what you're talking about," she choked out. She would not betray Matt, even though he had left her to face this beast alone.

"The man traveling with you."

"I don't know what you're talking about."

His gaze raked her again. "A lady doesn't travel by herself. Unless you're no lady."

"How dare you!"

A cry came from the other side of the wall. "She's fainted! Leave her alone!"

The man holding her wrist reached for her bag. "What's in this?"

"Just my sewing."

"Nothing else?"

She shook her head. "Nothing else."

"Open it up."

"My pins will fall out. They'll make a mess on the floor."

He laughed. "Won't that be too bad? Open it up."

"No!"

"If you won't, I will." He reached for the bag.

With a shout, she threw it under the table. He swore viciously, shoving her aside. She fought to stay on her feet. When he bent to pick up her bag, she took a deep breath and grabbed his arm as Thad had shown her.

She tugged. The man looked at her, shaking her off. She

gripped his arm again and, locking her knees in place, tried again.

Why wasn't this working? Thad had assured her the razzle-dazzle-1-2-3 would work with any opponent, no matter the size. She was doing everything right. Wasn't she?

The huge man turned to face her. With another curse, he bent his arm, catching her hands in the crook of his elbow before she could pull them away. He slanted his arm against his chest and laughed as she tried to free her fingers. She gasped when she bumped into the gelatinous wall beneath his filthy shirt.

"What do you think you're doing?" he growled.

She tried to answer, but fear clogged her throat. The razzle-dazzle-1-2-3 should have worked. Thad had promised her that it would. What had she done wrong?

"What are you hiding in that bag? Money? Jewelry?"

"Nothing."

He raised his hand. She drove her elbow into his stomach. His arm dropped, and she freed her hands. She whirled to run down the aisle. She skidded to a stop as the other robber, who was shorter than her but almost as round as the man chasing her, turned and pointed his gun at her.

The big man caught her by the waist, nearly lifting her off her feet. Seeing her horror mirrored in the faces within the car, she cowered as screams echoed off the ceiling. He dragged her into the other compartment. She fought to escape.

"Matt!" she cried. Where was he? Why didn't he help her?

Her flailing fists struck flesh. With a groan, the robber released her. He stumbled forward, and she seized his arm as Thad had shown her and shifted to her other foot, sending him rushing past her.

In amazement, she watched him careen into the other thief. Both men tumbled to the floor, hitting it with a thud. Blood trickled across the floor, and a woman shrieked.

A passenger jumped up and grabbed the gun slithering

down the aisle. Another ran out the far door, shouting for assistance.

Chandelle did not move. She simply stared. The blood was coming from the huge man's head. He must have struck one of the seats when she sent him crashing into his crony. Looking past him, she saw that the passengers were all standing on one side, except for Miss Southey, who was sprawled across a seat, senseless. A man sank to a seat, then another. Everyone began to speak at once, and none of their words made any sense in her throbbing head. One woman reached for a sack that had fallen from the first robber's hands and spewed stolen items across the floor.

Her bag! Where was it?

Chandelle grabbed her bag from the floor, holding it close to her chest as she leaned against a wall. Knowing she should go to help those hovering over Miss Southey, she could not force her feet forward. They seemed to have grown roots to the floorboards.

"Well done."

At Matt's chuckled comment, Chandelle gasped. He was still here!

She looked over her shoulder to see him lighting the kerosene lamps over the table. He grinned as he set the globes over the flames. Because he was standing so close to the light, she could not see more of his face than his satisfied smile.

"I couldn't have done better myself," he added, stepping aside as the conductor rushed through the car.

Chandelle edged back when the conductor turned to shout to another trainman and the porters who were trying to wake Miss Southey from her swoon. When Chandelle's knees wobbled, Matt guided her to a chair. She continued to hold on tightly to her bag.

"That was the most asinine thing I've ever seen in my life," Matt said as he sat on another chair.

"Yes," she whispered. "They should have known that robbing this train—"

"Not them, you."

"Me?"

He handed her his handkerchief. She looked at it, baffled. Taking it from her, he dabbed at her cheeks. Only then did she realize that tears were running down her face. Voices—some angry, some frightened—swirled around them, but she paid them no mind as she used the handkerchief to wipe away the unwanted tears.

"I couldn't let him take my bag," she murmured, not able to speak louder.

"Your quilt isn't worth your life." He scowled.

"Not my quilt." She shivered at the thought of losing the precious pieces of material that she had spent so many hours stitching together. "I have Captain Friedlander's address in my bag."

His eyes widened. "You risked your life simply for that?"

"Grandma is depending on me."

He put his hands on her cheeks, warming her icy skin. "You fool! Anyone in Philadelphia could tell you where the Friedlanders live."

"It's a big city. I didn't know if . . ." She closed her eyes. "I guess I wasn't thinking too clearly."

"If you had, you would have listened to me."

She had to concentrate on breathing. Everything she once had done automatically now seemed to require every bit of her attention. Struggling to remember what he had said, she looked directly at him. "Maybe I should have, but I couldn't leave without my bag."

"You do have a singular way of looking at things." He drew the bag down to rest in her lap. "I should have guessed you wouldn't do the sensible thing and scamper out of here while the hubbub kept them busy."

"You did."

He grinned wryly. "I thought I could, but I found I had to stick around and see how much trouble you actually could get yourself in without my help."

"You were here all along?" She could not believe the words even as she spoke them. Coming to her feet, she hooked her bag over her wrist. She rubbed her hands together, but nothing warmed them. "I can't believe you stood here and watched."

Hooking a thumb toward the kitchen door, which was swinging as one of the porters rushed out with a pot of coffee for the distressed passengers, he said, "I was on the other side of that door. I had a great view at the same time that I was out of sight."

"Why did you just stand there?"

"It didn't look as if I would be needed. You seemed to be handling things."

"Me?" She stared at him again, then a shudder exploded across her shoulders.

"I saw no reason to jump in while you had the situation under control." He grinned. "What do you call that fancy motion that you used to toss that mountain of a man into his accomplice?"

"Thad calls it—he calls—" She fought to speak. "He calls it the razzle-dazzle-one-two-three. He—" Her voice broke as she swayed.

Matt gathered Chandelle up against him. She quivered so hard, he feared she would shatter. Leaning her head on his chest, he said nothing as a new, hot stream of tears rushed down her cheeks and seared through his shirt.

He looked over her head to where the two robbers were being brought to their feet with little sympathy for their heads, which must be aching more than his had when he boarded this train in Asheville. The conductor handed the big one a cloth to hold over the bloody spot on his head and prodded them out of the car, using their own weapons to keep them from escaping.

He smiled when he heard Miss Southey's voice, albeit not as cheery as it had been. She must have recovered from her swoon.

Resting his cheek against Chandelle's battered bonnet, he said nothing while she sobbed. Everyone had a different way of dealing with danger. He should have guessed Chandelle would not collapse in a feminine faint. His mouth tightened into a straight line. He should have guessed as well that she would do something insane like fighting off a man twice her size for that blasted quilting bag.

If you told her the truth... No, it was too late for that now. Although she trusted him no more than he had trusted those two thieves, she would have every reason to fire him if she discovered what he had not told her. One way or the other, he was going to have to reveal enough of the truth so she would not jeopardize herself for something worthless. If she had not been scared completely free of her wits, she would have jumped more fiercely on his comment about everyone in Philadelphia knowing where the Friedlanders lived.

"Tea for the lady," he murmured as a porter glanced at him.

The man's face was a sickly shade of gray, but he tried to smile politely. "Here?"

Matt nodded. He doubted if Chandelle could have walked forward to her seat, for she wobbled with every breath she took.

When the floor shifted beneath his feet, he frowned. Then he smiled grimly. The train crew must be keeping the thieves somewhere away from the passengers until they could be turned over to the authorities at the next regular stop.

"Why don't you sit down, Chandelle?" he asked, easing her into the closest chair.

The train lurched, banging him into the wall. He cursed and rubbed his head as the car stopped again. What was wrong now?

Before he could ask, the conductor announced, "Sorry, folks. The locomotive was damaged by this band of thieves. It will be a slow trip to the next station, where we'll have to wait for another locomotive to be brought to continue on to Washington." His smile became as bright as his gold buttons. "You'll be glad to know that we captured three of them before the others ran off. They're under guard in the baggage car."

A cheer resonated through the car. Turning his back on the celebration, Matt knelt by Chandelle.

"Are you going to be all right?" he asked.

She did not answer.

"Chandelle, are you going to be all right?"

The only sound from her was sobs.

He frowned. Panic he could deal with, but not this gentle hysteria. This called for drastic measures, so . . . He took her hand between his and asked, "Are you going to be all right, honey?"

Her head snapped up. "What—what did you call me?"

Matt almost laughed, but that would make matters worse. "I asked if you wanted sugar or honey in your tea."

"I thought you said—Never mind." She looked at the cup of tea the porter had set beside her. "Either will be fine."

"Is this the woman?" asked the conductor as he strode toward them. He grasped the sides of the door when the train staggered a few more yards forward. "Are you the woman who saved this car?"

Matt rose and stepped aside while the conductor congratulated Chandelle on her exceptional courage. As the conductor extolled how she had managed to subdue both thieves by herself, other passengers crowded around to congratulate her and thank her.

Folding his arms over his chest and resting his shoulder against the wall, Matt watched in silence. He considered telling the fawning men to give Chandelle some time to regain her composure, but remained where he was. Maybe now she would understand why he had told her he had no intentions of playing the hero. In spite of the discomfort and embarrassment that added a pretty pink to her colorless face, he guessed it would take more than this one lesson to teach her that being a hero was a very dangerous business.

He hoped the next lesson was not her last.

8

CHANDELLE PACED IN FRONT of the single window in the small station north of Charlottesville. They should have reached Philadelphia after midnight tonight, but they were still hours away. Nothing had gone right since the beginning of this trip north. It was as if the closer she got to Philadelphia and the chance to obtain Grandma's coming home quilt, the more obstacles were placed in her way.

The clacking of the telegraph was muted by the shade drawn down over the window where tickets were sold. A single lantern burned by the cold stove that was pocked from where chewing tobacco had been spit at it. Odors of dust and sweat clung to the room, but, outside, a summer thunderstorm was throwing rain viciously at the station.

Lightning flashed through the room, illuminating the family huddled together on the other side of the stove. The woman, who was traveling with two small children, had introduced herself as Mrs. Dulles before she fell asleep at the same time the youngsters did.

Chandelle wished she could share their slumber. Her body ached from hours of sitting, and her head still rang from the big thief's abuse. All she wanted was to fall into a soft mattress and sleep until she could sleep no more.

All she wanted... Her gaze turned toward the office where Matt's silhouette was a dim shadow against the discolored shade. The thing that had gone most wrong since the beginning of this trip north was her peculiar attraction to Matt Winchester. How many times had Grandma warned her about the dangers that awaited the unwary woman who let herself be beguiled by a fast-talking man whose promises had about as much substance as the colors of a rainbow? She knew the dangers, but she was tempted to throw aside common sense for another kiss.

She looked out at the storm. Holding one of those lightning bolts in her hands would be smarter than letting him woo her into his arms again. So why was she thinking of nothing else? All her thoughts should be concentrated on how she would approach Captain Friedlander and request the return of her grandmother's coming home quilt.

Door hinges creaked. Matt emerged from the office where the telegraph operator was writing intently whatever message was coming over the wires. He wore a grim expression. She edged around the back-to-back benches in the middle of the station and went to meet him.

"Matt, I've been thinking that we should give my free room to Mrs. Dulles." That was one of the biggest lies she had ever spoken. She had not been thinking of anything but his warm mouth. Struggling to keep her gaze from flitting to his lips, she added, "I'm sure she can't afford to pay for a room in town, so that is why she is planing to spend the night here."

"Then she's going to have company." His voice was as gloomy as his expression.

"No, she can have the free room the train company gave me for tonight. We can rent two other rooms."

"A nice idea, but the hotel here by the station is full," he said softly.

Chandelle hesitated, then glanced at the woman, who looked only a bit older than her children. "All right. She can have my room, and I'll make other arrangements."

"You don't understand, Chandelle. The hotel is full without you. It seems that the other passengers took advantage of the train crew keeping you busy with their thanks. That free room the train line offered you in exchange for saving their passengers has already been rented for the night."

"Oh." She was not sure what else to say. She had been looking forward to a good night's sleep in a comfortable bed.

"There is another hotel about three miles from here if you want to walk." He scowled at the ticket office. "This town doesn't have a livery, and the stationmaster feels it would be bad for business if he woke someone up to take us out there. As you can see, this hero business isn't all that you might have thought it would be."

She sighed. As exhausted as she was, she could have been tempted to give in to tears if she had any left. She sank to sit on the bench in the middle of the small room. "I guess we're going to have to stay here, too."

"Maybe I should have bought us berths on the sleeper car."

"Are there any berths left?"

He shook his head. "The few that hadn't already been sold were going for a hefty premium even before we arrived here. I should have taken more notice of the bidding going on among the passengers and gotten the crew to promise you one of those for tonight."

"You should have."

"Now that sounds more like the Chandelle McBride I know." When he smiled, she let her shoulders sag from their stern stance.

"What else did the telegraph operator have to say?" she asked as he sat beside her.

"Another locomotive should be here before noon."

"Noon?" She groaned. "That means another day of traveling. Grandma will be wondering what has happened to me if she doesn't hear from me soon."

"Do you want to send her a telegram from here?"

She sighed. "No, because I told her I would send it when I reached Philadelphia. In her condition, it's probably better if she doesn't know about all this." She glanced out the window to where the train lurked like a dead creature on the rails. "Can't we sleep in our seats on the buffet car?"

"Apparently not. The roof has sprung a leak." He chuckled. "I heard folks saying it's your fault."

"Mine?"

"They were muttering about a bullet going through the roof when you attacked the robbers."

"But the gun never fired."

"True, but they've convinced themselves it did. Maybe it makes them feel better that they sat on their hands while you saved them." His smile disappeared. "The telegraph operator said something about the authorities needing to get in our car and that the crew has to clean it up. I get the feeling that the car will be left behind when we go on to Washington tomorrow." He relaxed against the slatted bench. "I assume they'll bring another car in with the locomotive. I've kind of gotten used to the comforts of a Pullman car."

"Robbers and all?"

"Those are the risks you face when traveling with the upper crust."

She faced him and smiled. "Do you take anything seriously, Matt?"

"I try not to, because then I might have to take myself seriously." He looked past her as a distant expression filled his eyes. "I once took myself and everything around me very, very seriously. Everything needed to be an impassioned success, a triumph over everyone around me. I couldn't win unless someone lost." His smile returned as he looked at her again. "I figured the odds were that I couldn't be a winner all the time, and I didn't want to be a loser, so I decided not to take the rules of the game seriously. Then there didn't have to be winners and losers."

"That's a very cynical attitude."

"An appropriate one for tonight." He grimaced as he ran his hand along the slats. "I don't think one can keep from being cynical when this is where one is going to sleep tonight."

"One should be grateful."

"*One* is because two are going to be spending the night here."

Chandelle flushed. Wishing she could halt the high color that rose up her face every time he made a crude remark, she knew it was futile. She had been able to tease her cousins about things like this and never once was bothered by their bawdy retorts. With Matt, it was different. Maybe because with her cousins, she had known that the jesting was no more than words.

The door to the station opened, and a man walked in. He pulled a watch from his pocket. Glancing at it, he looked at them and at Mrs. Dulles and her children. A frown lengthened the jowls on his sallow face.

"Wait here," Matt said as the man strode past them and went into the office where the tickets were sold. The sound of the telegraph filtered out before the door closed behind him. "I don't like the looks of this."

Chandelle wondered what he had seen that bothered him, but he was following the man into the station's office before she had a chance to ask. She chafed her tired eyes with her hand. They were heavy from being flooded with tears. How foolish she must have looked sitting there on the Pullman car with her eyes leaking like a rusty roof while everyone was lauding her!

Now she could admit that Matt had been right all along. She had been crazy to try to save her bag when her very attempt to sneak it away had convinced the robber that it held something he wanted. Yet she would probably do the same thing all over again, even knowing what she did now. She had not been willing to reveal to Matt how precious her coming home quilt was. She could endure his teasing about other things, but not this. Maybe he held nothing sacred, but this family tradition was her sole guidepost when she was traveling so far from home.

She brushed her hand along the bag that was stained from whatever had been in the corner of the buffet car. No one but a McBride woman comprehended the depth of the connection between a coming home quilt and the woman who pieced it together. It was an ongoing segment of a larger design, an endlessly written story of birth and growth and death but one without an end, because each quilt was created from one sewn before it.

Grandma had given her the quilt that she was using for the backing of her quilt on her fifth birthday. By then, Chandelle had learned most of the stitches needed to sew clothes, so Grandma had decided it was time for her to learn the family skill of quilting. With the quilt had come a half dozen patches that were already waiting for Chandelle to tack them together and quilt them to the backing. Those first, hesitant stitches were uneven, but that was part of the joy of a coming home quilt. The past was a part of the future. She enjoyed touching the special metal buttons that had been on one of the baby dresses her mother had made.

She had found a box of clothes in a trunk, and Grandma had explained that Chandelle's mother had sewn them from whatever scraps they could find as the war drew to a close. Although Grandma had suggested more than once that leaving the rather large buttons on the quilt would be a nuisance in the years to come, Chandelle had included them in her design as a remembrance of the mother she could not remember.

The office door slammed with a vengeance, and she looked up. She was about to chide Matt for risking waking the children when she saw his formidable scowl. Coming slowly to her feet, she wished he had looked like this on the train. She suspected this expression would have daunted the robbers without a word being spoken.

"It's official," he said. "The new locomotive won't be here until tomorrow morning."

"That's no surprise."

"This may be. The stationmaster wants to close the station for the night."

"Close the station?" She gripped her bag. "But where does he expect us to go?"

"The hotel."

She shook her head in disbelief. "Matt, you said there are no rooms available tonight. Didn't you tell him that?"

"I did, and he suggested that we get a room at the other hotel."

"The one three miles away?"

"One and the same."

"You told him that we'd have to walk in the rain?"

"I didn't say he was reasonable. He wants to close the station down, so he can go home to his cozy bed." He sighed. "Not that I blame him. Right now, I'd like to be in a cozy bed." His arm snaked around her waist, pulling her up close to him. "Do you want to be a part of my fantasy of being in a cozy bed, Chandelle?"

"You are horrible!" She slapped his arm, but he refused to release her.

"It's just a fantasy. There's nothing wrong with a bit of imagination." He pressed his cheek against hers, so his whisper rushed through her bonnet, tantalizing her ear. "You have fantasies, don't you, Chandelle?"

"Whether I do or not is none of your business."

"Ah, but you are my business."

Shivering as his warm breath swirled across her, bringing the memory of his mouth on hers, she drew back. His arm kept her from turning away. Lured to him by the promise of pleasure gleaming in his eyes, she could not keep her hands from curving up around his shoulders. That promise became the glitter of conquest in the moment before his lips found hers.

Her concerns evaporated away as she melted against him. His hard chest refused to yield when his arms tightened around her, holding her so close that she could not breathe. She did not want to breathe. All she wanted was the rapture of this kiss.

At the sound of a soft cry, Chandelle ripped herself out of Matt's arms. She whirled to see that the children were still asleep along with their mother. One of them must have whimpered while turning on the hard bench.

Matt put his hands on her shoulders, urging her to lean against his strength, to be captured anew in the seductive trap he had devised with his kisses. She shrugged off his hands and her own desire to cede herself to that craving, no matter the cost. Tossing aside everything that mattered to her in an unseemly public display could ruin more than her reputation.

"I think I should speak to the stationmaster myself," she said, brushing her abruptly cold hands on her gown.

"Chandelle—"

"Don't try to stop me, Matt." She knew she should look at him, but she was afraid to. Then she might see the whetted hunger he had created within her.

"I'm not trying to stop you. I saw how impossible that was on the train." He kissed her cheek lightly without turning her toward him. "For good luck."

Wanting to say something, Chandelle hurried around the bench to go to the office. Anything she said might complicate things more. If that was still possible. She had never guessed that her uneasiness about hiring Matt might lead to this overwhelming craving for his touch.

Grandma's coming home quilt! She must keep finding the quilt the only thing on her mind. Once she returned it to Grandma, then . . . She did not know what might happen then. Matt Winchester had made it very clear that he held all ties in contempt.

Chandelle pushed thoughts of that uncertain time from her head as she entered the cramped office. If someone had been selling tickets, it would have been too crowded for the telegraph operator to move his chair out from the counter where the telegraph was now silent. Slips of paper and tickets cluttered the shelf that ringed the room at waist height. In the corner by the telegraph operator's chair was a long stick with a forked end. A roll of string waited beside it. She knew it was for passing information about upcoming track conditions to trains that barely slowed on their way north.

"What do you want?" asked a disagreeable voice.

She affixed her warmest smile in place as she looked at where the stubby stationmaster was puffing on a cigar that was even thicker than his fingers. The gray smoke stripped away more life from his cadaverous face where his skin hung as if he had been recently ill.

Letting a sugary gentleness lengthen her drawl, for Grandma had told her often how Yankees were affected by a lady's tone, she asked, "Are you the stationmaster, sir?"

"I'm Carlson."

"A pleasure to meet you, Mr. Carlson, despite these distressful circumstances." She held out her hand. "I am Chandelle McBride of Asheville, North Carolina."

"Miss McBride." He dipped his head and glanced at the telegraph operator. "This is Fred."

"Sir," she said with the same polite nod in his direction.

The young man became as red as his flannel shirt and mumbled something before spinning in his chair as the telegraph began to click.

"Will we disturb him with our conversation?" Chandelle asked.

"No."

She hoped she could inveigle more than two words in a row from Mr. Carlson. Dabbing at her eyes as if they were filled with tears, she whispered, "I do need to speak with you."

"About the station's closing?"

He was direct, so she would be, too. "I know how agonizing the whole of this unfortunate situation must be to you, sir."

"Nothing a good night's sleep won't solve."

"I agree." She gave him a glorious smile. "And that's why I'm hoping you will allow me to get one."

"What do you mean?"

"I could not sleep tonight knowing that Mrs. Dulles and her children had no place to spend the night." Widening her eyes, she dropped her voice to a whisper. "Could you?"

He shuffled his feet on the dusty boards, reminding her of Thad scuffing the dirt with his bare feet. "Miss McBride, you have to understand that rules are rules. No one can sleep here when the station is closed."

"I understand, but . . ." She sighed deeply and watched as his gaze riveted on her breasts. She was glad that the telegraph operator was here, even though Fred was concentrating so deeply on the incoming message that she doubted he would have noticed anything short of a train coming through the wall. "This is so disconcerting. I swear I shall weep the night away at the thought of that poor woman and her children out in the rain."

"Miss McBride—"

She put her hand on his arm and pretended to wipe her eyes again. "Oh, dear, how can I stand the thought of them abandoned by the very ones who could help them?"

"There is the hotel on the edge of town."

"Would you send a mother and two small children out into that storm?" As if on cue, a roll of thunder shook the station like a passing train. A child's cry from the waiting room added the perfect touch.

Mr. Carlson's long jowls drooped, and she knew she had reached his heart. Taking a puff on his cigar, he looked over his shoulder. "Fred, stay here tonight in case a message comes from the Virginia Midland Railroad offices about the arrival of a new locomotive."

Fred faltered in his writing. "All night?"

"You heard me."

"Yes, sir." He bent to this task again, tapping on the telegraph.

Chandelle guessed he was asking for a repeat of what he had missed. She wanted to thank Fred, but did not want to interrupt him again. Instead she said, "I am so grateful to you, Mr. Carlson. Your generosity is heartwarming."

Muttering something, he opened the door. She took the hint and went out into the waiting room.

Matt stood as Chandelle walked toward him, smiling. He grinned, unable to mistake the sense of triumph in her light steps. That the stationmaster had not been able to turn a deaf ear to her appeal—both her words and the allure of her slender curves—was no surprise. No man on their travels so far had been immune to it, not even him.

Thunder thudded again against the station, tearing his gaze from her. Rain clawed at the window, as desperate to get in as he was to stay out of the storm. But even that storm was not as powerful as the craving gnawing at his gut when Chandelle was near. Too bad she insisted on holding on to her ladylike demeanor. The hints he had enjoyed of the passion that waited behind it made him eager for more. He guessed, if he were to suggest sharing more, he would get a slap across the face and no ticket to Asheville. As close as he was to Philadelphia and the chance to smooth over some of the rough spots in his past, he could not destroy that by trying to persuade Chandelle that this trip did not have to be all business.

Son of a gun! He should have listened to his own warnings two days ago that getting mixed up with this blond vixen was a shortcut to trouble.

"Good news," she said, grasping his hands. "We can stay here tonight."

"How did you manage that?" He tightened his hold on her hands. "You didn't promise something you shouldn't have, did you?"

As he had expected, she yanked her hands away. That sultry sparkle in her eyes was meant to be a warning of her temper, but he liked it. More than he should.

"Will you please remember yourself?" she asked in that prim tone that always made him grin. "There are children here as well as ladies."

"It was an innocent question. If you assumed otherwise, that is your mistake."

"I doubt if anything you have done for a very long time could be described as innocent."

He let a grin settle on his lips. "If you'd made that a bet, you'd have won again."

"I didn't think you liked winners or losers."

He recoiled at her pointed words. He had no more sense than a sow's suckling if he did not recall how skilled she was at throwing his own words back at him. Fool that he was, he should have known better than to give her ammunition. She was already too aware of too many of his shortcomings.

Chandelle was amazed when Matt walked away without a reply. As she was about to follow, Mr. Carlson came out of the ticket office. She sighed and sat on the hard bench.

Her retort had been aimed at wounding Matt because he had teased her about her grand victory. Although she wanted to blame her words on fatigue, she knew better. They must devise a truce before they reached Philadelphia. There, she might have to depend on him, even when he riled her into losing her temper.

She said nothing as Mr. Carlson went out the door, smoke from his cigar trailing like low-lying fog. A flash of lightning was followed closely by thunder, but not as close as it had been even moments before. The savage storm was passing. Now all she needed to do was find a way to ease the tempest brewing between her and Matt.

"No new tidings on when the locomotive will be here," Matt said as he came to where she was waiting. "He said we'd know when we heard three long blasts that the train was ready to pull out. That's how they plan to rouse everyone staying at the hotel."

"I'm sure we'll hear it when it arrives."

"I'm sure."

This was the conversation of strangers, and, although she was not sure how she would describe what they were, they were no longer strangers. Taking a deep breath, she said, "Matt, if I hurt your feelings—"

"Naw," he said in an easy copy of her drawl. "Just tired, Chandelle. Both of us." He sat beside her on the bench. "Are you sure staying here tonight was such a good idea? This bench is hard."

"At least it's not soaked with rain."

Stretching out his legs, he said, "Your way of looking at everything in a positive light can get real annoying."

"There's a lot about you that's annoying." She gasped. What had Grandma told her? *Think before you speak.*

"So I've been told." He grinned, then drew his hat forward over his forehead. Then he tilted one corner of the brim aside far enough so one eye peeked out. "But I bet you've never been told by a man, 'Snuggle up beside me, Chandelle, and get some sleep.' "

She bit her lip and stared at her fingers that were locked so tightly in her lap that her knuckles grew as wan as her spirits. Even though he was trying to tease her, his words taunted her with the fact that the war which had stolen her grandmother's coming home quilt had also taken Chandelle's father. No man had ever lived in their home, for her father had been gone before she was born.

Father... So often she had tried to imagine what her father looked like. She had spent hours as a child looking into a glass and trying to decide which of her features she might have inherited from him. His height, she guessed, because she towered over most of her cousins. Her light coloring and blond curls were like no one else's on the mountain, so they must have been a legacy from him as well.

She had tried to imagine him coming in the house after a long day's work and holding out his arms to pull her into a big hug. She had watched her cousins sharing a hug with their fathers as well as a special link of laughter and good-natured teasing. She had watched only, except for her dream of having a father of her own.

"What is it?" Matt asked.

Blast his eyes that never missed anything!

Letting anger coat her grief, she snapped, "Isn't it enough that you are teasing me with your crude comments? You could lower your voice so it didn't ring off the top of the station."

"Chandelle—"

"I know it bothers you to curtail your mannerless ways for even a heartbeat, but please keep your dismay about that to yourself."

"Chandelle," he said in a taut whisper, "you should at least give a man a chance to apologize before you jump down his throat."

"Apologize?"

"For obviously probing too closely to something that bothers you."

She stiffened. Somehow, she must have betrayed her true feelings. "It's nothing."

"If you say so."

"Let's get some sleep."

Closing her eyes, she tried to shut out the view of Matt's sympathetic face. Why couldn't he remain a bother instead of proving there was more to him than the ill-mannered ruffian who acknowledged that he would do anything for a few dollars?

Matt kept his eyes open. He was too exhausted to sleep. Listening to the incessant clattering of the telegraph and the snores from one of the children, he put his arm on the back of the bench, curving his hand around Chandelle's arm. He knew she must be asleep when she did not protest. Her head teetered, and he guided it toward his shoulder. The flowery aroma of her perfume swept over him as it had when he had sat next to her on the train. But then, while napping, she had rested her cheek against the shutters, determined to keep an appropriate distance between them. That seemed like months ago, although less than two days had passed.

He smiled. He was, he had to admit, glad he had taken this job. If he had sent her on her way, he never would have discovered the contradictions that were such a large part of Chandelle McBride. She was a gloriously beautiful woman and an artless child. She was a well-mannered lady, and she carried that flask of moonshine liniment and played cards like a sharper. She was . . .

She shifted in her sleep, her hand drifting across his thigh.

He sucked in his breath before his gasp could explode out, waking her. The fragile, innocuous caress of her fingers sent sensations that were anything but innocuous roiling through him. He gripped the iron arm of the bench to keep from sweeping her even closer and showing her that Sleeping Beauty's dreams had only begun to come true when her prince woke her with a kiss.

He grumbled a curse as her breath puffed soft heat against his neck. The pliant curve of her breast grazed his arm with each motion. Across his leg, her fingers splayed with the intimacy of a lover. Sleeping Beauty had never slept like this.

And he was no prince. He knew that all too well. How

many times had she lambasted him for lacking the manners of a gentleman? The only thing he cared about right now was how her hair curled up along his cheek and those fingers . . . those enticing, exciting fingers whose very ingenuousness and trust stoked the fierce fire eating at his gut. It was a hot hunger that had nothing to do with how little he had eaten tonight, but everything to do with this beguiling woman.

He slowly released his hold on the bench, watching his shadowed fingers rise toward her face. With a groan, he dragged his hand back.

The hushed sound must have reached Chandelle because she stirred, lisping words that made no sense, save for one.

"Grandma."

Unable to utter as much as a curse, he lifted her hand off his leg and edged away along the bench. He had promised to help her find that stupid quilt before her grandmother died. That was all he was supposed to do for her.

This was, he admitted as he tried to sleep, the very worst time to decide to play the sacrificing hero. He doubted if he could keep up the role much longer, even though he knew stopping might mean disaster for Chandelle and her grandmother.

9

"OH, MY!" CHANDELLE PAUSED in the middle of the train platform and slowly turned to look in every direction.

The building ahead of them was the largest she had ever seen, even grander, in her opinion, than the station in Washington, D.C. The arched glass over the tracks as they had entered the Pennsylvania Railroad's Philadelphia station should have warned her that the building would be as glorious. The gates into the station were wrought iron twisted in different patterns to complement the magnificent building and the powerful locomotives puffing with impatience beside the platforms.

"Stop gawking," Matt ordered, taking her hand and drawing it into his arm as they walked toward where her trunk would be waiting. "Some pickpocket will take note of you as a tourist and think he can relieve you of your money in no time."

"Pickpockets? Here? Where?" She scanned the busy platform. No one seemed to be paying attention to them. The other passengers rushed along as if trying to make up for time lost on the trip north.

He laughed. "My dear Miss McBride, they do not wear uniforms announcing their trade, you know."

"I can wait in the ladies' waiting room while you retrieve my trunk, if you think that is better."

"That may not keep you and your purse safe. Pickpockets come in all ages and both genders. Just because you are called the gentler sex does not mean that you do not have some among you who are far from gentle." He gave her a superior grin. "And when did I say that *I* would retrieve your trunk?"

She lifted her hand off his arm. "Forgive me. I forget that false gentlemen of your particular ilk come in all sorts of disguises as well."

"There's nothing false about me. I told you that I'm no gentleman."

"More times than I care to remember."

He halted her from walking away by stepping in front of her. As the other passengers flowed around them in a steady stream, he did not touch her. Something unseen connected her to him, again separating them from everything else.

"And what will you remember about me?" he asked, not needing to lower his voice because dozens of conversations flew across the platforms, passengers and train crews and station employees.

She should have a quick, sharp retort, something to flay that superior smile right off his face. She should pick some words that would remind him, once and for all, who was in charge of this quest to find Grandma's quilt. She should, but, when he took her hands in his, she was sure her gloves had dissolved to let the heat of his fingers burnish hers with molten pleasure.

"Shall I tell you," he asked, drawing her a step closer, so his words puffed against the wisps of hair escaping from her bonnet, "what I shall remember about this journey?"

"It might be better if you don't."

"I thought you wanted honesty from me."

"What I want and what I expect to get are two different things."

With a chuckle, he raised one of her hands to his lips and then the other. "That is the most honest thing either of us has ever said." He brushed her right hand with a more prolonged kiss as his thumb stroked her palm. "And that is also the saddest thing either of us has ever said."

"Matt, we should—"

"I know we should." His laugh was disarming, but his gaze was a steady flame she knew was dangerous. "But we shan't, shall we?"

How could he twist every conversation into an intimate debate where she must counter each remark and stand guard against his next parry?

Grinning, he placed her hand on his arm. "Red is such a charming color on your cheeks."

"One I'd rather not wear." She walked with him to the room where the arriving passengers could claim their baggage.

They were above street level, which surprised her. She had heard of raised rails, but train tracks seemed too massive to be lifted from the earth to cross the arches that reached from one concrete pillar to the next. Tempted to put her hands over her ears as one of the locomotives rang its bell and the sound resonated beneath the roof and bounced off the walls on either side, she hoped all of Philadelphia was not this noisy.

She was glad to see only one other person standing by the arriving passengers' luggage window beneath the brick arch with its thick keystone. So close, so close she was to getting Grandma's coming home quilt. Waiting here even a second longer than necessary was a torment.

"Whoa!" Matt said with a chuckle.

"What?"

"You act like a horse about to begin a race. Slow down, Chandelle. You've waited almost twenty years to get this quilt. A few minutes more won't be a problem."

"My grandmother may not have those few extra minutes."

He frowned. "Why are you assuming the worst? She could get better."

"I hope you are right, but I can't dally when you may be wrong. If—"

"Look at what happened to these!" The shout from the arriving passengers' luggage window rose over the other noise. "They are ruined."

Chandelle stared in dismay at the satchel and pair of bandboxes that were dented as if they had been placed on the tracks instead of within the baggage car. "Oh, my!"

"Don't worry," Matt said with a hearty chuckle. "I gave the porter in Asheville a good tip to make sure that your trunk wouldn't be included in any baggage-smashing."

"Baggage-smashing?"

He tapped the tip of her nose and laughed again when she drew back. "The lads on the train get bored. Sometimes they decide to see how many tosses it will take for a piece of luggage to break."

"That's horrible."

"Greasing the right palm keeps it from happening to your luggage." He stepped up to the window and leaned one elbow on the counter. "I believe those two shirts on the floor there also belong to this gentleman."

The porter rushed to pick them up and, with a sheepish expression that hinted he was trying not to grin, handed them to the furious man.

"Thanks, friend," grumbled the man as he stuffed the now dirty shirts into the broken box. He pumped Matt's hand and strode toward the gates into the station.

Chandelle looked into the luggage area and smiled as she saw her trunk was unharmed. When the porter glanced at her, she pointed to her trunk and said, "That one is mine."

"Good afternoon, miss," he replied with an accent that was oddly like Matt's.

She reminded herself that Northerners sounded much the same. "May I have my trunk please?"

"Do you have your tag, miss?" he asked.

"My what?"

"The brass tag," Matt said, "that the porter in Asheville gave you. Its number will match the one hooked to your trunk."

"It's in my bag."

"You need to get it out now, Chandelle."

She scowled as she opened her bag. Matt had no reason to speak in a tone that suggested she was an imbecile. The sleep she had snatched last night had not been deep, and the patchwork of dreams had been unsettling. Usually she was more alert than this.

Pulling out a section of her quilt to search under it, she was tempted to remark that Matt looked even worse than he had the morning they left Asheville. His cheeks were darkened by his beard, and there were lines in his forehead she had not seen before. It would serve him right if they remained, after he had glowered at her so often!

"Did you lose it?" he asked impatiently.

"It's in here."

The porter grinned. "Plenty of time, miss."

Now both of them were being condescending to her. She would have been tempted to give them a piece of her mind, but she was not certain if she could spare any now. Fishing through the bag blindly, she plucked out the brass tag. She handed it to the Pennsylvania Railroad porter.

"Thank you, miss." He looked again at Matt. "Do you have a carriage waiting, sir?"

"We'll be needing one of the railroad's carriages." He held out a coin to the porter. "I trust you can arrange that."

He tipped his cap. "It will be waiting under the arches for you, sir. I'll have your trunk delivered there."

"Thank you." Turning to Chandelle, he asked, "Would you like to refresh yourself before we leave the station?"

She would have liked to have taken a nap for about three hours, but she simply nodded. Splashing some cool water on her face might wash away the cloying fatigue.

As they entered the station, her exhaustion was forgotten. This station dwarfed all the others they had passed. Rows and rows of benches were set in the middle of the room that was bigger than Grandma's house with a ceiling that rose higher than many of the trees on the mountain. A huge map of the United States and its territories claimed one wall above the iron lamps that hung with the elegance of an ancient castle. The whole place reminded her of a picture she had seen in a storybook of a French château. Arched windows decorated with enough stained glass to fill every church in Asheville reached toward the fretwork in the ceiling.

"You're gawking again," Matt said, smiling.

"And you're not?"

"It is pretty gaudy, don't you think?"

"I think it's wonderful." She held her bag close as she slowly turned to look at the whole room. "I'm surprised people don't come here simply to enjoy it."

"Most of them are in too much of a hurry to get to where they are bound."

His words broke her free of the enchantment of this incredible building. How could she be standing here gawking, as he so inelegantly put it, when she should not delay collecting Grandma's coming home quilt?

"If the carriage is waiting for us," she began.

"It will take a few minutes for your trunk to be delivered down to street level." He pointed to a door across the waiting room. "The ladies' waiting room is through there. I shall meet you here in about fifteen minutes."

"Where are you going?" She hated how the question made her sound like a frightened child, but it had already escaped from her lips.

He squeezed her hand. "A man needs some privacy, too, Chandelle." Laughing as that blasted warmth warned her her face was aglow, he said, "I'll be waiting for you right here in fifteen minutes."

Crossing the waiting room, she skipped aside when two women in an obvious hurry almost ran right over her. Other people were rushing as swiftly through the waiting room. Was everyone north of the Mason-Dixon line late? No one stopped to chat as they would have in Asheville, and the expressions worn by everyone other than the children were decidedly grim. Edging around the outstretched legs of a man who was sleeping beneath a newspaper that fluttered on his face, she went into the ladies' waiting room.

Chandelle forced her feet forward as she stared around the room, amazed anew. This room was even more glorious than the other. A fireplace, large enough to heat the great hall of that French castle, was set into an arch in one wall. Colored tiles surrounded the firebox that was empty on this warm day. Curved ironwork marked the hearth to keep anyone from coming too near. Benches that reminded her of the pews in a church edged the wall on either side, and other chairs were scattered across the floor. Women were sitting and talking quietly or trying to entertain young children. No boy old enough for trousers was in the room, and she wondered if they were banished to the men's waiting room as soon as they were out of skirts.

Although sitting for a moment was a tempting idea, she walked into the alcove where sinks waited. She stared at her reflection in the glass. She looked as rumpled and exhausted as Matt. No wonder the porter had treated her with such concern. He probably had feared she would keel over at any moment.

Lifting off her bonnet, she tried to rearrange her hair so it did not look as if she had fought her way through a blizzard. Some of her hairpins were missing, although she had no idea when they might have popped out. She jabbed in place the ones she still had.

This was not how she had imagined she would look when she presented herself at Captain Friedlander's door. She scowled into the glass. Why should she care about making a good impression on Captain Friedlander? He had already made an impression on her family, and it was anything but good. She would be so glad to tell him how much he had devastated her family by stealing their food and trying to steal their souls.

As she came out into the general waiting room in the center of the station, she looked around but saw no sign of Matt anywhere. The clock showed that more than fifteen minutes had passed. Maybe he had gone down to the street to make sure everything was set with her trunk. She took a step toward the stairs leading to the street, then paused. He had told her to wait here. He had also told her that he would be here. Where was he?

"Do you need some assistance, miss?" asked a man,

tipping his hat toward her. His voice was far more polite than his gaze, which swept over her.

"I am fine, thank you." She hesitated, then added, "I'm waiting for my husband."

"Oh." He continued on his way.

The bad taste of the lie clung to her mouth as she edged toward a wall where she would not be so visibly alone. Where was Matt?

Maybe she *should* go downstairs and see if he had gone there. If he had not, she might find herself in a more uncomfortable situation. She knew nothing about Philadelphia, and tales she had heard of the lack of manners in the North she once had dismissed as lingering bad will. Now they all cascaded over her, each with a warning that no lady should ever find herself alone here.

A finger tapped her shoulder. She spun and gasped, "Matt! Thank God, it's you!" She flung her arms around his shoulders, then pulled back, shocked at her own outrageous actions.

"Now that's quite a greeting."

"I thought you might have gone downstairs, and . . ."

He smiled and lifted her hand to his arm. "I told you I would meet you here. I wouldn't leave you to wander all alone around Philadelphia."

A shudder bored through her.

"How can you be cold on a hot day like this?" he asked as he motioned toward the arched doors opening onto the great curving staircase that led down to the street. If he had made any attempt to repair the damage of the past few hours on the train, she saw no sign of it, because his hair was still mussed across his forehead and his cheeks were blackened with whiskers.

"I'm not cold."

"I didn't think you could be. Philadelphia in summer can have temperatures more unbearable than Asheville, much worse than the weather you have up on the mountains." He frowned. "You're shivering. Are you sure you're not cold?"

"No."

"Then why are you quivering like a sacrificial virgin?" He paused on one step and faced her. "You didn't think I would leave you here, did you?"

"I don't know." She was unsettled by having his eyes even with hers. When people pushed past where they stood by the ornate railing, she whispered, "I don't know you well enough to know what you would do."

"I told you I'd help you find your grandmother's quilt and get it to Asheville, and, no matter what you think, I keep my word."

"I didn't mean to suggest otherwise."

He took her hand, bringing her down to stand on the same riser as he did. "Then what is it, Chandelle?"

"I'm really here."

He laughed, the sound rising up to the roof high above them as they continued down the lazy curve of the staircase. "I cannot argue with that, but you still haven't explained what's making you tremble."

"I've been thinking about coming here for so long, and now I'm here. It's like a dream come true."

"A dream come true? I hope you're right, and it's not a nightmare come true." His face grew blank again, and she knew he had once again said something that he thought revealed too much. He need not have worried, because she had no idea what he was referring to.

As they reached the ground level, Chandelle's ears were battered by the noise of the street. Carriages and a horse-drawn trolley reluctantly shared the street with pedestrians and drays. Somewhere, men were hammering. Shouts from peddlers came from every direction. The shriek of a departing train drowned out all of it.

She looked out into the sunshine as she walked with Matt toward a row of carriages that were the same maroon as the Pennsylvania Railroad cars. Although there were many types of carriages from simple hansoms to elegant opera carriages, each one had "Pennsylvania Railroad Company" painted on its door.

"My, it's loud here," Chandelle said when they paused

by a hansom carriage that was large enough to carry them and her trunk.

"It'll probably be louder on the other side of the Schuylkill," Matt replied.

"Schuylkill?"

"The river on this side of the city. The Delaware River is on the other side."

"You seem to know a lot about Philadelphia."

"I lived here a while back." He handed her into the rented carriage.

"Why didn't you say something about that before?"

"It didn't seem important."

She gazed at the buildings visible through the large arches while Matt oversaw the storing of his satchel and her trunk in the carriage's boot. Setting her quilting bag on her lap, she hugged it as she smiled. She could not believe she was here. Even when she had stepped on the train in Asheville, she had not quite believed that she was on her way to Philadelphia and her best chance to recover Grandma's coming home quilt.

Matt opened the door to sit beside her. The carriage lurched as the cabbie climbed into the seat at the front.

"Are you staying in Philadelphia long?" the cabbie asked.

"I hope not," Chandelle murmured.

He must not have heard her, because he added, "You should take time to go out to the Centennial Grounds in Fairmount Park. Quite a thing that fair was."

Chandelle wondered what he was talking about until Matt leaned toward her and whispered, "In 1876, Philadelphia hosted a world's fair to celebrate our country's centennial. You must have heard about it."

"Maybe. I'm not sure." She looked out the window as the cabbie drove into the bustling traffic and toward the bridge over the river. "Where are we going?" She frowned when she noted a number on the street sign. "Isn't Rittenhouse Square in the other direction?"

"Yes, but the first thing we need to do is to find a place to stay."

"Stay? If we get the quilt today, we can catch the southbound train at noon tomorrow."

He patted her gloved hand. "I know that's what you want to do, Chandelle, but I'm warning you that it won't be that easy."

"Why not?"

"You're about to accuse a leading citizen of Philadelphia of stealing from a pair of widows. Friedlander isn't going to acquiesce easily."

"Maybe he'll be happy to give me the quilt and get me out of Philadelphia."

"Maybe, but things like this aren't ever simple. For once, listen to the voice of experience."

"Yours?"

He gave her a cocky grin. "Sad as it must seem to you, yes. Just be patient."

"You're asking for the impossible. I don't have time to be patient." *Or the money,* she almost added, but she could not let him know the sorry state of her finances. She knew money was not the most important reason they must hurry, but she did not want even to think that Grandma might die before she could return to Asheville with the quilt.

"I know." He put his hand over her clasped ones.

She wanted to rest her head on his shoulder as she had as she fell asleep last night. Then she could let her cares ooze away in a breathless moment of reveling in the hard comfort of his shoulder and the undeniably male scent of leather and bay rum.

"But, Chandelle," he continued, "I know you want to send a telegram to your grandmother. We can send her one from the Pennsylvania Railroad station or from the B&O station on Chestnut Street. But if someone wants to send you an answer, you need an address where it can reach you. For that, you've got to have a place to stay. Let's find that, and then we'll deal with getting the quilt."

It made sense. Complete sense, but her limited patience had expired when she stepped off the train in Philadelphia. All the time they had been traveling north, she had been able to tell herself she must be patient, because there was nothing she could do to make the train go faster. Here . . . She clenched her hands over her bag to keep from grasping the reins and ordering the horse toward Rittenhouse Square—wherever that might be—and to meet with Captain Friedlander to get Grandma's quilt back.

She was so close to retrieving it.

She hoped.

10

AS MATT HANDED CHANDELLE from the hansom carriage, he said to the cabbie, "Wait while we see if this is suitable." He rushed up the immaculate marble steps as if a vicious dog bit at his heels.

Chandelle followed more slowly. As much as he had teased her about being on edge since their arrival in Philadelphia, he seemed to be wearing a smile that was a tad too brittle. He had not looked once out of the carriage, even when she had pointed out interesting buildings. If she did not know better, she would say he was trying to hide. That made no sense. If he wanted to remain out of sight, why had he agreed to come to Philadelphia with her?

He had not at first. That thought halted her as she was about to step onto the risers. Only when she had mentioned Captain Friedlander's name had Matt decided to accept her offer of employment. That connection again, but she could not see what it was. She did not want to believe that Matt had deserted from Captain Friedlander's command. He would be risking imprisonment if he presented himself to a former commanding officer.

None of this made sense. There must be an answer. She wished she had some clue what it might be.

As if he had just noticed she was not beside him, Matt came down the steps. "Don't fall asleep on the street when you're so close to getting a room."

"I'm wide awake."

"Your eyes were all glassy, and you were staring at nothing."

"I was lost in thought."

"About what?"

She did not want to be false again, but speaking the truth was incomprehensible. "Too many things, Matt. I'm still overwhelmed at being here."

"Here? This boardinghouse?"

"You know what I mean."

"I know that *I* could use a few hours of sleep, and that carriage will start costing more than you can afford if we stand here jawing. This is a nice boardinghouse, and it should be cheap enough for you to get us a couple of beds." He gave her a wicked grin. "Unless you want to save some money and get one."

"You wouldn't like that."

"No?" He slipped his arm around her waist. "What makes you think so?"

"Because you complained about the seats on the train being hard and uncomfortable." She drew away and put her hand on the newel post. "I know you would find sleeping on the floor even worse."

"Not if I had something soft beside me."

"I shall see if the landlady has a dog."

He caught her hand as she climbed the stairs, halting her from reaching for the door. With a slow, deliberate smile, he stepped up beside her. "You didn't mind sleeping beside me last night." He caressed her cheek.

Closing her eyes, she delighted in that eager touch, which, if she wavered as her body urged her to, could be only the beginning of so much more. "Last night," she whispered, "was very different."

"Was it?" He slanted toward her, so she could see nothing but his eyes. His incredible eyes could flash with fury or with laughter. They could be breathtaking and as beguiling as a snake's. Now they threatened to scorch her with the heat that blazed within her at the brush of his fingertips. "Was it really so different?"

"We were well chaperoned."

"So if I invite the landlady to sit in our room, you would fall asleep again in my arms?"

"Matt! The carriage—"

"Blast the carriage!" He put his finger under her chin and tilted it so her lips met his.

She gasped as waves of sensation washed over her, drowning her in her own longing. When she swayed with the rhythms of desire overpowering her, her fingers rose slowly. The harsh lines of his face tempered with her first tentative touch. The sandy coarseness of his cheeks teased her, and his lips parted as her finger traced the curve of his mouth.

No! This was not right. Not here, not now when she should be thinking only of her grandmother's coming home quilt. She tried to force her body away from his, but her bones had dissolved.

She hastily dropped her arms to her sides, and his eyes crinkled with amusement. "I think we should remember we are in public." Frustration honed her words.

Rapping the knocker on the door, Chandelle hoped he would not retort. She was tired. That was what it must be. Otherwise, she would not allow this rogue to treat her like this. Once she had a good night's sleep, she would regain her equilibrium and would be able to concentrate on doing what she had come here to do.

The door opened. A short woman with hair as dark as Matt's peered out. "Yes?"

"Do you have rooms to be let?" Chandelle asked, disconcerted. She was used to having doors thrown open widely for family and strangers alike.

The woman tapped a sign by the door. Peering at it, Chandelle saw the sun-bleached wood was engraved with MRS. COATES'S BOARDINGHOUSE.

"Do you have rooms available?" she asked.

Mrs. Coates did not offer to invite them inside. Instead

she asked, "Did someone send you to me?"

"No," she replied.

"I seldom rent rooms to strangers." She started to close the door.

Matt stepped forward, firing a frown at Chandelle before he offered Mrs. Coates the charming smile that no one seemed impervious to. "We had heard that, but we heard as well on our journey north that your boardinghouse was one of the best in Philadelphia."

"And who told you that?"

"Thomas Borden, ma'am."

Her face softened from its hard expression. "Are you a friend of Mr. Borden's?"

"We have traveled on occasion on the same train, ma'am. He speaks very highly of your hospitality."

Chandelle bit her lower lip to keep her questions from bursting forth. She had not guessed, during the time Matt had been giving the other men a lesson in not trusting the odds, that he had been gathering information to help them. Recalling as well her acrid tone when she had paid him his dollar last night, she wanted to apologize.

Now was not the time, because Mrs. Coates was throwing aside her door to let them enter. The sounds of young children were muted, so they must be coming from beyond the door under the stairs that commanded the otherwise empty hall.

"If you'll follow me, I show you the room I have available." She stared at them. "You only have one bag?"

"Our trunk and another bag are waiting in the railroad cab." Matt's smile broadened. "We did not want to have them left on your walkway if you had no rooms."

"Wise of you. Follow me please." Mrs. Coates led the way up the stairs.

Striped green wallpaper was peeling in one corner where dampness had leaked past a window. Although the gray runner was worn, it was clean. Lovely friezes ran along the curve of the staircase, and she guessed this house had once been a fine, private home. Now it had settled for genteel neglect.

"Have you been traveling long?" Mrs. Coates asked as she withdrew a ring of keys from under her plain apron.

"A day longer than we had planned," Chandelle answered. "Our locomotive was damaged before we reached Washington, and we had to wait for another."

Mrs. Coates clicked her tongue sympathetically. "I know riding on a train is considered the modern way to get about, but I prefer a horse and carriage myself. Take good care of your horse, and it will never fail you. Those iron horses pulling trains are something I could never trust." She turned the key in the door and opened it. "Here you are . . ."

"Chandelle McBride," she answered quietly to the unasked question.

The room was, in truth, two rooms. The main room led to a small bedroom. Through the door, she could see an iron bed with a plain coverlet. In this room, a divan was sagging in front of a tall, narrow window with lace curtains. A pair of tables and one chair were set on a rug that had long ago given up any pretense of a pattern and had become as gray as the runner on the stairs. The room was not stuffy, and a lamp waited to be lit on one of the tables. Compared to what she had known the past few days, this was heavenly.

"My rules are posted by the door. If you have any questions, knock on my door downstairs." Mrs. Coates smiled. "Knock loudly, so I might be able to hear over the children, Mrs. McBride."

Chandelle opened her mouth, but her gaze was caught by Matt's. He shook his head in a silent warning. Her fingers clenched around the strings of her bag. How could he expect her to lie like this? He must have said something to Mrs. Coates to suggest that they were married. But what? She wished she was not so exhausted. Then she would be able to think.

Matt said, "This will be perfect, Mrs. Coates. I assume you rent by the week."

"I prefer by the month." She held out her hand. "That will be forty dollars."

"Chandelle?" Matt asked.

"I'm not sure—"

"I'm sure, if we continue to look for a place to stay, that we will be wasting time better spent in other pursuits."

She flinched. Although forty dollars would take more than half of the money remaining from what Grandma had given her, finding the quilt must be her first priority. Matt was right . . . again! She should forget how bothersome that was and remember what she was here to do.

Reaching into her bag, she drew out the money and handed it to the landlady.

Matt said, "You've given her too much, Chandelle."

Color soared up her cheeks. Why did she get so absent-minded when her mind was full of other things? Taking back two dollar bills, she watched Mrs. Coates stuff the money beneath her apron.

"As I said, Mr. and Mrs. McBride, the rules are posted by the door. The back stairs lead down to the well and the necessary. No liquor is allowed in the rooms. Laundry is picked up on Sunday evening and returned on Wednesday. Breakfast is at six, and supper will be served no later than seven. I'll tell your cabdriver to bring your things up." She was gone before either of them could reply.

"Quite the busy bee, isn't she?" Matt asked as he closed the door. He whistled. "Look at that list of rules. I haven't seen anything like this since I was in school."

"Why do you care when you'll probably break each one as soon you can?"

"Ouch! Certainly giving you a little kiss on the front steps doesn't rate such a nasty remark."

"That would have been enough," she retorted, although she was afraid her face was on fire again at the memory of that too public display, "but lying to Mrs. Coates about us being married is worse."

"She wouldn't have rented us these rooms if she thought we were not sharing a blissful marital state."

"But we should not have lied."

He sat and put his feet on a stool by the chair. Folding his arms across his chest, he need only pull his hat down over his eyes to look exactly as he had when she had entered his office. But she was no longer fooled by his pose. Even when he looked utterly relaxed and without a care, he was watching everything as closely as a cat eyed a mouse's hole.

"I did not think," he said, closing his eyes, "that you'd like to live on the streets. All that mud and the smell and the traffic make it difficult to sleep."

"There are boardinghouses that welcome ladies traveling alone."

"I'm sure there are." He looked up at her, his smile gone. "But do you want to waste time finding one of those or use the time to find your grandmother's quilt?"

Chandelle lowered herself to the chair. "Grandma's quilt, of course."

"That's what I thought, so I decided to use Borden's name to obtain us a place as quickly as possible." He grinned as he locked his fingers behind his head. "And, Chandelle, so you know, I didn't lie. She simply assumed."

"Oh."

Stretching forward, he put his finger under her chin as he had on the steps. "Honey, *you* have to stop assuming that I'm responsible for everything that distresses you."

"I don't." She frowned. "And don't call me that."

"Why not?" His finger spiraled up her cheek to the skin behind her ear. When she gasped at the unexpected thrill in that caress, he whispered, "Your hair is the rich gold color of honey, and I have discovered that your lips are as sweet." His eyes twinkled a warning only a heartbeat before he added, "And you sting like a swarm of maddened bees when your world is upset."

At a knock on the door, he stood. She stared after him, trying to regain her composure while the cabbie brought her trunk and Matt's bag into the room.

Coming to her feet, she watched the cabbie set the trunk at the foot of the bed in the other room. She reached for her bag.

Matt waved Chandelle's money aside as he paid the cabbie, adding a healthy tip for the man's hard work carrying that trunk up the stairs. He never had understood why a woman needed so many things for a short trip. After all, Chandelle had managed quite well with only the things she had stuffed into her bag.

"Thank you," she said as he closed the door again.

"I figured it was the least I could do since you've paid more for these rooms than you planned." He went to look out the room's single window.

The Philadelphia skyline had changed in the years he had been away. Buildings were taller. More of them spread farther away from both rivers, and some landmarks he had thought would stand forever had vanished. He wondered if they had been burned or torn down. Philadelphia, from what he had seen during the ride from the train station, was in the midst of re-creating itself. Maybe after all the work at the Centennial Grounds in Fairmount Park, folks had decided to modernize the rest of the city before the nineteenth century came to an end.

A new city hall, a train station for the Philadelphia & Reading Railroad Company, and dozens of other projects had been discussed with great enthusiasm in the Pennsylvania Railroad station. Soon, everything he had once known as Philadelphia would be gone.

Good! Too bad he could not tear down his memories of this city as easily. He had built new memories that had nothing to do with Philadelphia, but the foundations of what he had been remained.

"This boardinghouse is expensive, but I think we'll find it worth the price." Chandelle's voice made him face her. She had taken off her gloves and was reaching for the ribbons of her bonnet. "I noticed the streetcar line is only a block away."

"Exactly." He sat on the divan and set his feet on a table. "All the comforts of home."

"I'm glad you think so. It doesn't remind me a bit of home."

He looked around the room, glad she had not guessed what was underlying his sarcasm. He had to be careful. She was perceptive, and he did not need her latching on to the truth, because she was sure to try to unlatch it and release all kinds of memories he wanted locked away. Keeping his voice light, he said, "You're right. My rooms in Asheville are not as nice as this. Maybe I'll buy some curtains when I get back."

"How can you live like that?"

"I don't live there often." Weaving his hands together behind his head, he asked, "So what now, boss?"

"I suggest you shave and make yourself presentable while I unpack my things."

"Presentable? For who?"

"Captain Friedlander."

Had her desperation to find her grandmother's quilt completely unhinged her mind? "You want to go to Rittenhouse Square now? We just got off the train."

"Weren't you the one talking about how I didn't want to waste time looking for a boardinghouse?" With her shoe, she shoved his feet to the floor. She laughed when he scowled. "I don't intend to squander it by sitting here while you take a nap."

"You slept last night," he grumbled, slowly coming to his feet.

"And why didn't you?"

Matt was tempted to retort with the truth. Then the fire in her eyes would flash up her cheeks, making them even redder than the center of the bedraggled flowers on her hat. If he spoke of her enticing touch and the promise of delight in her breath through his shirt, she would assume that puritanical pose again. Her hands would be clasped prudishly in front of her, her chin raised with an expression best suited to a schoolmarm disciplining a recalcitrant lad, and her eyes as icy as a wintry storm.

Or would she? Maybe she would realize that her cool façade was in shambles and toss it aside as useless. He almost laughed. Chandelle McBride was as unswerving as a train on a single track. All she thought about was finding that silly quilt. It was all he should be thinking of, too, but he knew that was no longer possible when he grasped her elbows and pulled her to him.

"What are you doing?" she cried.

"If you don't know, I probably need to remind you." He nuzzled her neck. Her sharp intake of breath sent yearning to every muscle. "We aren't in public any longer, honey."

"Will you stop calling me that?"

He laughed. Sparks burned in her silvery eyes. She gasped when he held her even more tightly, and he saw a flare of yearning amid her anger. Her eyes closed as he bent to claim her lips.

When her soft breath grew ragged, her hands encircled his shoulders. He pressed his lips to her throat, tasting the luscious flavor of her skin. Greedily, he recaptured her mouth. This hunger only sharpened each time he kissed her, but he did not care. All he wanted was this pleasure.

He gazed at her as he lifted his mouth from hers. She was so lovely, so perfect in his arms. He had never held a woman like her, neither a woman of her height nor one of her unexplored passion. As her fingers stroked his face, he tipped his head to kiss her palm. He brushed her hair back and gathered her close again.

When he released her with a curse, she stared up at him with unfocused doe-soft eyes that teased him to give in to his yearning to discover each delight she had waiting for him. She whispered his name, and he reached for her before turning away and clenching his hands into fists. He repeated the curse as he walked to the window and stared out of it.

Was he out of his mind? She was, as he taunted her so often, every inch a lady. He was, as he told her even more frequently, no gentleman. Anything other than business between them was an invitation to the trouble he had spent the last few years trying to avoid. Keep things simple had been his motto since he left Philadelphia. It was about time he remembered that.

CHANDELLE TRIED TO KEEP her fingers from trembling as she walked down the front steps of the boardinghouse. The time was finally here when she had the chance to retrieve Grandma's quilt. No wonder she was shaking like a child with the ague.

But, as she watched Matt talking to a carriage driver about taking them to the Friedlander house on Rittenhouse Square, she had to admit that her fingers trembled with the power of the passion he had elicited with his kisses. If he had not stopped...

What was wrong with her? She had never had any difficulty in knowing the right thing to do, but no one had ever tempted her as Matt Winchester did. Tempted her to give herself to the delight of his touch, tempted her to learn more of the man he hid behind his sarcastic remarks, tempted her to fall in love with him. She *was* mad! Men like him did not fall in love, because they never stayed in one place long enough.

"All set, Chandelle," he called.

She tightened her grip on her quilting bag and hurried to the simple carriage that could have been the one they came from the railroad station in, except it did not have the lettering that announced it belonged to the railroad company. When Matt held out his hand to assist her in, she watched her fingers settle on his broad palm. Looking up at his face, she was startled to see regret in his eyes.

Regret? Because he had kissed her or because he had stopped? She could not ask here on the street.

"Why are you bringing your bag?" he asked quietly.

"I thought Captain Friedlander might be more amiable to listening to my request if I showed him my own quilt."

"More amiable?" His eyebrows rose. "I suppose it's possible. We need to hurry, Chandelle. The hour for calls is nearly over."

"You know the rules of making calls?"

"One must know the rules before one can break them." He assisted her in. Stepping up to sit beside her, he hastily released her fingers. He folded his arms over his chest and leaned against the wall of the carriage, putting as much distance between them as possible in the small space.

Chandelle looked out the other window. She should be glad that he realized, more clearly than she did, the absurdity of their situation. As soon as she got her grandmother's coming home quilt, she would return to Asheville and bid him farewell. She would be a fool to let him take her heart with him.

The clatter of the wheels on the uneven pavements urged Chandelle to compose herself. She was so close to her goal. She was wearing her best gown of light blue taffeta with its redingote whose lapels were edged with navy ribbons. The flounced skirt was pulled back to reveal the underdress that was pleated with the same navy ribbons. With mother-of-pearl buttons and lace at her wrists and the high collar, it looked like the one she had seen torn from a magazine whose name had been lost. Her kid gloves were not as stained as her slippers, which were thankfully hidden beneath her gown. Her attempts to fix her bonnet had been futile, so she had stitched the flowers to the brim to keep them from drooping down over her face. She looked her best, although she wondered if she could find a false smile to wear when she greeted Captain Friedlander and requested the return of Grandma's coming home quilt.

"Son of a gun!" Matt grumbled.

"Is something wrong?" That was a stupid question when so much was not right, but she was elated he had broken the dismal silence between them.

"I didn't think he'd turn up Chestnut Street."

"Is this the wrong direction?"

"No, it's the right direction, just the wrong way."

She faced him. Her hopes that he was wearing a grin to go along with his cryptic words faded when she saw his frown. He was not teasing her. "I don't understand."

"Wait a minute. You'll see."

"See what?"

"Look out your window."

Chandelle did and saw a collection of restaurants and businesses facing the street. The carriage paused to allow traffic to cross in front of it, then continued to the next block. With a gasp, she clutched the window so tightly the brads for the curtain dug through her gloves into her fingers.

The letters marching across the mercantile were as tall as the stack on a train. The lack of ornate design that she had seen on other stores they passed announced that this store needed no pretensions. It simply commanded the street.

FRIEDLANDER'S

She stared at the windows, which were filled with a variety of merchandise from furniture to elegant gowns draped next to a sign that stated, NEW FROM PARIS. Each window held something more wondrous than the next. At each of the doors, people were surging in and out in a rush to spend their money at Friedlander's.

"The store really grew," Matt said in a strained voice, "after the Civil War. There was some speculation that the Friedlanders used the war to line their own pockets, but that was never proven."

"I had no idea."

"I warned you that you were about to come face-to-face with one of the most powerful families in Philadelphia."

"Not the most powerful?"

His laugh was whetted. "Close enough. Commerce is what buys influence in this city. Like Rome, in the wake of Julius Caesar's assassination, the retail trade here is ruled by an uneasy triumvirate. Wanamaker has his big store at Chestnut and Thirteenth. Friedlander's is here, and . . ."

When his voice faded away, she saw what he was staring at. Another storefront, this one commanding an even larger portion of its block, displayed the name MATHESON AND SONS across its uppermost story. It had fewer windows, but the merchandise in them was beautifully and tantalizingly displayed. Every door opened and closed with a parade of patrons.

"They are situated so close to each other," Chandelle said. "You would think one of them would have put the other out of business."

"It hasn't been from a lack of trying." His smile returned as they continued along the street. "Rumors of underhanded tricks by both families to force the other out of business flitter about regularly. So far as I know, nobody has proven either guilty of illegal dealings. Money buys lots of loyalty."

"Did you work for one of them?"

"Yes." His gaze drilled her, daring her to ask her next question.

"And that's why you left Philadelphia?"

"Indirectly."

She dampened her lips. For too long, she had delayed in speaking of her suspicions. She could not curb her curiosity any longer, although she did not want to accuse him. "Matt, if you think it better that you do not come with me to Captain Friedlander's house, I understand."

"Do you?"

"Yes." She wished he would make things easy for her once. "I know you may be risking a great deal coming here with me."

"Risking a great deal?" His eyes narrowed.

Unable to halt the words that spilled from her lips, she said, "Lots of young men went through what you went through. Many of them made the same choice that you did."

"And what choice is that?"

"The choice to leave."

He grasped her shoulders. When she winced, he loosened his grip. "Who told you about why I left?"

"I figured it out for myself."

"How?"

She stared at his taut face. This was a stranger, not the man who had held her so beguilingly less than an hour ago. That man would not be lashing questions at her with the cruelty of a slave's overseer. "Matt, I tried to figure out why you were in Asheville although you are so obviously a Yankee. There was only one answer."

"Which is?"

Again she dampened her lips. "I won't turn you in, and you need not face Captain Friedlander if it will jeopardize your freedom."

"Chandelle, you are talking in riddles. Spit it out. What answer have you come up with?"

"You hate Captain Friedlander."

"That's a fact."

"So I surmised that you served with him during the War of Northern—during the War Between the States until you deserted." When he regarded her with astonishment, she hurried to say, "Matt, that's why you don't have to go in with me when I call on Captain Friedlander. If—"

"You think I deserted from the army?" His eyes glittered fiercely, but she could not guess with what emotion.

"You don't have to tell me if you'd rather not." She looked down at her hands folded in her lap. "You proved when the robbers came on the train that you wouldn't desert me, too."

The carriage slowed, but he did not reach for the door. His finger tipped her face up. When he grinned, she searched her mind for something to say. But what?

"Chandelle McBride, you are an amazing woman. I swear you were about to jump into the breach to protect me when more than once you hinted that you would gladly dunk me in boiling oil yourself. However, you are playing the heroine needlessly. I did not desert during the war. I was barely into short pants when it was over."

"But I figured it out. You would have been the right age, if—"

"I had been born a decade earlier." He laughed. "Let me guess. You were all flustered when you made this decision that I had a horrible, dark secret that would keep me far from Philadelphia. Every time you've been upset since we started this trip, you manage to make a massive mistake of any simple bit of figuring. So, all at once, I was old enough to be fighting with Friedlander. Then I've decided that I'd had enough of the war. Quite a leap in logic, Chandelle."

His finger pushed up on her chin, and she knew her mouth was gaping. Somehow, she choked out, "Oh, my! I didn't mean to—I mean, the thought got in my head, and I didn't bother to dislodge it, and . . ." She closed her eyes and sighed. "I'm sorry. I wouldn't blame you if you quit right now."

"Chandelle?" he whispered. "Open your eyes."

She did. "Yes?"

"We're too close to getting what you came here for, for me to quit now. I'm with you to the bitter end on this."

"I hope it's not bitter."

She expected him to chuckle, but he was silent as he opened the door and stepped out onto the walkway. Telling the carriage driver to wait, he handed her out.

"There," he said, pointing at the house across the street, "is where your buddy Captain Friedlander lives."

Chandelle swallowed a harsh gasp as she held her quilting bag in front of her like a shield. The house rose a full story above its neighbors, a consummate monument to the wealth of the family within. A trio of bay windows marked each level of the house. Lace that was finer than what she wore edged the windows, hinting at even greater treasures that were kept out of view of the street.

"Don't be intimidated by the façade, Chandelle," he said with a resurgence of that odd tightness that had filled his voice from the moment the conductor announced their arrival in Philadelphia. "It's just a house."

"Just a house?" She shook her head. "I've never seen anything like it. Those windows must be twenty feet high. The roof of our house in Asheville isn't that high."

"Maybe because you don't feel the need to impress your neighbors after you have robbed them at every possible turn."

She pulled her gaze from the house. His face was as expressionless as his voice. What was amiss now? Although she had known Matt less than a week, never had she seen his face so blank. With a cold shiver, she realized that, although he was not a deserter as she had persuaded herself so foolishly that he might be, there was still some reason why he had agreed to come with her to Philadelphia when she mentioned Esau Friedlander's name. The truth was probably right in front of her, but she could not see it.

He offered his arm. "As long as we're here, we might as well face the lion in his den."

"All right." Her fingers shook when she placed them on his arm.

"If you would rather not . . ."

"Don't be ridiculous!"

His smile was the warmest she had seen since they had left Mrs. Coates's boardinghouse. "Hold on to that fire, Chandelle. If you can keep Friedlander from dousing it, you may best him yet."

"I don't want to defeat him. Only get my grandmother's coming home quilt."

Again Matt did not reply as he led her up the wide steps to the front door that was as intricately decorated as a wedding cake. He lifted the knocker and let it fall once. When she was about to say that no one would hear a single knock in that huge house, the door swung open.

A slender, dark-haired man wearing an immaculate black frock coat appeared in the doorway. "May I help you?"

A nudge from Matt's elbow was an ungracious admonishment to answer.

"Good afternoon," Chandelle said. "I would like to speak with Esau Friedlander."

"Mr. Friedlander—" The butler faltered as he stared at them.

Wanting to make sure her dress was properly closed at the throat with the broach Grandma had given her on her sixteenth birthday, Chandelle instead clenched her hand on Matt's arm. She knew her dress was not the cream of fashion, but she looked her best.

And Matt looked dashing. His coat was as unsullied as the butler's, and his trousers and shirt did not reveal that they must have spent the trip north crammed into his bag. The tips of his boots reflected the afternoon sun, and, with his hair brushed and his mustache neat, he could have belonged in this house.

"Thanks," Matt said as he stepped up into the foyer, bringing Chandelle with him. "We'll be glad to wait in the parlor while you let Mr. Friedlander know he has guests who need to speak with him urgently."

The butler sputtered something, but, when Matt acted as if he had not heard, he rushed toward the back of the house.

A door closed somewhere, trying to steal Chandelle from her admiration of the magnificent foyer. She slowly turned to discover each wall was as wonderful as the one before it. A pair of columns opened up to where the stairs rose to the next floor before disappearing at a sharp angle. A tall-case clock stood beneath the steps leading up to the third floor. Unlike the door, this space was almost devoid of decoration. Even the lines on the columns were simple and the pediments had no design. Rugs woven with flowery patterns were spread across the dark wood floor.

Two sets of double white doors were embedded in the walls on either side of the foyer. Both were closed, but Matt went to one pair, as if he were the master of this house, and threw them open. When she did not follow, he grasped her hand, tugging her into the room beyond.

Matching bay windows demanded her attention. Crimson drapes flowed from either side of the glass, leading her gaze up to the ceiling that was painted with a pattern of flowers that gathered in the center where a crystal chandelier hung from a plaster medallion. The furniture was clumped by the walls, making the room appear even larger. A grand piano, its legs enveloped demurely with a fringed shawl, held court within one bay. The other was filled with a collection of wildly sprouting ferns.

Chandelle walked to the hearth where blue tiles followed the curve of the firebox, which had been closed in with cast iron to burn coal in it. Shaking her head in disbelief, she wondered why a man who had a home like this would have taken her grandmother's simple quilt. It made no sense.

"Close your mouth, Chandelle," Matt said, "before someone comes in and decides you are a candidate for the mental hospital."

She scowled at him.

"And that frown will not make a good first impression either." He smiled tautly. "After all, you are about to accuse the patriarch of the Friedlander family of a heinous crime. It would behoove you to win him over with a smile before you call in the law."

He was right. She knew that, but why did he have to phrase his suggestions with that frigid flippancy? This was no game. Finding Grandma's coming home quilt was the most important thing she had ever done.

"Why don't you sit?" Matt asked as he went to stand in front of a settee that was upholstered in a brilliant gold. Clasping his hands behind his back, he stared up at the painting of a country house hung over it.

"Do you think I should? I mean, it's beautiful, and if I—"

"Enough, Chandelle!" He whirled so fast that his frock coat billowed like an ebony shadow behind him. "If you're so overwhelmed by this show of trinkets, there's no sense in staying to talk to Friedlander. You'll probably end up giving him your coming home quilt, too."

Frowning, she went to the settee in front of the fern-filled window. She sat, placed her bag on her lap, and met his anger with her coolest smile. "I forget that you have little use for honesty. I will try to curb my admiration for this lovely room."

"Try to curb your assumption that the people within this house will somehow be as pleasant as their surroundings. Gilt on a weed does not make it a rose."

"I know that. Do not treat me as if I'm witless."

"Just have your wits about you." His mouth worked as if he were about to be ill, but he said, "You'll need all of them before this is over."

"If you know so much about Captain Friedlander, then tell me what you know. Anything may help."

"Nothing *I* know will help you now."

Angry voices came from the hall, shattering the dignified silence. A man strode into the foyer, looked both ways, then stormed into the room. When he stared at her, Chandelle came to her feet, silencing her apology for being so brazen as to sit before being invited to.

His scowl deepened. She wondered who he might be. Although he was dressed with a casual affluence that matched this house, he could not be Captain Esau Friedlander, for he could not be more than a few years older than she was. His pale hair under his black bowler hat was a shade darker than his thin mustache that emphasized the straight line of his lips as he locked eyes with Matt.

"Who let *you* in here?" he growled. He pulled off his gloves and handed them, his hat, and his walking stick to a young woman who appeared as if he had given a command.

"Your butler," Matt replied, his smile returning.

Chandelle wished it had not, because she recognized that grin. He had worn it when he was about to collect his winnings at the card table. Then he had been delighting in trouncing those who dared to challenge him. But why was he wearing that smile now?

Pushing aside her curiosity, she stepped forward. "Good afternoon. I am Chandelle McBride, and I wish to speak with Captain Esau Friedlander."

"I think not." He brushed at the sleeves of his double-breasted coat as if she were a wearisome gnat he was shooing away.

"You think . . . ?" She bit back the rest of her amazement as she saw the man's lips curl in a smile as icy as Matt's. "May I ask why not?"

"If you wish to waste your breath."

She was not sure how to reply to such overt rudeness. Glancing at Matt, she discovered his face was lost in the glare coming through the bay windows. She resisted the impulse to ask him to move so she could read his expression. *Think before you speak. Speak before you act.*

"Thank you for your warning," she said, keeping her voice pleasant. "However, I shall, as you put it, waste a bit of my breath to ask your name, sir."

"I am Jakob Friedlander."

When he added nothing more, she guessed he believed the name would explain everything. It explained nothing, except that he was related in some way to Captain Friedlander. He might be a son or a nephew.

"Mr. Friedlander, I would very much like to see Captain Friedlander."

"I think not, as I said before." He locked his hands behind his back and bowed his head with the merest of respect. "And as I bid you good day, Miss McBride, I would offer you some advice."

"But—"

"Be wary of what companions you choose, for you shall be judged by them." He turned. "Good day."

Chandelle gasped as he walked out. Before she could take a single step to go after him, Matt's hand on her arm halted her.

"Don't lower yourself to chasing after *him*," he murmured.

She nearly recoiled from the loathing in his eyes as he stared at the empty doorway. She had been right. There was more to this than what the few words had suggested.

"Matt—"

"Not here." His nose wrinkled. "C'mon. The stench is getting to me."

"But Grandma's coming home quilt may be somewhere in this house."

He put his hands on either side of her face and tilted it so her eyes were right below his. "Whether it is or not, you're not going to get it today."

"I can't go home to Asheville without it." She wanted to rest her head upon his strong shoulder and pretend they were traveling, even now, on the train and that this was nothing but a horrible dream.

"I'm not telling you to." When his wry grin returned, she saw the Matt who had been by her side through all the complications of getting here. "You hired me to help you get your grandmother's quilt. That's what I intend to do, but it's not going to be today. Now you know, as you had to, what you are up against here."

"But why wouldn't he let me see Captain Friedlander?"

"Spite, I'm sure. He knows you want something, and he has the power to deny it to you. Let him exult in that for a day or two—"

"A day or two!" she cried. "Matt, Grandma may not have that much time."

"We'll get her quilt. Don't fret. This was only the first confrontation. Now that you see what is ahead of us, we can devise a way to find out if your grandmother's quilt is here."

"I know it must be here still."

"If it is, I will get it for you, Chandelle." He stepped away and held out his arm. As she put her hand on it, he led her to the door where the butler was waiting.

"Good day, miss," he said as he held the outer door open for them. His voice shook as he added, "Sir."

Matt hurried her down the steps. When the door closed resoundingly behind them, Chandelle let her hand linger on the railing. Seeing a curtain pulled aside a finger's breadth on an upper floor, she grasped Matt's sleeve.

"Matt—"

"Not here." He peeled her fingers off his coat and drew her hand within his arm.

"Someone's watching us."

"I guessed that. I'd be shocked if it were otherwise." Leading her to the carriage, he handed her in. He leaned against the dash, his back to the house as if he feared someone might see what he was saying. "This went exactly, I'm sorry to say, as I guessed it would."

"Then why—?"

He put his finger to her lips. "I'll explain everything when this is over, Chandelle. For now, you have to trust me."

She swallowed, trying to dam the tears that wanted to flood from her eyes. A hollow emptiness consumed her, as if nothing remained within her but those hot tears. All her hopes, all her expectations, all that had happened on their trip north, all the things she had planned to say once she could hand Grandma her coming home quilt . . . all had been for naught. "I'm not sure I can trust you or anyone else now."

"I'm not asking you to trust everyone. Just me."

"I'm not sure I can."

"You must." He glanced at the house, then climbed into the carriage. "You must, or any chance you have to get your grandmother's quilt will be gone."

12

CHANDELLE COUNTED OUT THE money to pay for the telegram to let her grandmother know that she had arrived safely in Philadelphia. Why did she feel like such a liar? She had not said anything about meeting Jakob Friedlander, keeping the message to the fact she was here and what her address was.

As she was about to set the money on the counter, Matt reached over and added another two bits. She flashed him a weak smile and set the money in front of the telegraph clerk. The rumble of an arriving train made the station quiver, but the clerk continued with his work as if he did not notice.

"I guess I shouldn't have to ask," Matt said when they reached the street again. "Miscounting the money upstairs warns you are really upset. How are you doing?"

"I'm not really sure." She looked both ways along the street to see which direction the trolley might be coming in. She could not afford to pay over a dollar to hire a carriage to return to Mrs. Coates's boardinghouse when the streetcar was less than a dime. "I imagined a lot of things, but not that I would be refused the chance to speak with Captain Friedlander."

"You seem very calm."

"Do I?"

"Too calm." He put his hand on her elbow and stepped in front of her. "You've got me worried, Chandelle."

"That's a change."

He blinked at her sharp tone, and his smile became rigid. "Do you want to explain that?"

"I don't see any need to when you know as well as I do that you were happy to leave me alone to face those robbers on the train."

"Chandelle, you don't know—" Matt realized he was talking to her back. Blast this woman! When he tried to help her, she threw his assistance in his face. When he let her try to work things out by herself, as she had requested, she became even more furious.

Trotting after her like an obedient pup exasperated him, but he was not about to let her storm back to Rittenhouse Square and make things worse. She had no idea what she was facing there. He did. Or he had. Since he had left Philadelphia, he had cut himself off from everything that was going on in the city. Some things had changed, but he was sure that more had not.

He walked along the street in Chandelle's wake, pausing to buy the day's paper from a newsboy on the corner. He folded it and tucked it under his arm as he caught up with her. Slipping his other arm through hers, he gave her a smile.

She glanced at him and quickly away, but not before he saw the shimmer of tears in her eyes. He scowled. He should be thrilled that she was not all weepy and weak. Having her throw her arms around him and sob would gain them nothing. Yet the quiet desperation in her expression and in her tight steps unsettled him.

"Give the trolley a chance to reach the stop here," he said, slowing his steps so she had to as well. "If you try to outrun it, you'll be exhausted by the time you return to the boardinghouse." With a grin he did not feel like wearing, he added, "It's too hot to be racing about."

She stared at him for a moment, as if she could not

fathom the meaning of his words. Then she stopped. "I guess I hadn't noticed."

"Your flowers have." He tapped the blossoms on top of her hat. "They are wilting again."

Pink tarnished her cheeks, surprising him until she said, "No wonder Mr. Friedlander looked at me as if I were no better than an urchin."

"I suspect he regards everyone as beneath him." He glanced past her when he heard the smooth sound of the trolley's wheels on the track and the clip-clop of the horses pulling it. Seeing the route posted on it, he smiled. "Perfect."

"This is our car?"

"It is now." His grin broadened when she asked what he meant. Instead of answering, he handed her into an empty seat on the open-sided trolley, which was only about half full. He did not wait for her to fumble with the pennies for the fare, handing them to the trolley driver himself. Sitting beside her as the trolley continued along the track, gently rocking from side to side, he said, "As I recall, there is a nice milliner's shop on this route."

"Milliner's shop?"

"I thought I might buy you a new bonnet."

Her head snapped up, and she looked at him directly for the first time since they had left Rittenhouse Square. The sight nearly took his breath away. Her silvery eyes were brightened even more by her unshed tears, her cheeks with their powdering of soft rose, her lustrous lips that teased him to cover them with his own... He dared not look beyond her face, or he doubted if he could keep from pulling her into his arms and kissing her until she was as soft against him as tar on a summer street.

"A new bonnet?" she asked. "Are you crazy?"

"Probably." He rested his arm on the back of the seat, although he did not touch her. It did not matter. Being so close to her made his skin prickle as if he had grabbed the end of a telegraph wire. It was more of an effort than he would have guessed to keep his voice even. "But there's nothing else we can do right now, so we might as well let

Borden and company buy you a new hat to go with that pretty dress."

"I should . . ."

"You have nothing else to do right now."

"But worry."

He could not halt his finger from reaching up to brush her cheek. "Honey, you can worry and let me buy you a new bonnet at the same time."

"No, I must not. It wouldn't be right to accept such a gift from—from—"

"A stranger?" He laughed quietly. "I don't think we are exactly strangers any longer." When she opened her mouth to answer, he added, "And don't consider it an unseemly gift from someone you deem less than a gentleman. It's business. Purely business."

"In what way?"

"You can't look like a street urchin when we go back to Rittenhouse Square, can you?"

"We're going back?" The lustrous glow of joy in her eyes sent fiery sparks erupting through his gut. Next job, he told himself, his boss had to be uglier than sin. How much more temptation could he take?

"Of course. You still believe your grandmother's quilt is there."

"If we go back now—"

"We'll be shown the outside of the door." He tapped her nose and then wished he had not. Even that fleeting touch of her skin against his added to the tempest of need roiling within him. Fisting his hand on the seat, he said, "Let me check with a few people here in Philadelphia who might be able to give me a hint how we should proceed."

"What people?"

"I asked you to trust me, Chandelle."

A smile finally returned to her face, lighting it as if the sun beamed through it. "And I told you how impossible that might be."

"Do you have any other ideas? Do you think we should break down the door or barge in there like the robbers on the train?"

"Shh!" She looked anxiously about the trolley.

"No one's paying us any mind."

She relaxed against the hard seat. "You're right. I'm sorry I'm so jumpy."

"You have a right to be."

"I wish there was something we could do other than talk about breaking into the house. That would have to be a last resort."

Matt stared at her, amazed. He had not intended for her to consider that as a serious suggestion. "Have you ever broken into a house?"

"Yes."

"Yes?" Laughter burst from him, bringing admonishing glances from two ladies at the front of the car. "Chandelle, you can't be serious."

"I am. It was only once, when I was about seven or eight. One of my cousins—"

"Of moonshining fame?"

She nodded. "One of those cousins and I wanted to see inside the Old Burley Mansion. It had been abandoned since before the war, and it was rumored to be haunted. I reckon we were more afraid we would not see a ghost than we'd see one. I was taller than Jeb, so I tore aside the shutters and hefted him in. He found a way to get the door unlocked, and we had a wonderful time sneaking about the place, scaring ourselves half out of our wits."

He stood as the trolley slowed. "Here's our stop." Taking her hand, he stepped down from the trolley. He quickly paid for the transfers they would need for the rest of their trip, then drew her hand into his arm. As the trolley pulled away, he said, "Chandelle, right now I'd rather buy you a new bonnet as a weapon to help you obtain your grandmother's quilt."

"You really shouldn't—"

"Let's not argue about that again."

Chandelle realized it was worthless to respond when Matt walked her along the street to where a small hat-shaped sign announced MISS VARNER'S MILLINERY SHOP. Looking along the street, she was surprised that they had returned to Chestnut Street. She wanted to ask him why they were not going to one of the street's large department stores that would be less expensive than this small shop, but he had opened the door and was ushering her inside.

A bell rang over the door, and she flinched. She should not be here among the bolts of lace and the lovely hats waiting to be tried on when Grandma was depending on her to bring back her coming home quilt. Every second delayed might be the very one that made her too late in returning to Asheville.

From behind a mirrored door, a chubby-cheeked woman appeared. She smiled broadly. "Welcome to my shop. How may I assist you?"

Matt offered her a smile. "Miss McBride's bonnet was ruined when we were caught in the rain. She would like to replace it with something appropriate for calls."

"Of course." Motioning toward a table where several hats sat, she said, "I have the very thing for a lady with your coloring, Miss McBride. It is de rigueur, the most fashionable style to come from Paris this year."

"Paris fashion might be—"

"Perfect for you, Chandelle," Matt finished before she could say the hat would be too expensive.

Miss Varner gave neither of them a chance to add more. Seating Chandelle in front of a mirrored door and taking Chandelle's battered bonnet, she chattered like Miss Southey. Chandelle wondered if the milliner had ever considered becoming a hello girl, but she pushed that silly thought away as Miss Varner set a frothy confection of flowers and straw on her hair.

"What do you think?" asked the milliner.

"I—"

"Yes, I agree." She pulled it off and reached for another. "You would do better with something a bit less diaphanous. As pretty as you are, you want the hat to draw attention to your face, not away from it." She laughed. "I have some patrons who are quite the opposite, although I would not tell them such a thing." She set a blue hat with an explosion of flowers on Chandelle's head and whipped it away before Chandelle could do more than catch a glimpse of it. "No, no, that is all wrong, too. Where is my head today?" She laughed again. "I know. I have the perfect thing. Wait here." Pulling open the door, she vanished into the back of the shop.

Matt chuckled. "We do attract prattlers, don't we? I wonder how."

"Must be luck and clean living."

"For you maybe."

Again Chandelle had no chance to reply. Miss Varner rushed into the room and placed another hat on Chandelle's hair. "Perfect," the milliner announced.

Chandelle stared at her reflection. Miss Varner was correct. The pale pink velvet ribbon accented the simple stovepipe style of the straw hat. A single daisy, its center the same color as the ribbon, gave it a jaunty air, and the gilt edging the daisy's leaves was a delightful surprise. She reached up to touch the narrow brim, needing to assure herself that she was really wearing such a lovely hat.

About to ask Matt what he thought, for he never seemed to be at a loss for an opinion, she could not get the words past her lips when she saw his reflection in the glass. He was turned mostly away from her as he stood by the store's window. His gaze was focused farther along the street toward where Friedlander's store tried to overwhelm all its competitors. Was she seeing sorrow in his eyes, or could it be regret, or was she misreading his expression altogether, painting him with a coat of her own disquiet?

Once more she paused a moment too long, for Miss Varner called, "Sir, do come and look at this hat. Is it not perfect for Miss McBride?"

A smile returned to Matt's face. "Yes, indeed. It is perfect. Don't you agree, Chandelle?"

"I like it very much."

"Is there something wrong with it?" he asked, and she knew her dismay had crept into her voice.

How could she ask him what was amiss when he was acting as if he had no more cares than a child enjoying a favorite treat? Even if she found a way, would he be honest with her? He had asked her to trust him, but she doubted if he trusted her. Or anyone, for that matter.

"It is lovely," she replied, for there was nothing else she could say. *Except the truth.* She silenced the taunting voice while Matt went to pay Miss Varner.

Looking into the mirror, she wondered how she could demand that Matt be honest with her when she could not be honest with him or with herself. She lowered her eyes from the condemning stare of her own reflection. Admitting the truth of how her heart thundered when he stood near would make her too vulnerable. She would not be seduced by a man who would leave her—as her father had left her mother. Not even by Matt, who had already staked a claim on her heart whether he knew it or not.

THE SUN BECAME AN eye-searing scarlet as it dropped into the river to the west. Chandelle was grateful for the brim of her new bonnet when they walked up the steps of Mrs. Coates's boardinghouse. Exhaustion weighted every motion she made. Glad for the pastries that Matt had purchased from a street hawker, she decided she would have one of those instead of dinner. She doubted if she could climb up and down the stairs twice without collapsing.

Their rooms were several degrees hotter than the street. Matt went to open the window as she took off her hat and put it on the closest table. With a sigh, she sat on the sofa. She closed her eyes, ignoring the sound of Matt's footfalls as he took off his coat and hung it by the door. The rattle of his newspaper tempted her to open them again, but they seemed sealed in place.

"You might want to look at this, Chandelle."

She did not want to look at anything. She wanted to drift to sleep where she could enjoy dreams of what seemed to be impossible. Dreams of handing her grandmother's coming home quilt to her, dreams of her grandmother saying she would not need it for years longer, dreams of Matt standing beside her and holding her in his arms as she wept with joy.

"Chandelle!"

Wanting to tell him to leave her alone with her dreams, she forced her eyes open. He was holding one page of the newspaper close to her face. His finger jabbed at one column of the small print. She started to ask him why he was bothering her when she saw the headline above his finger.

"Oh, my!" She pulled the paper out of his hands and stared at the bold type.

Jakob Friedlander announces that he will be running for Philadelphia City Council. She scanned the article, which went on to say that Jakob Friedlander, son of Esau Friedlander, decorated veteran of the Civil War, had decided to enter city politics.

"How much more complicated can this get?" Matt asked, sweeping his hand through his hair and leaving it spiked and falling across his eyes. "That explains why Friedlander *fils* refused to let you speak with his father. Any taint of past crimes could destroy his political aspirations."

"Maybe if we were to explain the situation and agree to say nothing if they would return the quilt to us—"

"A Friedlander never keeps his word, so why should he expect us to?"

Closing the paper, she rose and set it on the table. "You act as if you know them well, and Jakob Friedlander clearly knew you. Have you associated with him before?"

"If you mean, have we socialized, the answer is no. Friedlander would have no use for the likes of me. He—"

A rap on the door halted him. When he opened it, Mrs. Coates bustled in, a smile on her face. "This arrived for you while you were out, Mrs. McBride."

Taking the folded page, Chandelle managed not to wince at the landlady's mistaken assumption. "Thank you."

"Gave the lad a nickel for delivering it."

A nickel? That was an outrageous amount when she soon would be down to her last pennies.

"Allow me, Chandelle," Matt said as he fished a coin out of his pocket. He dropped it into Mrs. Coates's hand.

The landlady gasped. " 'Tis a dime you've given me."

"For your time and quick delivery to Chandelle." He gave her that effervescent smile that always charmed folks.

And it did again because Mrs. Coates giggled like a girl and hurried away.

Matt turned to Chandelle. "What does the telegram say?"

"Telegram?" Her fingers suddenly shook. "Is that what this is?"

He nodded. "Do you want me to read it first?"

"No, I can read it myself." She dampened her lips as she opened the single page. "Oh, no!"

He held out his hand, and she gave him the telegram as she clutched her hands together. When he began to read aloud, she tensed more.

"Hurry home with quilt. Grandmother worse. Marnie."

He dropped it on the table.

"I wish you hadn't done that," Chandelle murmured.

"Done what? Put it on the table?" He picked the page up and offered it to her.

"No, read it aloud. That makes it all too real." She took the telegram and stared at it.

Matt cursed under his breath when a shudder rippled through her, nearly throwing her off her feet. Pulling her into his arms, he leaned her forehead against him. He willed some of his strength to sift into her. How could he forget how fragile she was? As delicate as a lark, she hid her reactions behind the unremitting determination of a hawk.

Her forehead pressed on his shoulder, but no tears dampened his shirt. Why didn't she cry? Heavens, he would if he had received such news. Wouldn't he? He wondered, after so many years of training himself to feel nothing, if he could ever respond to anything but sarcasm again.

Yes, he could, for within him ached the knowledge that he could do nothing to ease Chandelle's grief. He could only help her to the sofa and sit beside her. There must be something he could say to help. He wished he knew what it was.

"I'm sorry," he whispered. That was stupid!

She raised her head, and his breath caught, serrated and hot within him, as he was captured by the pain bared by her face. Nothing masked the grief in her luminous eyes. His hand curved along her face, and he was bending to kiss her before he knew what he was doing.

Her arms encircled his shoulders as she answered his yearning with her own. Her lips offered everything he wanted from her. Hungrily, he explored her exquisite mouth. His hands settled on her waist. As they glided up her back to press her to him, she gasped against his mouth.

The sound was like a slap. He released her, knowing that, if he took advantage of her grief to seduce her, she would never forgive him. She might even give him his walking ticket, and then she would have no one to help her with the Friedlanders.

Standing, he lurched to sit on the chair on the other side of the table. The more distance between them, the better it would be for her. For him? He wanted nothing between them but the sweaty caress of their bodies.

Chandelle stared down at her hands, which moments before had been splayed across Matt's back. Locking them together so they could not betray her again, she tried to think of something to say.

"Is this Marnie staying with your grandmother?" Matt asked in a rough voice. He must be as overcome as she with how easily they had almost surrendered to passion.

"She would if nobody in the family could, but I doubt if she'll need to." Speaking of prosaic matters was so much simpler than admitting how much she yearned to be in his arms.

"You have a very close family."

"I'm sorry you don't."

His forehead rutted. "Why do you say that?"

"You never speak of your family."

"You speak of yours all the time. I believe I know the name of every cousin on your mountain and who's married to whom and how many children they have and—"

"Matt, you're doing it again."

"Doing what?"

"Changing the subject. You do that whenever we speak about anything you deem private." Although she knew she should stay far from him, she knelt by his chair and folded her hands on the arm. "Why won't you speak of your family?"

"I figure if I don't say anything bad about them, maybe they'll give up saying bad things about me."

"What a horrible thing to say!"

He draped his hand over hers and smiled. "If you think the truth is horrible. I'd rather not talk about them."

She would not let him end the conversation like this. "Do you have siblings?"

"A brother and a sister."

"Oh, how wonderful! I always wanted a sister and a brother. It seemed empty sometimes in the house with just Grandma and me."

"Even with all those cousins?"

"You're trying to change the subject again. We're talking about your family, not mine." She rested her chin on her crossed arms. "When did you see them last?"

"Them?"

"Your brother and sister."

"Five or six years ago." He frowned. "No, I guess it's been closer to eight years. I didn't realize it had been so long."

"You never think of them?"

"Probably more than they think of me." He came to his feet. "Stop probing, Chandelle. You grew up in the center of your family, loved and adored. I grew up with the perfect children, who were willing to be groomed for the life of privilege that is due the progeny of a robber baron. Not once did they question where the money came from and who had paid to put it in our father's coffers."

"Your father is a robber baron?" She stared at him. This explained so much, his obvious education, his ability to fit in with anyone, his knowledge of the ways of uppermost society.

"That's what his friends call him. I wouldn't repeat what his enemies call him."

"And what do you call him?"

He laughed coldly. "You'd be all a-twitter if I said that in front of you. You look tired, Chandelle. Why don't we make this an early evening? I'll even be a gentleman for once and let you have the bedroom while I sleep on the sofa."

Chandelle did not move. "And you were unwilling to be the perfect child of a robber baron?"

"As well as questioning everything." He chuckled and tapped her nose as he sat and began to loosen his boots. "Much as you are doing now."

"I wasn't taught to swallow my opinions at home."

"Only in public?"

"A lady should remember her manners at all times."

"Then why are you anything but reticent with me?"

She opened her mouth to answer, then closed it. To be honest would mean admitting how he had become so much a part of her life in the past few days that she had begun to treat him with the informality of family. She must not tell him that.

She started to stand, but he put his hand over hers, pinning them to the chair. Irritated, she snapped, "I might treat you politely if you ever offered me the least hint of civility." She tried to slide her hands away, but his fingers clamped over them. "Let me go!"

"I would if I thought you really wished to go." He leaned toward her, his smile vanishing as his voice grew low and rough. "Why don't you be honest? Your eyes reveal the truth when they glow like gas lamps each time I touch you."

"I don't know what you're talking about, and neither do you." She gasped when his fingertip traced the corner of her mouth.

His hand molded to the curve of her cheek. "There it is! If I had a mirror, you would know. I guess you'll have to see that bright flame reflected back to you from my eyes."

She slowly stood. To savor the passions that so brazenly gleamed in his ebony gaze, she would have to abandon all sanity. She could not. Not when Grandma had told her so often how her mother had been fooled into loving a man who left her to fight his war. Matt had so many battles of his own to wage. If she gave him her heart and herself, she feared she, too, would be left behind to mourn a lost love. She must keep the pattern of desolation from being repeated like the stitches in a quilt, even if it meant breaking her heart.

∞

MATT SAT UP AND grimaced. How many different ways could these cushions on this sofa torment him?

You could be more comfortable at home.

Cursing, he banished that thought from his head. Yes, he might be able to get a better night's sleep if he crawled back to his family's home, but the cost to his pride was not worth it. He kneaded his back.

Thoughts of the pangs at the base of his spine were eclipsed by a soft sound. Coming to his feet, he swore again when his toe struck the table's leg. He ignored the sharp pain and hurried to the bedroom door.

He pressed his ear against it, holding his breath and willing his heart to skip a beat or two so he could hear past its steady thump. Yes! The sound came from within. What could have gone wrong now?

He opened the door, making sure the latch's click was almost silent. He realized he was worrying needlessly, for the sobs were as loud as metal wheels on a cobbled street—resonant and in a broken rhythm.

"Chandelle?" he whispered.

She did not answer.

"Chandelle?"

The sobs continued as he inched, hobbling on his sore toe, toward the iron bed, that, with a washstand, almost filled the room. He paused and let his eyes adjust to the moonlight creating a milky path across the covers.

Chandelle was, he discovered, asleep. The strong will that had sustained her this evening had fallen away, leaving her defenseless against the grief that he had seen in her eyes and tasted on her trembling lips.

He came around the bed and reached toward her. He jerked his hand back. Was he out of his mind? Chandelle would be horrified to wake and find him here, as well as mortified that he had overheard her weeping.

But it was not *her* reactions that halted him. It was his own. If he had not fought to control himself tonight, they both would have been sleeping here. How much more would she have cried when he told her that he had no place in his life for her, that he had been burned once by daring to care for those he thought cared about him and that he would not be so foolish again?

When her sobs drove through him like a whetted blade, he gazed down at her. With her golden hair turned silver by the moonlight, her damp cheeks held the dewy sparkle of a night garden. He turned away, knowing he had never seen any woman more beautiful or any woman he wanted more.

But must never have.

13

CHANDELLE CAME OUT OF the telegraph office at the train station. Checking her quilting bag to make sure her purse was secure inside, she wished she could share the enthusiasm of the message she had sent. The truth had been stretched to the point of shredding. Yes, it was true that she had met with a member of Captain Friedlander's family and that she planned to return for another call soon, but she had not mentioned that she and Matt might never be received again at the house. Nor did she mention that her heart teased her to give it to Matt. Grandma had no use for Yankees, even after nearly two decades. If she discovered Chandelle was falling in love with a most outrageous one, she would be so furious that she could do worse damage to her failing heart.

It was best to keep Grandma in the dark on some of the details of this trip.

How many times had Chandelle told herself that? How many times had guilt coiled around her? She could not change a word now, because the telegraph operator had been preparing to send the message as she left the office. Once the message reached Asheville, it would delivered to Grandma. *If she is still alive.* Hating her own apprehension, she said nothing as she walked to where Matt was standing by the trolley stop.

She wanted to pause and admire his dapper appearance. He must have purchased the straw boater when he was out on errands earlier this morning. It added a lightheartedness to his appearance, but his face still wore its rigid lines.

He had not said more than a few words to her this morning, once again the terse stranger he had been when she'd first entered his office. But then he had met her eyes boldly. Today he did not. She wanted to ask him why, but that was certain to touch upon what they had discussed—and how they had touched—last night.

"Shall we wait for the trolley?" Chandelle asked.

"I thought we would walk."

"All right."

He glanced at her, and she knew he was amazed that she did not ask why. There was no reason to when his explanation, even if he gave her one, would be brusque.

The day's heat was unrelenting as they walked toward the center of the city. A low haze clung to the river, warning there might be another thunderstorm later in the afternoon. Matt had been right when he warned her that the weather in Philadelphia might be more uncomfortable than in her aerie outside Asheville.

When he paused on a corner and looked both ways, he frowned. "I must have taken a wrong turn. I thought this led to Spruce Street."

"I thought you knew this city well. How long did you live here?"

"Too long." With a chuckle, he put his hand on her arm. "All right. I know where I am. We don't want to go that way, Chandelle. Down this street."

She could no longer resist asking, "Where are we going?"

"To see Jesse, an old friend of mine who runs a cigar shop on Fitzwater Street near Eighteenth. He might have a way for us to see your old friend Captain Friedlander without resorting to breaking into his house."

"I never intended that to be a real alternative."

"I know you didn't." The twinkle in his eye warned that he considered it as an optional plan if nothing else worked out.

Anything for money. The echo of her own voice haunted her. Such a challenge had been easy when Matt Winchester was a stranger with a less than polished reputation. Now . . . now she needed her grandmother's coming home quilt desperately, but she did not want to see him risk himself to get it.

"This friend Jesse," she said as they stepped down off the curb to cross the street, "is trustworthy, I assume."

"He can be."

"And expensive?"

"He can be. However, he owes me a few favors. He—" He swore vividly at shouts from along the street.

Her eyes widened as she saw a driverless dray careening toward them. The horse was gaining speed with every step. She grabbed Matt's arm. "Run!"

She pulled on him, but he whirled in the opposite direction, swinging her toward the sidewalk. She struck a lamppost and fell to her knees. Scrambling to her feet, she shrieked as the dray bounced up on the walkway and hit him. It sent him sprawling on the street.

She ran to him and knelt. Fiery pain flashed through her, but she ignored her scraped knees as she touched his shoulder. His eyes were closed. Was he senseless or . . . ? No, she could not even think that he might be dead.

"Matt?" she whispered. She could not speak louder. This could not be happening. *Dear God, let him be alive!* She did not want to lose him.

Shouts filled the street, but she did not look up as she tore open the collar of his ripped shirt. She pressed her fingers to his neck. When she discovered the slow beat of his pulse, she sat on her heels and looked up at the growing crowd.

"Send for a doctor!" she called.

A man squatted beside her. "Are you hurt, miss?"

"I am fine," she lied. Her sore knees were not important. "But Matt is unconscious!"

The man waved down an open carriage. Rushing up to it, he said to the driver, "We have an injured man. Can you help?"

Chandelle did not hear the answer as she bent over Matt to keep the dust from the slowing carriages and wagons out of his face. Never had she seen him so lifeless. When he had been asleep on the train, she had known she could wake him with a light tap on his arm. Now it was as if he had gone somewhere where she could not reach him.

Fear closed around her like a gray, damp fog, clinging to her. She had learned so little about Philadelphia in the two days she had been here. Without Matt, she was unsure where she could go for help.

But it was more than that. Without Matt, her life was as bitter as the bile in her mouth. In the past few days, his acerbic comments and honeyed caresses had become such an important part of her life. Without them . . . No, she would not think of that! He was alive. She must make sure he stayed that way.

Opening her quilt bag, she pulled out her coming home quilt. She could almost hear him laughing that she was using what he derided as her burial shroud to keep him alive. She paid no attention to the dirt as she spread it across him. When she saw blood on the ground, she pressed her hands over her mouth. He must be hurt far worse than she had guessed.

A policeman bent toward her. "Do you know this man, miss?"

"Yes. He's Matt Winchester. He's my . . ." She swallowed past the fear in her throat. "He's my friend." It was a weak word to describe her feelings for him, but it was the best she could do.

"What happened?"

"A runaway dray almost ran us both down. Matt was hit."

The policeman stood and blew on a whistle. The sound bounced through her aching head. Another police officer rushed up. While one began to control the traffic, the other directed several men to help lift Matt into the carriage that had been stopped.

A man helped Chandelle to her feet. She whispered her thanks as she tried to move a few steps without limping. Her scraped knees could wait until she was sure that Matt was not seriously injured.

She watched, as silent as the street had become, while several men lifted Matt. Although he sagged between them, they carried him to the open carriage as gently as if he were their own child. They placed him on the seat as best they could, leaving him at an awkward angle.

Chandelle whispered her thanks when someone handed her into the carriage. Tucking her quilt around him, she sat facing him.

"Where do you live, miss?" asked the policeman as he handed her Matt's straw boater that somehow had not been broken.

She hoped she had Mrs. Coates's address right. No matter, once they reached that neighborhood, she would be able to find the house. She hoped she would.

"I'll have a doctor sent there to meet you," the policeman said.

"Thank you." She was not sure if he had heard her because he turned to signal the carriage driver to go.

Chandelle was pleased to see several of the men who had helped lift Matt into the carriage following. Without their help, she could not get Matt up the marble steps in front of the boardinghouse or up the steep stairs to their rooms. She put her hand on Matt's chest as one of the wheels dropped into a chuckhole.

"Careful," came a weak grumble.

"Matt, you're awake." She wanted to jump with joy, but doubted if her stiffening knees would allow that.

"I hope not." He opened one eye only a slit. "I'd rather this pain was a nightmare."

"Hush." She folded his hand between hers and stroked it. "Don't strain yourself. Lie still."

"Then stop doing that." He put his hand over hers. "Lying still is impossible when you caress me like that."

"Hush!" She glanced around, hoping no one else had heard his low voice. How much more impossible could this man be? His quiet whisper sent a pulse of urgency through her, bringing forth sensations and thoughts she should not be having when he had so nearly been killed.

"You sound fine." He opened both eyes, but his expression remained dazed. "Thanks for pushing me right into the path of that dray."

"I did no such thing!" To think that moments ago she had been lamenting about missing his caustic comments. She must have been completely out of her mind. "I tried to get you out of the way. You ran the wrong way. If you had half the sense of that horse . . ." She sighed. "I'm not going to argue with you now."

His eyes widened. "Am I so close to death?"

"No, of course not."

"Sounds that way if you're not going to argue with me. And I'm all wrapped up in a quilt. Not a good sign around a McBride woman." He squeezed her fingers weakly.

Chandelle smiled. Although he had been banged about, his sense of humor was as undamaged as his new hat. That was good, because she suspected he would need it—and she would need hers—during his recovery.

∞

MRS. COATES STOOD BY the stairs, wringing her hands in her apron. Over and over, she repeated, "Be careful there. Watch where you are stepping. Be careful."

Chandelle opened the door to their rooms. She watched as the men assisted Matt to the sofa. He had insisted on climbing the stairs with their help instead of being carried. Hoping his pride was not going to add to his injuries, she had managed to get up the stairs without anyone noticing her tentative steps, each one sending pain outward from her knees.

"Does someone need a doctor here?" asked a painfully thin man with graying hair, as he paused by the door.

"Come in," Chandelle said. "Mr.—" Mindful that Mrs.

Coates might be within earshot, she hastened to correct herself to say, "Matt was struck by a runaway dray. He's there on the sofa."

The doctor pushed past the crowd of men who were trying to get out the door.

When Chandelle thanked the men and reached to open her bag, the man who had halted the carriage tipped his hat and shook his head. "Our pleasure, ma'am. Hope he gets on both feet soon."

"So do I." She closed the door behind them and went to the sofa to get the doctor's opinion on Matt's injuries.

"Dr. Horndale," the doctor said without looking up or pausing in his examination. He held a stethoscope through Matt's torn shirt to his chest. He had Matt take off his coat and roll up his sleeves to look at his arms and hands. Next, Matt removed his boots and wiggled his toes.

Muttering to himself, the doctor pulled out some lint bandages and wrapped them around Matt's head. The blood she had seen on the street must have come from the cut by his temple. The doctor set a small packet on the table by the sofa.

"Take a small spoonful in tea until it is gone. It is for the headache you've probably got," Dr. Horndale said.

"It's a big one." Matt tried to smile but grimaced.

"I'm sure. However, in a week, the bruises should be pretty much healed." He patted Matt's shoulder. "If you want to brag to your friends about being a hero and saving this young lady's life, you'd better do it quickly."

"I wasn't being a hero." He winced, and she knew every word hurt his head as much as it did hers. "I was trying to get myself out of there."

The doctor chuckled and closed his bag. Motioning toward the door, he started for it. He paused when Chandelle tried to follow. "Are you hurt, too, young lady?"

"I shall be—"

"Chandelle," Matt said in his most imperious voice, "let the doctor check you, too, if you are hurt." Looking past her, he added, "This is the most stubborn woman you'll ever meet, Doc."

Dr. Horndale did not reply. Taking Chandelle's arm, he seated her across from the sofa. A moan slipped through her lips as she bent her knees. It was followed by a gasp when she saw the bloodstains on her gown. Not from the street, she knew, but from her own injured knees.

"I will need you to raise your skirt high enough for me to see the damage," the doctor said as he knelt beside the chair and opened his bag again.

"But—" She looked to where Matt was watching, the roguish gleam in his eyes once more.

The doctor's voice became impatient. "Madam, I can assure you that I am a man of medicine. Your husband is right here, so you need fear nothing improper will take place."

She wanted to protest that she would have no problem with this examination if Matt truly was her husband. To admit that might guarantee that they were tossed into the street by a righteously appalled Mrs. Coates. But to say nothing . . . She foolishly glanced at Matt again. As it had so often and with ever increasing enchantment, his gaze tangled with hers, weaving them together in a tapestry of sensations that wrapped around her, refusing to release her even if she had wanted it to.

Slowly she drew her skirt up past the top of her shoes and along her stockings. When Matt continued to look at her face, his eyes not flickering once toward her legs, a warmth like when he had held her in his arms surged through her. The quick rise and fall of his chest showed that he was fighting to hold his gaze steady.

She bit her lip when the doctor put some salve on her knees. It stung fiercely, but the pain was muted by the happiness soaring through her as Matt continued to stare into her eyes until Dr. Horndale had bandaged her knees and lowered her skirt over her shoes.

Standing, the doctor handed her the jar of salve. "Put some of this on your knees twice a day until they are healed. Both of you are lucky, you know. We had a man run down and killed a day or so ago by a dray. It happens too often."

"Thank you, Doctor," Chandelle said.

When she started to stand, he shook his head. "Stay where you are. I shall tell your landlady that she is to deliver your supper here tonight and some hot tea to you as soon as she can. I will have my bill sent to you tomorrow." He left before either of them could say anything else.

Chandelle looked at where Matt was lying with his eyes closed on the sofa. Was he asleep? As if he had heard her ask, he opened his eyes and gave her a flimsy smile.

"Thank you," she whispered.

"For what? I almost got both of us killed."

"You know what I mean." She was abruptly shy, a most unfamiliar feeling. She did not want to speak of how much she appreciated him not ogling her legs, because she wanted to keep the warmth of his kindness close for as long as possible.

Instead of nodding, he pushed himself up to sit. He touched his forehead cautiously, and she knew it must hurt horribly. "I didn't plan on the expenses you'd have on this job to include a doctor's visit." One corner of his mouth tipped his dark mustache. "I think I said that on my last job, too, and the one before that."

"Maybe you should consider a different way of earning a living."

"What? Riding the rails as a trainman maybe?"

"You could go back to your family."

He shook his head, then swore. "I don't want to talk about that now. Or anytime. Leave me be, Chandelle."

"But—"

"You heard the doctor. I should be fine in a day or two. Until then, you are going to have to be patient and heal yourself, too."

"While we're recovering, I shall write a letter to Captain Friedlander and have it delivered."

"You'll do nothing of the sort."

"I can't do nothing."

"You must."

She clutched on to the arms of the chair. "Matt, be reasonable. Grandma needs her coming home quilt right away."

"I know." He stretched out his hand. When she put hers in it, he whispered, "And I know if you do anything now, you may ruin everything I hope to have in place by the time I get better. If all goes well, I can guarantee you that, assuming the quilt is at the Friedlander house, you'll have it back."

"And if all doesn't go well?"

He did not answer as he released her hand. When he looked away, she knew that he feared that if his plan did not succeed, nothing would. Then, all hopes of retrieving Grandma's coming home quilt might be gone.

14

THE NIGHT LURED THICK shadows from the corners of the room as Chandelle opened the door. Mrs. Coates might run an excellent boardinghouse, but her cooking was less than wonderful. When Chandelle had groused about that last night, Matt had told her that she could not expect the spicy flavors and variety of food she had taken for granted at home.

Today had been wonderful, even though she was not sure if they were any closer to getting Grandma's quilt. First had come a telegram from Asheville that her grandma's condition, though grave, was no worse. This afternoon, she and Matt had taken their first walk since the dray had almost run them down three days ago.

More than once, Matt had stopped to speak with someone along the street. The conversations were innocuous, but she had learned that, with Matt, things were not always as they seemed. Asking him had gained her nothing, for he had prattled on as endlessly as Miss Southey about how friendly Philadelphia had become.

She frowned as she sat on the sofa. Her knees were better, but they still balked on every step. Sitting the rest of the evening would be the best thing she could do. She picked up her quilting bag and lifted out her coming home quilt. Yesterday, she had washed the dust out of it, so she could do some more stitching on it tonight.

Matt drew off his coat and placed it on the peg by the door. His motions were careful, although he had gotten rid of the white bandage around his forehead that had made him look like some wounded knight of old. Crossing the room, he leaned on the chair. She wondered if he was as exhausted as she was by their outing.

She smoothed the quilt across her lap and reached into the bag for the strip of flannel where she kept the old needles that she used for quilting. A new straight needle was best for sewing other things, but when it became curved with continued use, it was perfect for quilting. For as long as she could remember, the ladies at the church at the bottom of the hill had saved their old needles and given them to Grandma. With her needle threaded and knotted and her thimble on the first finger of her right hand, she was ready to begin.

"Show me how you do it," Matt said as he came around the chair and sat beside her.

"You want to learn to quilt?"

"Why not? It's such a large part of your life."

She touched the buttons sewn into the quilt. "You're right. It is."

"This must be a red-letter day. We've been in agreement all day long."

Folding her quilt, she reached for her bag. "Must you always ruin things with your irreverence?"

"No, not always." He put his hand over hers. "I'd really like to know more about your quilting."

"Really?"

"Yes."

Her resistance melted at the hushed sincerity in his voice. She had never imagined sharing this part of herself with him, although she had imagined so many other sorts of sharing in her dreams. Grandma had warned her that her future husband would probably have little interest in this important tradition and that it would be Chandelle's task to keep it alive by sharing the precious legacy with her daughters.

"What do you want to know?" she asked.

"Everything." His voice dropped to a timbre that made her tremble, as if he were a perfect note and she a tuning fork.

She laughed. "That's a tall order."

"All right. Just tell me what you are doing here."

Forcing her eyes away from his enticing warmth, Chandelle said, "A coming home quilt is different from any other. Most quilts have the top pieced together, then are quilted on a quilting frame."

"But that would not be possible with this quilt."

"No. I stitch on it when I can, sewing each piece of the top together, then basting it to the old quilt until I can continue the diamond pattern of the quilting."

"Why not just pin it?"

"I got tired of jabbing myself on the pins, so this was easier."

He ran his finger across where the quilt flowed over her lap. She sucked in her breath to keep from gasping. The touch was so gentle, yet so questing that it seared the layers of the quilt and her gown and undergarments away until she was sure his fingertip brushed her skin. Or maybe it was nothing more than her craving to have him touch her like that.

"It looks more like seashells."

"I call it a round diamond, but it may look like shells. I have never seen the ocean."

"You would love it," he murmured as he settled his arm behind her on the sofa. "We summered there every year when I was a child. Cape May. Before the war, there were as many Southerners in Cape May as folks from up this way. I must have gathered a thousand shells each summer." He touched the quilt again. "And so many of them were shaped like this."

"I thought I had devised something original, but apparently not."

"It was original for you. Tell me something else. How

do you decide which pieces of your life to include?"

She smiled. "There are no hard and fast rules, Matt. Whatever strikes my fancy is included."

"Like my handkerchief." He tipped the middle of the quilt across his lap to examine how she had stitched it to the rest of the quilt top. "When did you add this to your quilt?"

"Last night after Mrs. Coates brought the clean laundry upstairs." With a laugh, she said, "You aren't the only one who can work quickly."

"So I see." He plucked the thimble off her finger. "Teach me to do the stitching."

She chuckled again when he tried to put the thimble on his much wider finger. Taking it, she said, "I'll warn you that it is more difficult than it looks. See this piece?" She lifted the corner where she had started her quilt when she was a child. "The stitches are uneven and about as straight as a snake."

"Maybe you'd prefer that I didn't add anything but my handkerchief to your quilt."

Chandelle wanted to answer him, but the words refused to form on her lips as his hand curled around her shoulder, leaning her toward him. Even more, she wanted to let his shoulder cushion her head as she closed her eyes and savored the dream that filled her nights with endless delight and her days with unending frustration.

His eyes narrowed, and she knew he was wondering why she had not answered. Handing him the needle, she pointed to the section of material next to the handkerchief. "Push the needle through there."

"Like this?"

She adjusted his grip on the needle. "I think that's right. Your fingers are so much broader than mine."

"All the better to hold yours, my dear."

"That sounds like the wolf in *Little Red Riding Hood*." Laughing, she said, "The wolf didn't have to worry about sewing when he chased Grandmother out of her house and donned her nightgown."

"He didn't have to worry about this ache to kiss someone either."

Her breath raced in her ears. "He could have kissed Little Red Riding Hood instead of trying to devour her." She sensed his reaction to her fingers lingering atop the orange-speckled handkerchief on his lap.

"True, but I'd like to think I'm smarter than a wolf." His hand combed through her hair, loosening it to fall about her shoulders. When she reached up to it, he slid her closer. She recoiled as she brushed against his coat.

With a wry smile, he reached under it and drew out his pistol. He set it on the table and pulled her closer. "See, I'm smarter than that silly wolf." His voice deepened to a fervent whisper. "And I suspect you taste much better than Little Red Riding Hood."

His kiss was slow and deep, not a kiss of mastery, but of exploration, seeking all the pleasure waiting for both of them. When his tongue outlined her lips with moist flame, she let the quilt fall, forgotten, to the floor.

He pressed her against the cushions, his tongue darting past her lips in a dazzling caress. It had become a brand which lit every bit of the delight within. Held between his steely arm and the rugged planes of his chest, she let herself sink into the mushy cushions. She drew him with her, keeping him so near, she was no longer sure where her body ended and his began. That did not matter. All that mattered was satisfying this persistent craving that rippled through her and settled in all the places she longed for him to touch her.

When he lifted his mouth from hers, she groaned in denial. She wanted it upon her lips, upon her face, upon her, adding to the thrill that dimmed what she had savored in her dreams.

His hands framed her face as she slowly opened her eyes to find his only the breadth of a shadow away. "It's your choice."

"Choice?" She smiled. That was easy. She wanted him to kiss her again and again.

"If you and I will become lovers tonight." His voice

throbbed with the passion she had discovered in his kiss.

"Lovers?" She started to put her hand over her heart, but his chest pressed over her.

He grazed her forehead with a tender kiss. "You sound surprised. You must know how much I want you."

Yes, she knew, for she wanted him as much. She lowered her eyes. "You know there's no real choice."

"Honey, there are always choices." He tipped her face to look up at his. "See? I have chosen to touch you here, although I would rather be touching your bare skin as I peel away your gown by undoing these buttons." He ran his finger down the ornamental buttons on her bodice.

She clamped her hand over his, intending to halt him before she was utterly lost in the rapture. Instead, his hand spread across her breast, a tender seeking that sent the luscious sweetness coursing through her anew.

"Tell me what you want," he whispered.

She steered his mouth to hers. She wanted *this,* this indescribable ecstasy that dimmed all her fantasies, this giving that brought such joy in return, this being with him while the cloak of sarcasm and half-truths was stripped away.

When he drew back once more, she stared up at him in amazement. His eyes glowed with ebony flame, the same fire that scalded her with each caress.

"*Tell me* what you want," he murmured.

The heat that flared through her was not pleasant. It came from the very idea of giving voice to the dreams that haunted her each night. How could she speak of her yearning to savor his rough-skinned hands on her? It was as inconceivable as it was to give voice to her curiosity about the soft hair on his chest. She wanted to slip her fingers through it and follow it along him. Yet she could not say that.

"Matt, I would . . ." She lowered her eyes, for she could not speak the words that would push him away or would bring him so much nearer.

Sitting, he leaned toward her. "It sounds as if you've made your choice."

"I—I—" Closing her mouth, she came to her feet. She gathered up the quilt and stared down at him. "How did you know?"

Slowly he stood. He did not touch her, and she guessed he knew as she did how easy it would be to be swept away by desire. "I've always considered myself a good judge of people. That's part of my job, and I know it's as unthinkable for you to shed your ladylike ways as for me to assume the fancy feathers of a gentleman."

"But those sound like a gentleman's words."

"You have no idea how difficult they were to speak." He tipped her head forward and kissed her nose. "Good night, Chandelle."

"Matt, I don't want you to be angry with me."

"I'm not." He smiled sadly. Turning away, he said, "You'd better go to bed before both of us do together."

Her hand started to raise to touch the stiff line of his shoulders. Why were the words that flitted through her head with every unguarded thought so difficult to say? She gripped her quilt as her grandmother's admonition echoed in her mind. *Don't be a fool like your mother was and end up alone.* Matt had said nothing of love or of a future together beyond tonight's pleasures.

As she backed away one step, then another, the pain in her heart was worse than her sore knees. She turned and went to the bedroom door. Pausing as she opened it, she waited for him to face her. He continued to stare at the opposite wall.

She went into the bedroom and shut the door, her hand lingering on the knob. The rattle of carts from the street was the only sound she could hear, for she dared not release the breath burning in her chest. Maybe, if she held it a moment longer, her heart would slow from its frantic beat. Maybe she might convince her arms not to ache with the need to pull him close. Maybe . . . Her breath exploded out of her with a gasp.

Staring down at her fingers on the knob, she jerked them away. Was she out of her mind? So much of the time, she found Matt Winchester intolerable and arrogant. His sense of humor turned from self-deprecatory to taunting in a single breath. And he thought the most important tradition in her life was idiotic.

But he could be gentle and kind and make her laugh, and his touch turned her to liquid rapture. She knew she would never meet another man like him, no matter where she sought. No other would light her soul with this enticing, excruciating desire.

With a half-sob, she went to the simple iron bed. She spread her quilt across the bed. The quilted top was not large yet, for, as Grandma told her so often, she had so much of her life ahead of her. Smoothing out the wrinkles in the fabric, she faltered when she saw the monogram on the handkerchief that Matt had given her. Drawing her fingers back as hastily as she had from the doorknob, she sank to sit on the bed. For the first time ever, holding her quilt gave her no comfort.

∞

CHANDELLE TRIED TO RUB the sleep from her eyes as she opened the door to the hall. All night long, she had fought to fall asleep. She must have won the battle before dawn and the arrival of the teamsters making deliveries along the street. The wheels and the drivers' shouts had shattered her fragile hold on slumber.

The aromas of breakfast climbed the stairs. Knowing she should have something to eat, she doubted if she could swallow more than a few bites. Her stomach had tossed and turned as much as she had during the night. She had come so close to surrendering everything she held dear for the chance to hold the man she loved.

Why was she so stupid? She should not love Matt Winchester. So much about him drove her insane. That changed nothing. She loved him.

Lost in her thoughts, she collided with someone on the back stairs. Her hands touched bare skin. She pulled back and bumped into the wall. Her breath exploded out of her as she stared at Matt's naked chest in front of her.

The muscles she had touched through his shirt shifted smoothly as he put his hand out to steady her. She must look as faint as she felt. Her fingers tingled with the memory of that brief contact, urging her to caress him again.

"Sorry, I wasn't watching where I was going," Matt said, buttoning his shirt. "Are you all right? You look a little dazed."

"Just trying to wake up." That much was the truth. Touching him had been like a waking dream. Now she must push that tantalizing memory aside and concentrate on keeping him away while they got Grandma's coming home quilt.

"Why don't you rest today?" He bent to pick up the shaving soap and razor he must have been carrying. "This morning I thought I'd try to speak with someone else who may help us."

"Matt, how many more people are you going to need to talk to before we can go to Rittenhouse Square?"

"He's the last." He smiled as he pulled his suspenders over his shoulders. "You need to have patience, honey. You need to trust me to know how to do things here. It's different from the way you do things on your mountain."

"I'll try." She turned away, pretending that she was as calm as he was. Going into their room, she gathered up the blanket he had used last night and folded it over the sofa.

"How about some breakfast?" he asked.

She was not sure if his cheery voice was sincere or feigned because she did not dare to look at him. If she did, she doubted if she could keep from throwing herself in his arms and begging him to spend the day teaching her about the ecstasy they could share. She was tired and afraid of her own feelings and afraid of losing her grandmother and afraid of losing Matt.

"I'm not hungry."

"All right. I'll grab something on my way out the door." He kissed her cheek and whispered, "I hope you're not going to have to be patient much longer, honey."

Or you. She prayed she had not spoken those words

aloud. When the door closed behind him, she knew she had heard them only in her head.

She bent and picked up his pillow. She pressed it to her face. His scent remained, taunting and too tempting. Closing her eyes, she wrapped her arms around the pillow. Then she tossed it onto the sofa. She could not avoid the truth any longer. She was in love with this irascible, irresistible man. He was the very man Grandma had warned her to avoid.

And she should. She knew of only one way.

Taking a deep breath, she walked into the bedroom. She needed to get her grandmother's quilt and return to Asheville without delay. That would be the smartest thing she could do. It had not been Matt who had delayed the inevitable confrontation with Captain Friedlander by trying to find them an ally. She had hired him. She could have insisted that they go back to Rittenhouse Square right away. She could have reminded him that he had vowed to do whatever was necessary to retrieve Grandma's coming home quilt.

No longer. She could wait no longer. Grandma needed her, and she needed the quilt.

And Chandelle needed to get away from Matt's magic before she was lost within his spell completely. The only way to do that was to get the quilt and return home.

Now.

∽

IT HAD BEEN EASY coming to Rittenhouse Square at exactly the hour when calls should be coming to an end, so that no one would take note of her.

It had been easy so far, Chandelle cautioned herself while she set down her quilting bag by the bay window in the small office on the second floor of the lovely house on Rittenhouse Square. The butler had not recognized her, which should have been no surprise. A bit of rice powder had covered the dark circles under her eyes left by the loss of a night's sleep, but, even so, she must have looked much more bedraggled on her first call here. In her stylish new hat and her black gown, she had hoped to present a better image. She must have because the butler had brought her here and asked her to wait in this office with its imposing cherry desk and bookcases while he let Captain Friedlander know he had a caller.

Looking at the portrait over the hearth, she wondered if the handsome man was a member of this family. He had some resemblance to Jakob Friedlander, but his face was narrower and his eyes had a distant expression, as if the man had been thinking of other things while sitting for the painter.

Chandelle whirled as she heard footsteps approaching. A mistaken thing to do, she realized, when her corset cut into her side. Matt was right. She was a mountain girl who had no idea how to act in the city.

A man appeared in the doorway. His silvery hair complemented the dove-gray of his morning coat. "Good day," he said in an impatient tone. "I understand you asked to speak with me."

"Are you Esau Friedlander?"

"Yes. Who are you?"

She did not answer as she struggled to believe she might finally be at the end of her search. So often she had thought of this moment. Now that it was here, she was so overwhelmed that she was unsure what to say first. Dozens of thoughts demanded to be spoken.

Captain Esau Friedlander was older than she had expected, for she guessed he could claim almost as many years as Grandma. But he had none of Grandma's warmth in his smile. Matt was right. This family had nothing but their account books on their minds.

"I would like to speak to you of Lorraine McBride," she said, folding her hands primly in front of her.

"Lorraine?" Captain Friedlander's face grew pale. "Lorraine McBride?" Groping for the chair at his desk, he sat. His motion for her to do the same was more from the drilling of good manners than conscious thought, she guessed, for he was looking through her as if she had vanished. "It's been so long since I've heard that name."

"She's been dead for almost twenty years."

He nodded slowly. "So I understand." His eyes focused on her again. "However, I did not understand that your call was to be about what happened two decades ago. You sent word of a desperate need to speak to me?"

"Yes." She was glad she had resisted the yearning to surrender to the pity washing through her when he spoke her mother's name. His voice was icy cold, warning her that he would have little sympathy for her.

"I wish to speak to you of Lorraine's mother, Elitta McBride."

"Why? I recall little of her, save that Elitta McBride was a formidable woman."

"She still is."

"She is still alive?"

It was Chandelle's turn to choke as she whispered, "I hope so."

He seemed not to hear her, for he came to his feet, shaking his head. "Yes, a formidable woman. Even if the rest of the area around Asheville had laid down their arms in surrender to us, she intended to fight until she got her way. I never understood how Lorraine could be her daughter and be so different."

"Do you mean that you found her to be so willing to surrender?" Chandelle came to her feet. How dare he speak of her mother like that! "Maybe because she believed she had no alternative."

He faced her, astonishment glowing from his eyes that matched the shade of the ones in the painting behind him. "You speak with rare fervor. What business is this of yours?"

"More than you can guess."

"What did you say your name was, young lady?"

"Chandelle McBride."

Again he choked, this time asking, "Chandelle?"

"Yes." Fighting that weakness to offer him pity, when he deserved none, she said quietly, "Lorraine McBride was my mother."

He stared at her, his mouth agape, for so long she feared he had been taken in death and frozen like that. Then, something flickered in his eyes, and his scowl returned. Did he ever smile?

Don't be frivolous! What do you care if he smiles or spends every day trying to intimidate his servants and his employees with his glowers?

"Impossible!" He slammed his fist onto his desk. Picking up a handbell that was set on top of it, he rang it furiously.

"Captain Friedlander—"

"Be silent!" Looking past her, he ordered, "See this woman, who calls herself something McBride, to the front door and make certain that she never steps foot in this house again."

His butler nodded. "Miss?"

Chandelle was not going to be thrown out of this house again, especially not by this low-down, lying scoundrel who had tried to destroy her family. He had succeeded by stealing her family's home during his months in Asheville, but she would not let him defeat her today.

Crossing her arms in front of her, she stood still and met his glare. The butler put his hand on her elbow, but she shook his fingers off angrily. When he cleared his throat with anxiety, she did not dare to look away from Captain Friedlander's fury.

"I have come to say something to you, Captain Friedlander," she stated in the imperious tone Matt frequently used. "I shall not leave until I have had my say."

"I have no interest in hearing more of your lies!"

"Lies?" That shocked her. "I've only told you the truth."

"Impossible! Lorraine McBride could not be your mother. She had no children when we met."

"When you commandeered her house, you mean!"

"Miss—whatever your name is, I warn you that I have tried to treat you with the courtesy a young lady deserves, but that outburst suggests to me that I may have been misled by your fine feathers to label you as something you clearly are not."

Fury choked her. "Captain Friedlander, your outburst suggests to me that I have *not* been misled by my grandmother when she said you were a beast!"

"Dowdle," he called, although his butler stood right beside her, "I want her taken from this house immediately and not granted entrance again."

"Miss?" the butler asked, bowing toward the door. "If you please, Miss McBride . . ."

Captain Friedlander flinched as his butler spoke her name. "Before you go, tell me why you have tried to succeed with these obvious lies."

"I haven't lied to you." She blinked back tears. She would not weep in front of him, although she had no idea how she would get Grandma's coming home quilt now. Why hadn't she listened to Matt and waited until he found allies to assist them? "Lorraine McBride was my mother. She died when I was born. The winter was hard that year, my grandmother tells me, and my mother was so weak from lack of food that she died on Christmas Eve, only two days after I was born."

"Christmas Eve?" Again his face lost all color. "What year was that?"

"I was born in December 1864."

"December?"

"Almost nine months to the day my father left to fight in the last battles of the war, my grandmother told me." She wanted to wipe away the tears clinging to her lashes but would not let him see her weakness. "My father was already dead by the time my mother discovered she was going to have a baby. I never knew either of them, because, as I said, my mother died two days after I was born, although I doubt if you care."

"*December 1864?*"

"She died without her coming home quilt, sir, because you stole it from her. You stole her most precious possession as well as my grandmother's. Wasn't it enough that you forced yourself into their home and into my mother's bed when she must have been grieving for my father?" Her voice almost broke as she spoke of the shame that her grandmother made sure no one mentioned on the mountain. "Did you have to steal our special heritage, too?"

He surged around the desk with the speed of a man his son's age. She backed away, exchanging a horrified glance with the butler. Captain Friedlander must be bereft of his mind! No wonder Matt had warned her to stay away from this house and let him handle this.

Captain Friedlander grasped her arm. With a quick motion, he sent her hat careening across the room. It crashed against a lamp, but his gaze was fastened on her. His jaw worked as if he were trying to decide what to say.

The butler took a hesitant step forward. "Sir! Sir, what are you doing?"

Captain Friedlander ignored his butler and Chandelle's gasp of pain as he gripped her chin. He squinted, tipping her face toward the light.

"Dear God, why didn't she let me know that she was pregnant?" he demanded.

Chandelle stared at him. "She? Who?"

"Lorraine."

"Why should she tell you anything?"

"Because, if you were born in December 1864, you are my daughter."

15

THIS WAS MADNESS! HE must be insane. She must be as well to listen to this.

Chandelle grabbed her quilting bag from by the window. Pushing past the butler, she went toward the door. When Captain Friedlander shouted, the butler stepped in front of her with an apologetic smile.

"Miss McBride, Mr. Friedlander wishes to speak with you a bit longer."

"I shall not stay and listen to this." She turned to Captain Friedlander, who was staring at her in amazement. "I trust you will have my grandmother's coming home quilt sent to me posthaste. I shall leave my address with your butler."

"Don't leave yet," Captain Friedlander said. Again the butler edged between her and the door.

She shook her head. Then, realizing her hat was gone, she hurried to pick it up. "Oh, no!" she moaned when she saw the brim was broken. "I've never had a hat as pretty as this one, and you ruined it."

"I fear," Captain Friedlander said with a sigh as he sat on the corner of his desk, "that I have ruined many other things for you, Miss . . ."

When he paused, she whispered, "I told you. My name is Chandelle McBride."

Shock burst into his eyes. "Your name truly is Chandelle?"

She had not expected Captain Friedlander to ask such a question. Captain Friedlander or her father? Could they be one and the same? No, that was impossible. Grandma had told her that her father had left to fight in the war before her mother knew she was pregnant.

She was a fool to fall in love with a soldier who cared more about winning his war than staying with her.

Grandma's voice was as clear in Chandelle's head as if she stood in this room. But, for the first time, Chandelle realized her grandmother had not said that her father had gone to fight for the Confederacy. Chandelle had simply assumed that. Could it be true? Could this man who had stolen from her family when they had so little and then left her mother to die, pregnant and unmarried, be her father?

She did not want to believe that. It no longer mattered. All she wanted was to find out about Grandma's coming home quilt. Hoping that if she humored Captain Friedlander, he would be honest with her, she said, "As I understand it, a man living on our mountain before I was born spoke French. My mother learned some and chose this name for me."

"*Chandelle* means candle."

"Yes." Why did he go on staring at her so unceasingly? Maybe he was trying to decide if she believed his unbelievable tale. "Because, as my grandmother said, I was a bright spark of hope in a dark time."

"I suspect you were." He smiled sadly. "Lorraine spoke so often of wanting many children."

"I was her only one."

Captain Friedlander stood and crossed the room to her. Taking her hat, he set it on a chair. She reached for it, but he caught her hand in his that was as dry as the old pages of the family Bible.

"Chandelle, I know you don't want to hear this," he said, "but I was the man who spoke French on your grandmother's mountain. I taught your mother to speak some French, as well as the little song from which I suspect she took your name."

"What song?"

He glanced at the butler, who was struggling to maintain his poise as he listened to the strained conversation. "Dowdle, I shall call you when I need you."

"Yes, sir." The butler bowed his head and walked out.

"Close the door!" Captain Friedlander called.

Dowdle glanced at Chandelle, but she could not read his expression before he shut the door.

She looked at Captain Friedlander when he said, "The song was 'Au Clair de la Lune.'"

"I'm sorry. I don't know what that means. I don't speak French."

He laughed. "That is no surprise. Your grandmother had no use for what she called a barbaric tongue. She believed that everyone in the world should speak exactly as she does, the drawl included." Motioning for her to sit, he drew his chair around the desk. "Sit, Chandelle. You and I need to extricate what truth we can from this convoluted collection of lies that have been spun for both of us by your grandmother."

"Grandma would not lie."

"She would if she chanced losing you to one of the hated Yankees, as she did your mother."

Chandelle knew that was true. She sat and wished she had waited for Matt to come with her on this call. Right now, she would have appreciated a dose of his irreverent humor, a bit of the ridiculous that would remind her that nothing was as serious as it might appear. But this was serious. If Captain Esau Friedlander was her father, everything she had believed was true was not.

"*Au clair de la lune* means by the light of the moon," he said. "It is a nursery song. I whistled it often then." His forehead wrinkled more deeply. "I don't remember the last time I whistled it." Shaking his head, he sighed. "One of the lines includes the word *chandelle*. Lorraine thought the word was lovely and was most amused when I told her how the French said *voir trente-sixe chandelles* when they spoke of looking at the stars."

"As I said, I don't understand French." She knew she sounded cold when his eyes widened, but she was not sure what to say. Grandma should have been honest about the identity of Chandelle's father instead of hiding what might be the truth all these years. No wonder Grandma had insisted no one speak about Chandelle's father. She shook her head. Why should she believe this man who had stolen her grandmother's precious coming home quilt?

"*Voir* means to see." He folded her hands again between his, and she could not free them without a sharp yank. "Or to behold. To behold all those candles in the night sky, twinkling down on us and reminding us of a time when war did not scar our lives. Your mother was the sole moment of sanity amid that insane time. She taught me that I could love again, for I feared I could not after my wife died. That spring was magic, something I've never known before or since."

He looked past her, and she knew he must be the young man in the painting. The same search for the faraway filled his eyes. Had he been thinking of her mother then?

"Forgive me," he said. "I am babbling on and on, but there is so much to be said between us."

"There is only one important thing to be said."

"I did love her, if that is what you want to know."

Chandelle could not silence a gasp. She had not expected him to say that. Wanting to denounce him as a liar as he had her only moments ago, she could not doubt the sincerity on his face. "Then," she whispered, "how could you leave her to die?"

"I had no choice."

"There are always choices." This time, it was Matt's voice that rang in her mind, reminding her how her fear of her love for him had persuaded her to come here so precipitously.

"Not then. The war took precedence over everything else. I had to obey my orders and go."

"Taking my grandmother's coming home quilt with you. Do you remember?"

"A quilt? Yes, I know of what you speak."

"You do?" She would gladly concede that her grandmother had lied to her about her father if she could hold Grandma's coming home quilt in her hands. Then she would rush to the nearest telegraph office and have a message sent posthaste to Asheville that she and the quilt were on their way, that she had found it without Matt's help.

Matt . . . No, she could not pause to consider what he would think of this unexpected tangle.

"Yes, I remember your mother giving it to me."

"My mother gave you a quilt?"

He nodded. "Two actually. A large one, and one that she had been working on. She feared I would take a chill while camping in the late spring mountains. I will never forget her kindness. I kept those two quilts with me all through the war."

Chandelle tried to steady her hands from quivering, but she could not. "Do you still have it? The larger quilt?"

"It's possible."

"Here?"

"It's possible." He frowned. "Why is that quilt so important to you that you came here when you had every reason to hate me?"

Quickly, because she had repeated the story so often, she explained what the quilt meant to her grandmother and how she needed to get it to Asheville. She finished with, "Now you can see why there must be no delay."

"I'm afraid there will be." With a sigh, he stood. He turned, so his profile was silhouetted by the light coming through the bay window. The wrinkles on his face became invisible, and she could easily imagine his hair the same gold as hers. She glanced at the portrait on the chimneypiece. He had been a handsome man, who had somehow found his way into her mother's heart.

"But why?" she asked, reminding herself she must think only of her grandmother now. "Grandma must have it as soon as I can get it to her."

"If it is still here, Chandelle—" He smiled as he spoke her name and put his hand on her shoulder. "If it is still here, it must be in the attics. I can have them searched, but not until after this evening. The staff will be busy until then preparing for the party where the formal announcement will be made of Jakob's plan to run for city council."

"Jakob?" She had forgotten him in the midst of all this. He was, if what Captain Friedlander said was true, her half brother. And he was Matt's enemy. She knew that from how the two men had spoken with each other during her first call here.

"My son." Captain Friedlander's smile broadened. "He shall be very surprised to hear that his sister has arrived in time for his gathering. Unfortunately, he is at the resort in Bryn Mawr making plans for his campaign. He will not be back until the party this evening. You will join us, won't you, Chandelle?"

Coming to her feet, she picked up her quilting bag. "I think it would be better if I did not. I have rooms at Mrs. Coates's boardinghouse."

"That section of the city is no place for my daughter." He frowned. "You shall stay here until we can figure out how best to share the news of your identity. I think it would be a good idea for you to attend the gathering this evening. Then people will become accustomed to seeing you here."

Chandelle gasped. "But I have nothing appropriate to wear!" It was the most insipid excuse she could have spoken, but it was the first one that burst from her mouth.

"My dear young lady, I own the finest store in Philadelphia. Maybe on the whole east coast." Pride filled his voice. "Within the hour, you shall have a half dozen Paris frocks to choose from." He eyed her up and down. "You are quite tall, aren't you? I shall have some of our seamstresses come here as well to tailor the gown you select for yourself."

"But—"

"Chandelle," he said, his voice becoming a plea, "let me do this small thing for you. I do want to help you find your grandmother's quilt. But more than that, I want to get to know the daughter I never knew I had. Once you have Elitta's quilt, you will be rushing home to North Carolina. Don't deny us this one evening to learn more about each other."

He refused to listen to her protests. She agreed, because she would agree to anything now to get the quilt. When he offered to have someone go to retrieve her things at the boardinghouse, she almost asked if that person might search for the quilt instead. Then she realized how little she knew about the hierarchy of servants in a fine house.

"Just a message, if you would," she said. "My things can be brought later."

"A message? To whom?"

Knowing she must be careful not to mention Matt's name until she discovered if Esau's opinion of him was the same as his son's, she said, "To Mrs. Coates. She will need to know that I am not going to be there for supper and where to send any telegrams that might arrive from Asheville."

"Very well." He smiled. "Is that your quilting, Chandelle?"

She held the bag close to her, but nothing could shield her heart from this jumbled mess. If only Matt were here . . . She was certain he would find some way to help her navigate through these treacherous waters as he had before. With his arms around her and his heart beating beneath her ear, she could let his strength bolster hers, which was failing her now.

"Yes, this is my quilt."

"I would like to see it someday if you would show it to me. Perhaps by you sharing your memories with me, it will make it seem more as if I had the chance to be there to share those days of childhood with you."

She nodded, wondering how her grandmother could have hated this man. He could be icy cold. She had seen that for herself when she had first arrived, but there was a gentleness about him. *Her father!* From her earliest memories, she had wanted a father to smile at her as her cousins' fathers smiled at them. Now that longing had been fulfilled.

Longing . . . Her breath caught beneath her breasts as

Matt's face filled her mind. This longing was a serrated knife cutting into her even as she imagined his hands sweeping along her, urging her to soften against him. She forced her feet not to rush her out of the house and take her to Matt so she could share this unexpected twist with him. She wanted to share everything with him.

Chandelle flinched when Captain Friedlander tugged on a bellpull, and a woman in a plain, gray gown appeared at the door. "Lois, will you take Miss McBride to a guest room where she may prepare to select a new dress for this evening's gala?"

"Of course, Mr. Friedlander." The maid smiled at Chandelle. "This way, Miss McBride."

"If you want anything, ask," Esau said. "I want you to feel at home here, Chandelle."

Again she nodded. What she wanted was to understand why all she had believed to be true was not. Even though she wanted to denounce Esau's assertion that he was her father and that her mother had *given* him the two quilts, she could not. His irritation had been genuine when he had been about to throw her out of his house. His delight at discovering she was his daughter had been as honest.

Chandelle followed Lois up the curving stairs to a room on the floor above. Trying to hide her amazement with the bedchamber decorated in a sunny yellow that was splashed everywhere from the wall covering to the coverlet on the huge tester bed, she listened as Lois pointed out where the bowl and ewer were and where she might find extra pillows if she wished to rest and how to ring for assistance.

"Will there be anything else, miss?" the maid asked.

"No. No, thank you."

Chandelle let her strained smile fall away as Lois closed the door behind her. Wrapping her arms around herself, she went to peer out the grand bay window.

It would not be dark for several hours, but the lamps were being lit across the street, looking as if the lamplighter had captured a handful of stars and was tossing them along the walkway. The light breeze through the raised windows promised a gorgeous summer evening fit for strolling and chatting and enjoying the cool breath that signaled a comfortable night to come. On nights like this, Grandma liked to sit on the front porch and gaze down at the city being swallowed by shadow. She would rock and tell stories of the family, stories that she had seen in her own grandmother's coming home quilt or sewn into her own.

"Why didn't you tell me *this* story?" she asked as she sank to sit on the silk chaise in front of the window.

CHANDELLE WAS GRATEFUL THAT Esau Friedlander simply introduced her to his son's guests as "Chandelle, who is visiting us from North Carolina." That kept her from having to explain the relationship she still had a difficult time believing herself. He insisted, however, that she would address him as "Father" when others were not about. On this, he was adamant.

She used every excuse she could devise to remain near the door to the hall. As the other guests mingled beneath the hiss of gaslights set in the chandeliers hanging from wide medallions in the ceiling, she remained close to the walls that were covered in emerald silk only a shade darker than her dress. Touching the skirt that had fewer flounces than most of the others that had been brought from the store, she tried to believe she was here in her father's—*her father's* house and dressed in a gown that only months ago had been sewn in Paris. She could not believe any of this, but it was all true.

She watched the women in their glorious gowns of every possible hue flirt with the men who were dressed in ebony coats and trousers. Among them, the servants in their unobtrusive gray livery offered drinks and tidbits.

Wincing, she was sure there must be a pin still in the left side of her gown. She should have checked it before Lois helped her dress. As much as she had sewn, she knew how easy it was to miscount the pins.

Her stomach growled. Instead of remembering that she had skipped breakfast and had only a light supper, she should be enjoying this party. She had been introduced to city leaders and the *élite* of Philadelphia society, but all she could think of was her wish that one of the trays would come closer so she might sample some cheese or fruit. The waiters could not get through the press of women who seemed impressed that she had traveled all the way from North Carolina aboard the train.

"Unbelievable that you survived such a long trip," announced a woman who had identified herself as Mrs. Strauss. Her full face was as friendly as a kitten's. "Where is your traveling companion, Miss McBride?"

"Traveling companion?"

"Certainly you did not travel that distance alone."

Chandelle smiled. Every lesson that Grandma had taught her could be forgotten tonight, save for the most important one. *Think before you speak.* "The train was full, Mrs. Strauss. Much of my time was spent helping a young mother with her two children." She flipped open the fan that Lois had handed to her in a box before she came down to the gathering.

A gift from Esau Friedlander and Friedlander's Store had been printed on the card enclosed in the box. As Chandelle had stepped out into the hall, she had seen two more boxes filled with beautiful hats. She knew these were an apology for breaking the brim on her new hat.

Pushing Esau's unexpected generosity from her mind, she knew she must not give this busybody a chance to ask another probing question. "They were so adorable. The little boy was not even a year, but he was as friendly as a pup." She smiled at the others, who were making no effort to hide their eavesdropping. "I believe he wiggled as much. The little girl was only a year older. The perfect age, don't you agree, Mrs. Strauss?"

"I—"

"Entertaining them so their mother might get some sleep made the miles pass with unbelievable speed."

"There you are!"

At the male voice, her heart leaped, but just as quickly she realized it was not Matt's voice. He must have learned from Mrs. Coates by now that Chandelle had not returned to the boardinghouse.

She managed a smile as Esau—no, she had to think of him as Father—came toward her. Her expression faltered when she saw who was with him. Jakob Friedlander wore a simpering smile, but she could not doubt that his true feelings were in his narrowed eyes as he looked at her with a viper's venomous glare.

"Do excuse us, ladies," Father said with a smile that suggested they would be doing him a favor to agree. As the women edged away, he added, "Chandelle, this is my son Jakob."

"We've met." Jakob's voice was as cold as his eyes.

"When?"

"Miss McBride called earlier in the week to speak with you."

Father frowned. "You said nothing of that, Jakob."

"It quite slipped my mind in the midst of all the preparations for this evening." His smile returned. "I do think that is the mayor trying to get your attention, Father. Why don't you go and see what he needs while I speak with Miss McBride?"

"Chandelle," Father corrected with a smile. He gave her arm a squeeze. "We all shall be one very happy family, if I have my way."

"And when haven't you?" Jakob muttered as their father went to greet the mayor. Turning to look at Chandelle, he added, "So now I am to understand that you claim to be my sister. How did you devise this fabrication? Or did you create it alone? Maybe you were helped by—"

"I am as surprised as you by the whole of this." She met his cold gaze evenly. "I had believed my father died fighting for the Confederacy."

"I have worked too hard for this, Miss McBride, to have you come here and destroy my reputation."

"Your reputation is not the one in question if what your father says is true."

"No?" He laughed without humor. "You are disgustingly naïve if you believe that. When I consider what my political enemies will do when they learn of my illegitimate half sister, I shudder." He eyed her with a stare that froze her so much she could not shiver. "And a bumpkin, unrepentant Johnny Reb illegitimate half sister, who has no manners to speak of."

"That you speak as you do is proof that your manners are as despicable as you accuse mine of being." She raised her chin, refusing to knuckle down before his insults. "If you wish me to speak as plainly, I can tell you that I am as distressed as you to think that we share a father."

"You insolent—"

"Miss McBride," came a young voice from the doorway, "you have a caller."

Chandelle turned, resisting the temptation to thank the maid for intruding. Her words vanished as she saw Matt standing in the doorway, but a Matt she barely recognized. He was dressed as elegantly as the other gentlemen in the room. The black of his coat was not marred by a single mote of dust, and his shirt was eye-searingly white in the light from the chandeliers. With his hair combed neatly out of his eyes, she could not avoid his intense expression.

Before she could speak, Jakob said, "I thought I told you not to come here again. If—" His name was called from across the room. He hesitated, then added, "Leave now before you're sorry you didn't listen to me." He strode away.

Matt glanced at the maid, who excused herself. Only then did he say, "Good evening, Chandelle."

"I was beginning to fear that Mrs. Coates hadn't conveyed to you where I was." She reached to take his hand, needing the comfort of his touch.

He locked his hands behind his back and regarded her without his usual smile. "She could not wait. Imagine! One of her guests is now welcome at the Friedlanders' house on Rittenhouse Square." He arched a single brow. "I don't remember seeing that fancy gown among your things, Chandelle, although I seem to recall seeing it in the window at Friedlander's."

She brushed her hands together, fighting the urge to reach out to him. "You might have."

"I thought you were nearly broke. How could you afford to buy this?"

"I didn't buy it. My father gave—"

"*Father?* Didn't you tell me that your father died before you were born?"

"I need to speak with you."

"About what? Gifts from beyond the grave?"

Putting her hand on his arm, she whispered, "Matt, lower your voice. People are staring at us."

"My voice level has nothing to do with it." His smile returned but was strained as he scanned the room, battering back the curious looks in their direction. "Everyone is intrigued about why I am in Philadelphia after all these years and why I'm *here.*"

"What are you talking about?"

"You're right. We need to talk." He grasped her hand and pulled her out of the room at an unseemly pace. Hearing rumbles of questions behind her, she knew no one by the door had missed their hasty exit. She was not sure what might result, but she guessed it would be trouble. And why not? Trouble had been her companion since leaving Asheville.

Chandelle said nothing when Matt led her to another set of pocket doors beside the stairs. Opening them to reveal emerald portieres dripping with thick, gold fringe, he gave her a mocking bow. She went into the small parlor. It was as beautifully decorated as the other rooms she had seen in this house. Artwork covered the walls between intricate molding. Chairs were scattered about, offering an invitation to sit and admire the moonlit garden beyond the tall windows.

When Matt crossed the room and stared down at the fire burning needlessly on the hearth, for the night was warm, she tried to reconcile this image of him with the dust-covered office in Asheville. This once must have been his world, for he had admitted that he came from a wealthy family. Something had propelled him out of this comfort into the rough life he seemed to love.

"Why would anyone be shocked to see you in this house?" she asked when he remained silent.

"As you could see, Jakob Friedlander harbors no pretense of friendship toward me."

"Either of us." She went to him and put her hand on his shoulder. She wished he would face her instead of leaving her alone to speak the words that were almost impossible because she could not believe them completely herself. "But Jakob will have to accustom himself to both of us until I can take Grandma's coming home quilt to her."

"It's here?" He turned slowly, his eyes narrowing. "Has Friedlander admitted that?"

"He said it might still be here. He brought it to Philadelphia with him."

Matt shook his head. "I probably shouldn't ask how you persuaded him to admit that."

"I simply asked him."

Taking her hand, he seated her on a white satin settee. "You should have waited for me before you burst in here. There are ways of discovering the truth instead of being inundated with lies."

"He's not lying to me."

He sat beside her. "I know you want to believe that, but why should you believe him?"

She stood and looked out into the garden. She did not want to see his face when she said what she must. If she saw pity there or, even worse, hatred, she would not be able to endure it. "I believe him, Matt, because he is my father."

"Your father?" His voice was choked. "Your father is Esau Friedlander?"

"It seems so." She wanted to look at him, but she did not dare.

"I thought your father was dead."

"I thought so, too." She bit her lower lip, then whispered, "I don't know why Grandma lied to me."

"Are you sure she did?"

She spun to face him, her hands becoming as icy as his voice. "She told me that my father was dead, and that can't be true."

"All you know is that Friedlander told you something different. Who will you believe—your beloved grandmother or the man who stole her quilt?"

"I stole nothing," answered a deep voice before she could answer.

The sound of her gown's rustle as she whirled was overly loud. She looked from Esau Friedlander's face to Matt's. They could have been carved from the same rough marble, for both of them wore uncompromising frowns.

Esau—Could she ever think of him as her father?—stepped into the room and drew the pocket doors closed. Brushing aside the fringe on the portieres, he strode to the middle of the room. She noticed he kept more than an arm's length between him and Matt. Did he fear that Matt would strike him?

"I do not recall your name on the guest list," her father said coldly.

"I'm sure you do not." Matt folded his arms in front of him and smiled with the lack of warmth of his frigid retort. "However, as Chandelle and I had some business that was not completed—"

"My daughter has no business with you."

"Quite to the contrary, I am currently in her employ. To find her grandmother's quilt that disappeared at the same time that you took your leave from Asheville. She believes it was stolen."

Chandelle wanted to caution both men to restrain their tempers. "I told you—"

"Allow me to deal with this," Matt answered with that same cool smile. "I have learned how to deal with this type of snake."

Before she could reply, Esau said, "I know about her grandmother's missing quilt, and I have promised Chandelle that the attics will be checked on the morrow."

"After your son's little political gala to garner himself all the votes your money can buy?"

"See? Everything is going to turn out perfectly." Chandelle tried to sound cheery as the two men glowered at each other, but her voice had a brittle edge. "It's as I told you. Captain—" She amended when her father cleared his throat and frowned at her. "Father told me the quilt is here. I'll be able to get it to Grandma soon."

"So you truly believe he is your father?"

She wanted to ask him why he was posing this question in front of Esau Friedlander. Didn't Matt understand that she would agree to say she believed anything if it would get her grandmother's coming home quilt? If she spoke of her doubts now, Captain Friedlander might order her out of his house and not listen to her pleas for the quilt. Nothing must keep her from getting it. Why didn't Matt understand that? If he loved her as she loved him, he would know she had no other choice.

There are always other choices.

No, not now there wasn't.

Chandelle raised her chin and said, "Yes, I believe he is my father."

Matt scowled at Chandelle so savagely, she took a half step back. "So you are exactly like the rest of them, aren't you?"

"I don't know what you mean."

"I thought getting that coming home quilt to your grandmother mattered more to you than anything. More than your own safety. Even more than your feelings for me."

Her father growled, "Don't flatter yourself. My daughter would have no feelings for the likes of you."

"Can't you speak for yourself any longer, Chandelle?" Matt fired back. "Or are you already Friedlander's puppet, doing only what he says you should, speaking only when he allows you to? His son who will be on the city council if he can buy enough votes, his daughter who will converse only with those he decides are proper."

She took a step toward him, then faltered. How had everything become so confused? If Matt realized that she would do anything to obtain her grandmother's quilt, he should understand that this was part of it.

"I think you should go before I have to call the police," Esau said. "Send me a bill for all that Chandelle owes you for the job she so foolishly hired you for."

Matt's smile became sly. "I wouldn't charge her for *all* that I've done for her. Some things, like last night, have been my pleasure."

Chandelle gasped. "Matt, don't! I—"

"I have suffered enough from his crude behavior." Esau pointed toward the door. "Get out, and do not call here again for any reason, Matheson."

"What did you call him?" she asked, turning to her father.

He did not answer, because the pocket doors rolled back, and Chandelle knew the raised voices had carried through the thick mahogany. Seeing Jakob in the doorway, she clutched her hands together when half the guests appeared behind him.

Matt glanced at the guests. "I have seen this family push around the rest of Philadelphia for too many years. I shall not be a part of that again." He paused in mid-step, holding out his hand, and asked, "Chandelle, are you coming?"

She started to raise her hand, then paused. She could not leave as long as there was a chance that Grandma's coming home quilt might still be within these walls. "I can't. Matt, please understand—"

"I understand all too well," he said, bitterness in every word. "I hope you get all you deserve."

Desperately, she cried, "If you leave now, you're fired."

"Honey, you're too late." His taunting smile was scarce warning before he added, "I quit."

Chandelle gripped the back of a chair as he strode past the shocked guests, slamming the door to the street in his wake. She had not guessed that the cost of finding her grandmother's coming home quilt would be so high.

16

CHANDELLE WAS APPREHENSIVE WHEN Esau asked her to join him in his office while Jakob saw to bidding the guests good evening. In the wake of Matt's departure, nobody seemed anxious to remain. Maybe now she would get an explanation of what had caused the harsh words between Matt and the Friedlanders. It was time she knew the truth.

When she said as much to Esau as he filled a pipe and lit it, he nodded. "Sit down, Chandelle. I'm not sure how much pap he has filled your head with, but you're right. You deserve to know the truth about Matheson."

"Matheson? Who is Matheson?"

He gave her an odd look. "Matheson is the man who just quit working for you."

"His name isn't Matt Matheson. It's Matt..." She swallowed roughly. "Are you saying Matt's last name is Matheson?"

"Although it certainly is no surprise, I believe he has been less than honest with you about many things other than his name. However, it is clear he lied to you about that. His family's surname is Matheson." He sat at his desk and tapped his pipe against the chair. "What name did he give you?"

"Matt—Matt Winchester." She could barely speak. All the time Matt had been asking her to trust him, he had been lying to her. As Grandma had. She feared she could trust no one now.

"Winchester? Not surprising, for Winchester was his mother's maiden name." Esau puffed on his pipe and sighed. "So you had no idea that his family and yours are business rivals?"

She almost blurted out that her family had no business but their farm that would soon be taken by the bank, then she realized he meant the Friedlander family. Her eyes widened. "Matheson? Like the store Matheson and Sons on Chestnut Street?"

"The one across from our main store?" He nodded. "I had understood that the name was going to be changed when young Matheson walked out on his family, but obviously it was deemed too expensive to do that simply because the older son was not fit to join the family business."

Chandelle rose. The memory of the pain on Matt's face when he had spoken of his family refused to be forgotten. It had been as genuine as the desire in his eyes each time he kissed her. Of all that had happened, she dared to believe that passion was real. How ironic that the one thing her heart had not trusted might be the most honest part of what they had shared!

But that proves he is no better than the Friedlanders think he is.

She shook that thought out of her mind. It came from her shattered heart. Matt had drawn back last night, giving her the chance to choose. No matter what else he might have done, no matter what other lies he might have told her, no matter what truths he had not revealed, she could remember his reluctant sacrifice at that moment.

"I know this is painful for you to hear," Esau murmured, "because it is clear that you considered him far more than a friend."

"What he said suggested—"

He came to his feet and put his hands on her shoulders. "Chandelle, I will believe what you tell me, not what Matheson said. Be honest with me. Did he seduce you?"

Footsteps paused by the office door, and Jakob stared at her and his father. He was smiling, although she had no idea why.

"Chandelle?"

She looked at Esau. "I kissed him, no more." That was a lie, for she had given Matt her heart, whether he wanted it or not.

Jakob's laugh had a rusty edge on it as he entered the office. "Matheson's very public announcement led our guests to believe otherwise."

"I trust," his father replied, sitting again, "you persuaded them that they were mistaken." His smile became cool again. "The hallmark of a great politician is to convince the people to believe what you wish them to."

"It was not easy, but I managed it by reminding them that no friend of this family would have anything to do with a Matheson." He held out a large stack of cash. Smiling when Chandelle drew in a deep breath at the sight of enough money to pay off the liens against her grandmother's land, he said, "Apparently I convinced them of many things very well. Donations to my campaign, Father."

Esau took the money and smiled. "Excellent, Jakob. Maybe you do have the makings of a politician, after all." He opened a desk drawer. Dropping the money inside, he went on, "However, it is only a beginning. You need to continue to win their support."

"I shall as long as we don't have any other incidents like tonight." Jakob propped himself against his father's desk and glared at her. "You understand, don't you?"

Chandelle recoiled from his rancor. When Esau scowled at him, Jakob only smiled. What sort of family was this? In her family on the mountain in Asheville, they spoke plainly, but never with such snide expressions.

"Jakob, I shall say this but once." Esau pushed himself to his feet, his face florid with anger. "Chandelle is your sister. You will treat her with the respect she is due as your sister."

He bowed his head toward her. "I meant no disrespect to you, sister." He made the word sound like the most vile epithet. "I simply wanted to acquaint you with what we in Philadelphia consider good sense. You are judged by your companions."

"So you mentioned before." She would not let him browbeat her with his slimy insults.

"Chandelle knows that she will not see Matheson again," Esau stated as if his were the last word on the subject.

It was not.

"I never agreed to that," she argued.

"You must." Esau's taut face smoothed as he put his hand on her arm. "Chandelle, you are as sweet and as eager to forgive wrongs done to you as your mother was, but you aren't on your mountain any longer."

She clenched her hands, but uncurled her fingers when she noticed that Jakob had done the same when Esau mentioned her mother. "I know things are different here, but that changes nothing. All of the things I brought from Asheville are at Mrs. Coates's boardinghouse."

"I shall send someone to retrieve them," he said.

"No, that wouldn't be a good idea." When his face reddened again as it did whenever someone resisted his dictates, she added, "One thing seems to be the same here in the North as back home in North Carolina. People enjoy gossiping. If you send one of your servants to Mrs. Coates's boardinghouse, it is sure to cause talk. If I go by myself, no one will take note."

Jakob pushed himself away from the desk. "And it will give you opportunity to help Matheson undermine my campaign."

"Jakob!"

Chandelle watched, amazed, as Jakob seemed to shrink before his father's roar. The respect that Esau demanded his son show her was something he did not show his son.

"Chandelle," he continued without looking at her, "you are excused. I will discuss this with you tomorrow. Right now, Jakob and I must speak. Alone."

"But—"

"I said you are excused."

Every fiber rebelled at knuckling under to his orders. This was not a family, but an armed camp with Captain Esau Friedlander still very much in command.

"Sleep well, daughter."

Chandelle nodded, although he could not see her as he continued to stare at his son who was no match for him, for Jakob sat obediently at his father's order. Hurrying out into the hall, she climbed the stairs at a near run. She rushed into her room and closed the door behind her.

She did not want to be here. She wanted to be somewhere where she was loved, not merely a pawn in a game she could not begin to comprehend. Esau Friedlander intended to force his son to accept her as a member of this family, instead of allowing his children to come to know each other slowly.

Or was it something else, something beyond her ken? She could not miss Jakob's reaction at the mention of her mother. Esau must have seen his rage, too. She had been thrown into the middle of a fast-moving river and was being swirled about by currents she could not comprehend.

"A good night's sleep is what you need," Chandelle said to herself as she went to the large bed. Before she could wonder what she would wear to bed, she saw a beribboned nightgown spread across the pillows. She knew, without looking closer, that it came with a card imprinted with the name Friedlander's, a gift from Esau.

Setting her fan on the table by a stack of boxes that had not been here when she went down to the gathering, she loosened her shoes and drew them off. She was sure she could ring for a maid to help her get ready for bed, but right now she needed to be alone. Maybe some inspiration would pop into her head, and she could find a way out of this maze.

Her breath caught as the glint off one of the buttons on her coming home quilt poked her in the eyes. Tiptoeing to the bed, she stared at the orange-spotted handkerchief that was still unquilted. She touched the monogram on it. The filigree around the letter had not misled her. It was not a *W*, but an *M*. For Matheson. Matt had asked her to trust him while he spun his web of lies for her.

She reached for her scissors. She should excise every hint of Matt Winchester—or whatever-his-name Matheson—from this quilt. He had done nothing but lie to her from the beginning. Why would she want to remember *him*?

The scissors fell to the bed. She could cut the stitches holding the handkerchief in her quilt. It would make no difference, for how could she ever forget him?

∞

THE GLORIOUS CARRIAGE WAS as out of place on the narrow street as a ribbon on a pig. Chandelle had warned Esau of that when he surprisingly granted her permission to return to Mrs. Coates's boardinghouse to bring her things to Rittenhouse Square. She wondered what had been said by father and son after she left.

"I shall not have you in that section of the city on your own," Esau had insisted as they sat together in the breakfast room beyond the grander dining room.

"But yesterday—"

"Yesterday, we did not know that you are my daughter." He did not lower his newspaper as he picked up his cup of coffee and took an appreciative sip. Nor did he look at her. "I will not have my daughter wandering about Philadelphia unescorted, so you will take the carriage."

"Thank you." She doubted if anything she said would change his mind.

"I shall send Anthony, who is my best coachman, with you. If there is any trouble with Matheson, he will be there to protect you."

"Matt probably won't be there by the time I arrive."

As she had guessed he would when she said that, he put down the newspaper and smiled. "Where do you think he will be?"

"He's quit working for me, so he'll need to find another

way to make some money. He'll probably take the midday train to North Carolina."

Esau's smile widened. "Excellent. The sooner he is gone, the better." Raising his newspaper again, he asked, "How long will it take you to pack your things?"

"About an hour." It would, she knew, take less than half that, but she hoped if Matt was there, they might begin anew the conversation that had been brought to such an angry end last night. She did not want to believe that he would leave Philadelphia so quickly, but he had no reason to stay. He hated this city. She wondered now why he had agreed to come with her. To tweak the noses of the Friedlanders? If that had been his plan, it had failed miserably.

Esau folded the newspaper and stood. "Very well. I have let the manager of the ladies' department know that you shall be there exactly at eleven this morning."

"Ladies' department?"

"At the store." He gave her a beatific smile. "I'm certain that Miss Weigley will be delighted to show the best that we have to offer from the fashions that have recently been delivered from Paris."

"But I thought we would be looking for Grandma's coming home quilt today." She smiled. "I can do that instead of going to get my things."

As she had hoped, the thought of her not going to the boardinghouse tempted him. Then his smile returned as he said, "Let's see how long it takes for you at the store."

"But—"

"Chandelle!" His harsh tone warned her that she had overstepped the bounds he had established for his family. "I will not have you wandering about Philadelphia looking like a ragamuffin. Going to that horrible neighborhood where you have been staying is one thing, but you cannot receive callers here in the same dress day after day."

She wanted to ask who would be calling on her, but she was learning the only way to persuade him to change his mind was to agree. "I can look in the attics after I'm done at the store."

He beamed another smile at her. "That's possible. I have

an important appointment this morning. If all goes well, I shall see you when you arrive at the store. Don't fret about which frocks to select. I have already sent instructions to Miss Weigley about what I want you to have." He turned toward the door, then paused. "Chandelle, I believe it would be more prudent at this time, in light of Jakob's plans to run for city office, if we kept your place in this family to ourselves."

"But why?"

"There is no need for needless questions, is there?" He had bent and kissed her cheek before walking out of the breakfast room.

Chandelle sighed as she looked out the carriage window. She was not accustomed to someone else making decisions for her. Somehow, she must remind Esau that she was not a child, even though he seemed determined to make up for the years of her childhood that he had lost by showering her with more gifts than she had ever seen. The boxes in her room contained all sorts of clothing, including some she had no idea how to wear or what they were for.

As the carriage slowed, she reached for the door. She pulled back her hand as she recalled the polite scold the coachman had given her about allowing him to open and close the door for Mr. Friedlander's guests. Apparently a well-to-do woman did nothing for herself, because Lois had given her much the same chiding for not letting Lois help her dress this morning. That Chandelle had dressed herself and brushed her own hair every morning since she was three seemed irrelevant.

Chandelle stepped from the carriage. Curious gazes came at her from every direction on the street. Along the sidewalk, people paused to stare at the carriage. Curtains in many of the windows were drawn aside. She could almost hear the whispers through the open windows. Esau should have listened and let her hire a carriage instead of insisting that she take the elegant closed carriage that did not belong here.

As she climbed the steps, Mrs. Coates swung the door

open wide. "Good morning, Mrs. McBride. That is a grand carriage you're riding in."

"Isn't it, though?" Maybe by agreeing, as she had with Esau, she could put a halt to any further questions.

A silly hope, she discovered, when Mrs. Coates asked, "Does it belong to a friend of yours?"

"A family friend." She despised lying, but she did not want to chance the trouble that might come if she disregarded Esau's order to say nothing about being his daughter.

Mrs. Coates walked with her to the stairs. "Does Mr. McBride know about this friend?"

"Yes."

She frowned. "Mrs. McBride, you should know that Mr. McBride was in a foul mood when he came back here late last night. Very late. Stamped up the stairs so loudly that I heard him in my own rooms down here below. When I came out to see what might be wrong, he didn't answer a single one of my questions." She gripped the railing. "I was worried about him, Mrs. McBride." She lowered her voice to a whisper. "I was sure I smelled hard spirits on him."

Chandelle looked up the stairs at the closed door to the rooms she had paid for such a short time ago. Forcing a smile, she patted Mrs. Coates's hand. "I hope he didn't say anything spiteful to you."

"No, quite the opposite. He was blistering mad, but he was polite as always. A real gentleman." Again her voice dropped to a wispy whisper. "I wanted to warn you. Just in case."

Chandelle nodded. The landlady had made her point. Mrs. Coates guessed that Chandelle had spent the night with a lover, something that Matt had discovered so he had soothed his loss in a bottle.

"Is he still here?" she asked, trying to keep each word from trembling.

"I don't know. He didn't come down for breakfast."

Climbing the stairs before Mrs. Coates could ask another question, Chandelle drew her key out of her bag. She did not dare to falter while the landlady was watching.

As the key rattled in the lock, she heard, "Come in, Chandelle. It's not locked."

Her heart cramped with joy. Matt had not left yet! Her hand quivered when she turned the knob. Until now, she had not suspected how much she had feared Matt would be gone.

She looked about the room as she entered. It was empty, but she saw her open trunk by the bedroom door. Everything she had brought with her had been tossed into it. Where was Matt's bag? It was usually by the sofa. She bit her lip when she realized it was not there. Maybe he had left already. No, that could not be. She had heard his voice. It had not been her imagination bursting from her heart which held on to the hope that all could be as she had dreamed.

"In here."

She followed Matt's voice to the bedroom door. By the bowl, he was shaving. She clutched on to the door molding as she gazed at his naked back. It was as if the past day had never happened. Again she was a prisoner of the craving that ached inside of her, longing for him to satisfy it with his eager touch. Beads of water clung to his nape. She wanted to let her fingers connect one to the next as she delighted in the wonder of her skin on his.

Setting down the straight-edge razor, he reached for his shirt that had been tossed atop his bag by the washstand. He buttoned it as he turned. If he had been drinking last night, she saw no sign of it on his face. She saw no sign of anything, because it was as blank as the mirror when no one stood in front of it.

"Good morning," she said, unable to think of anything else.

"Good morning, Chandelle." He walked toward her, then past her as he came out into the main room. Settling his suspenders on his shoulders, he said, "I didn't expect you'd come here this morning."

"I came to get my things." *Don't do this, Matt. Don't hate me because you hate them.*

"I thought you'd send the servants over to do that little task for you."

She stopped kneading her fingers and looked at him directly. "Why are you being so horrible? Nothing has changed."

"No?" He sat on the sofa, shoving the blanket out of the way. "You are no longer Chandelle McBride. You are Chandelle Friedlander."

"You slept on the sofa last night?" The words burst from her before she could halt them.

"It's where I sleep."

"But..." She glanced over her shoulder at the bedroom.

"I wasn't sure if you might be coming back last night."

"Mrs. Coates said you didn't come back until very late."

He laughed, but his mouth remained straight. "If she told you I smelled like a brewery, she was right. I stopped to speak to several people last night to let them know I wouldn't be needing their help any longer to get your quilt. They spend their evenings at a tavern a couple of blocks from here."

"You don't owe me an explanation."

"But you owe me one."

She took a step toward him, then hesitated. "Matt, I had no idea that Captain Friedlander might be my father."

"I have to admit that you couldn't have made things more difficult for your new big brother. Your arrival before his party must have been a huge shock for him." He patted the sofa. "I figured I might as well sleep here, because I thought he might make things difficult for you and you'd be back."

"He tried."

"But your precious father is so delighted with his new toy that he would ruin even his ambitions for his son to keep you here."

She sat beside him on the sofa. "Matt, why didn't you tell me your real name?"

"Matt Winchester is my real name now."

"But your family is here in Philadelphia. You didn't tell

me that or that they owned the big store across from Friedlander's."

He stood, as if he could not tolerate being so close to her. "This has been about your family, not mine, Chandelle. And, as it seems you have found more than you expected waiting for you in Philadelphia, I'm not sure you need me any longer."

"How can you say that?" She jumped to her feet. *That was not what I meant to say.* Or was it? She needed him, not just his help, but his kisses. "Matt—Should I still call you Matt?"

"It's still my name."

He was not going to make this easy for her, but then he had not made anything easy for her during their journey north and their time together in Philadelphia. Nothing had been easy but falling in love with him.

She tried to ignore that thought. "Matt, I hired you to help me get my grandmother's coming home quilt. I still don't have it."

"You fired me last night."

"I didn't mean to." She clenched her hands. "Matt, you made me so angry!"

A hint of a sparkle swept through his eyes, gone almost before she had seen it. "You're a real spitfire when you get your dander up, Chandelle. If you didn't want to fire me, you shouldn't have said so."

"And you shouldn't have quit."

"You don't need me. You have your new father to help you get your quilt."

"He doesn't seem too interested in helping me."

He laughed tightly. "That's no surprise. Don't you see, Chandelle? You are the prize that he has won in his final years, a beautiful daughter who can be used to forge new alliances for the Friedlander family in an effort to gain more power in this city."

"You don't know what you're talking about."

"Oh, but, honey, I do. I saw the very same thing happen to my cousins."

"Cousins?"

"Not as many as you, and probably few of them very happy with their arranged marriages. But the Matheson family benefited with each one of those marriages, gaining control of one of the shipyards and valuable land around the city and beyond."

"That's awful!"

"That's the way things are among the robber barons of Philadelphia. I'm sure your father will think he is doing his best for you."

"I'm not a commodity to be bought and sold."

"As the daughter of Esau Friedlander, you are, honey. But do you want to know what is really awful?"

"No, I don't think so."

"I think you do." He grasped her wrist. "None of my cousins in those arranged marriages will ever know the pleasure of honest, uncontrollable desire."

She gasped when he pulled her against him, and yearning flared amid the anger in his eyes. Her own eyes closed as he tilted her mouth beneath his. Her heart ached to believe that he loved her as she loved him, that she could trust him with both her quest and her heart.

He teased her with light kisses and laughed against her neck when she shivered beneath the power of her need. She forgot everything else as she exulted in the pleasure. As his lips traced scintillating delight along her throat, she discovered there was nothing she wanted more than him caressing her with his mouth and his hands. No, there was. She wanted to touch him, too. She was shocked and pleased by her audacity when she slipped her hands beneath his loosened shirt to curve up his smooth back.

He leaned her against his arm as his mouth slid along her. Its moist warmth banished all thoughts of anything but him.

So lost was she in ecstasy she did not realize he had lifted her into his arms and carried her to the sofa until the cushions surrounded her. He held her to the sofa with his lips against hers.

Brushing her hair back from her face, he whispered, "Why can't I stay angry with you?"

"Probably for the same reason I can't stay angry with you."

He kissed her cheek. "Stop fleeing from me, honey," he whispered against the half circle of her ear. She quivered where he touched her. "Let me love you. You want that as much as I do."

"Yes!" She did not hesitate. She did want this. She knew she risked everything as her mother and grandmother had when their husbands left to fight their wars. She was tired of fighting the demons hiding in her heart. The grief and fear of being left utterly alone would resurface to haunt her when he was gone, but they could never frighten her when she was with Matt.

"Then come with me." He held out his hand.

She smiled impishly. Without a blush of self-consciousness, she reached up to the buttons on his shirt. "No, you stay here with me."

"You are a Friedlander." He chuckled. "Giving orders already."

"Don't speak of that. I don't want to think of that." She let her fingers enmesh in the hair on his chest. "I want to think only of this moment with you."

"Yes," he whispered, a rough edge to his voice. "But not here. Nor on that narrow bed in the other room."

Pulling the blanket from the sofa, he spread it across the floor. He sat and drew her down next to him. As he teased her earlobe with the tip of his tongue, she undid his shirt.

He pushed his sleeves along his arms, and she explored the breadth of his chest, sighing with eagerness. He leaned her onto the blanket. She did not notice the scratchy wool as her hands curved up his back, bringing him to her. The gentle pressure of him over her acquainted her with every inch of his hard, male body.

She was unprepared for the passion on his lips. It stripped away her breath and every thought. Each gasp brushed her breasts against his chest.

His gaze held hers as his fingers loosened the hooks along the back of her gown. A smile played on his lips as he lowered it to reveal the silk beneath. Fingering the lace across her breasts, he chuckled. "I like you in your father's French fashions, honey."

For once, she had no quick answer to his jests, for she could not think of anything but his hand on her. When it slipped beneath the silk to cup her breast, she moaned and arched toward him. She wanted to feel him with every bit of her. His thumb swept up her breast to tease its very tip. Writhing with the craving she could no longer control, she pulled his mouth down over hers. His tongue parried with hers, each motion matching his daring fingers.

Drawing away, he brought her to her feet. Her gown fell about her feet. With a laugh, he loosened the ribbons on her petticoats and swung her up into his arms, sending them and her dress flying across the room. He silenced her laugh when he pressed his lips over hers.

Slowly he set her on her feet and reached for the narrow straps of her chemise. He did not release her gaze as he pushed first one strap of her chemise, then the other below her shoulders.

She lifted the chemise off over her head and threw it to one side atop her dress. Her laughter became a soft cry of delight when he pulled her against his naked chest, her skin on his sending an explosion of sensation through her.

His mouth left hers, coursing along her neck before pressing over her thundering heartbeat. When it followed the curve of her breast, she clutched on to his shoulders as he knelt. She moaned when his tongue toyed with her breast, flitting across it like a hot summer rain searing eager earth. She sagged against him, too weakened by passion to stand.

She whispered his name in a desperate plea for what he ached to give her. He brought her down on the blanket again. Quickly he pulled off the last of her clothes as she unbuttoned his trousers. He stood to let them fall away. She smiled and held up her arms as her gaze wandered along him in open admiration. Her fingers ached to touch him. Leaning over her, he introduced her to the sturdy strength of his bare body.

Her mouth surrendered to the ecstasy conjured up by his.

Heat burned deep within her and would not be eased. Her hands slid along his hard body as his arm encircled her waist. Her fingers lingered on his hips until he took them with a smile and led them to discover every inch of him. Her breath caught as his eyes closed with pleasure. She fought to release it, but could not when his fingers rose along her legs and discovered the site of this unquenchable fire. His mouth melded with hers.

A craving so powerful that it burned like fiery ice overpowered her. She heard his voice murmuring against her mouth, but none of the words reached her fevered brain. She looked up to see him rising above her. She held out her arms to welcome him. They tightened around his shoulders as he sought pleasure in her.

With his mouth on hers and their bodies one, she moved with the rhythm he was teaching her. A quiver raced through her, showing that all other pleasure had been only a prelude. Like a waterfall down a mountainside, her passion surged forth, unstoppable.

Her body answered his, wanting to give as much as she took. Wanting more. Always wanting. The fever consumed her. Lost in the acute agony of needing and wanting, she clasped his shoulders. She was clay remolded about him. In the fire of his passion, she shattered into a million shards of rapture she could share only with this man she loved.

∞

CHANDELLE SMOOTHED MATT'S HAIR from his forehead. When he turned his face to kiss her fingers, he whispered, "You are wondrous, honey."

His mouth on hers halted her answer as it had every time she had started to reply. She knew she should ask him why he was keeping her from speaking. She did not care. She wanted only to savor this soft twilight of their passion.

"Matt, I love—"

"Don't talk, honey," he whispered, but she sensed the tension that tightened his body. "Just let me hold you for as long as I can."

She put her hand to his chest to push herself away so he could not discover how her heart was breaking within her. She loved him, but he wanted only her body.

When she sat, he did, too, drawing her back against his chest. "What is it?"

"I told Esau that I would only be a hour." How easy it was to fall back on the habit of half-truths! "If I stay here much longer, the coachman will come to see what is wrong."

"You don't have to go back there, Chandelle. Stay with me. You know you want to."

"Yes, but I can't." She wished he had continued to quell her questions with his kisses. Then she could pretend nothing else mattered, not even her heart that refused to accept that Matt Winchester had been so hurt by those he once had loved that he did not dare to love again.

"You're really going back to Rittenhouse Square?"

"Only long enough to get my grandmother's quilt."

"It still might not be as easy as you hope." He traced her brow before his finger coursed along her cheek. "Friedlander seems to be in no hurry to help you."

"Then we shall have to find it."

He shook his head sadly. "I'll only be a handicap for you now. I won't be allowed into the house."

"We'll have to see about that." She grinned. "In case you've forgotten, I am Esau Friedlander's daughter."

His smile faded. "I never forget that, honey, although I wish I could."

Standing, she held out her hand. "Matt, even though our families are rivals, I still need your help. Will you help me?"

"For the usual pay?"

She could not help laughing. "For a dollar a day plus expenses and all the trouble I fear we soon shall find ourselves in."

"I hope your words aren't prophetic."

An icy shudder slid down Chandelle's back, but she said nothing as she dressed. When Matt hooked his collar to his shirt and pulled on his coat, she noticed it was not the fancy one he had worn last night, but the dusty frock coat that was smudged from their ride on the train.

The coachman looked horrified when Chandelle came out of the house with Matt. He said nothing as she asked him to have her trunk brought down to the carriage.

"Are you sure you want to have your things over there?" Matt asked as he handed her into the carriage.

"I want to keep things simple, and, to do that, I need to bring my clothes to my father's house."

He grumbled, but she did not answer. She could not change who her father was any more than he could change his. Slipping her hand into his, she tried to smile.

"All set, miss," the coachman said, peering into the window.

"Then back to Rittenhouse Square." She let her shoulders sag against the thick cushions of the seat.

"With him?"

Chandelle glanced from Matt's cool smile to the coachman's perplexed expression. "Yes. Please hurry. I told Mr. Friedlander that I would meet him at the store by eleven. I don't want to be late."

As she had hoped, at the mention of his employer's name, the coachman hurried to climb into his seat.

"Rank does have its privileges, doesn't it?" she asked, smiling.

"Not enough to make up for noblesse oblige. The duties that go with money eat at one's soul until there is nothing left."

"Is that why you left Philadelphia?"

"Partly."

She waited for him to go on, but he added nothing else. Instead, he gazed out the window as if he had never seen these streets before. Wishing she could reach past the barriers that he kept so closed around him, she looked down at their entwined fingers. He was not shutting her out completely.

Chandelle savored that thought as they turned onto Rittenhouse Square. The traffic here was less, and each carriage was as magnificent as the one they rode in. A few drays rolled along the street, making deliveries. When they stopped in front of the Friedlanders' house, she offered Matt a smile.

He brushed her cheek with his lips and tilted her face toward his. When he did not kiss her, she opened her eyes. Was this another of his jests?

The answer was clear on his taut face. He was staring past her to the other side of the street. She turned.

Another carriage waited there. As its coachman jumped down, she pressed her hands over her mouth. He wore the same uniform as the man driving this carriage. Her father should be at the store by this hour, so it must be Jakob. She hoped he would remember his political aspirations and not make a scene.

She choked back a gasp when the door was opened, and a man emerged. The sun glinted silver off his hair. Esau! He crossed the street as Matt assisted Chandelle from their carriage.

"Are you mad, Chandelle?" Esau shouted as loudly as the teamsters farther along the square. "I told you I wanted you to have nothing more to do with Matheson."

"He offered to continue helping me find my grandmother's quilt." Lying would gain her nothing now when she suspected as many curious gazes were coming from the houses around them as when she had arrived at Mrs. Coates's boardinghouse.

"Chandelle," Esau ordered, "go into the house and stay there."

"Very well. We shall spend the rest of the morning looking for the quilt." She held out her hand to Matt.

"Don't touch her, Matheson," Esau warned in a clipped voice. "She will have nothing to do with the likes of you."

When he struck Matt's arm with his walking stick, she gasped, "Are you insane? Stop that!"

"Chandelle," Matt said softly, "do as he says. Go in the house." When she opened her mouth to protest, he repeated, "Go in the house. Now!"

She nodded when she saw Matt's stilted smile. She recognized it. He was trying to keep her from causing any more trouble for herself. Climbing the steps, she strained to hear what her father was saying to Matt. The teamsters' yelling drowned out their words. The front door opened, but she did not go in.

She forced back a scream when her father raised his walking stick again. Matt stepped aside, and the cane hit the carriage with a sharp crack. Her father turned and strode toward his carriage. Matt called something, but the words were lost in a shriek from the far end of the street.

Horror choked her as a horse raced along the street, its wagon bouncing wildly behind it.

"Look out!" she cried.

More shouts came from the house. She ran down the steps. She called out another warning as she stumbled off the curb. Arms kept her from falling. When she tried to pull away, they twisted her against Matt's chest. He pressed her face to his shoulder. Nothing could halt the sound of a man's scream and a thick thud.

"Let me go!" she gasped.

"No," he whispered, his cheek on hers. "I won't."

"But Esau—"

His voice was as unsteady as hers. "Esau Friedlander is dead."

17

CHANDELLE SAT ON THE divan in the front room of the Friedlander house and stared straight ahead. She wished she could erase from her memory the image of Esau Friedlander's crumpled body on the street. Although Matt had kept her from witnessing the horrible accident, she had seen the street as he hurried her into the house.

Esau Friedlander—*her father*—was dead. Before she had had a chance to know him, her father was dead. His life had come to an ignoble end, run down by a frightened horse. Gone.

As she sat on the divan, despair surrounded her. And guilt, for even more appalling than her father's death was that she was more paralyzed by the thought that Matt could have been the one dead out in the street. She had watched him being struck by a dray only a few days ago. He had survived, but, if he had followed her father into the street to continue their argument, Matt would have been dead, too.

"She saw nothing. You don't need to speak with her now." Anger rang through Matt's voice.

Chandelle looked toward the doors leading to the foyer. They were half-closed, but she could see Matt and two other men. Men with policemen's uniforms. She should get up. She should go and talk to them.

"Sir, we need to speak with Miss McBride." That must be one of the police officers speaking. Her mind was working so slowly, lost in a morass of molasses.

"I told you. She saw nothing." Matt's voice remained impatient. "She's in shock at the moment."

"It will take only a minute."

"Not now. Give her a chance to compose herself."

"Sir, we need to do our job."

"And you can, but give her some time. For the love of heaven, her father was just killed."

Chandelle came to her feet as she heard the policeman choke, "Father? She's Esau Friedlander's daughter?"

Matt should not have revealed that. She must explain that to him. Pushing herself away from the divan, she started for the door. She had gone only a step or two before the floor began to sway. From somewhere, she heard a scream. Her voice? Someone else's? She had no answer as the room vanished into darkness.

∽

"SLOWLY. OPEN YOUR EYES slowly." The words were hushed.

Chandelle was glad to obey. Although she feared light would leap through the windows to stab her eyes, the room was dim. Had she fallen asleep and let the day pass unnoticed? Her head ached with the steady pounding of a locomotive climbing a steep incline.

Matt bent over her, and something wondrously cool settled on her forehead. She sighed and sank deeper into the cushions to enjoy the unexpected relief from agony.

"You scared the devil out of us," he whispered. "Keeling over in a faint."

"McBride women don't faint. We're stronger than that."

He smiled, and she did, too, for her voice was as weak as a summer breeze. "If that was not a faint, it was a very good copy of one." He sat beside her. On a stool, she guessed, because the cushions beneath her did not shift. "The police are gone, but they will want to talk with you."

She gazed up at the fancy ceiling. "I know."

"I told them you didn't see anything."

"I know." She closed her eyes. "And you told them that Esau was my father."

"I figured I should before someone else did." His curt chuckle was hushed. "If you think any of the servants in this house don't know what's going on, you don't know much about servants."

"I don't know anything about servants. I don't know anything about this life."

He took her hand. "I know. That's why I think you should move back to Mrs. Coates's boardinghouse where I can keep an eye on you."

She sat. "I couldn't do that. Going there with you now would create even more gossip."

He stood. "Oh, I see. Now that you're the fine Philadelphia lady, you don't want to do anything to risk what you've gotten for yourself."

"You know it's not that." She lowered her eyes from his accusing stare. "Matt, my father welcomed me here as if I were the prodigal son."

"Which must have pleased his other son to no end."

"I doubt if Jakob will ever accept me as part of this family, but I can't change the past." She looked up at him as she whispered, "Even if I wish I could."

"If Friedlander lied about you being his daughter—"

"Why would he lie?"

Matt opened his mouth to answer, then shook his head. "I have no idea, but I know that anyone who trusts a Friedlander is doomed."

"Matt, I'm a Friedlander now."

He drew her to her feet. He crushed her mouth beneath his as if he could force every drop of Friedlander blood out of her. Slowly his kiss gentled from anger to the longing that coursed through her. His lips teased her with an invitation to more rapture. When he whispered her name in her ear, she quivered. Her mind fought this onslaught of pleasure while she struggled to think of a way to convince him of the madness of his plan.

When she eased out of his arms, he murmured a soft curse. She understood all too well, because she wished she could lean against the wall of his chest and let him lead her again to ecstasy. How simple her life had been even a few days ago! Then, she could gaze up into his dark eyes and watch them close as his lips claimed her waiting flesh, setting her aflame with his touch.

Grazing his cheek with the back of her hand, she bit her lip when he grasped it like a drowning man, pressing it to his mouth. They were adrift, lost from everything that had seemed so straightforward on their way north.

"Chandelle, come with me. I don't want you staying in this place."

"My grandmother's quilt is here."

"Maybe. Friedlander seemed in no hurry to look for it. Maybe he knew it wasn't here."

She pushed away from him. "Don't even suggest that. It has to be here." Her voice broke as she sat again. "I don't know where else to look."

"There may be no other place to look." He knelt beside her. "It may have been destroyed a long time ago. Friedlander may have known that, but, if he had told you the truth, you would not have stayed."

Coming to her feet, because she could not sit still, she said, "You don't know that for sure. He told me the truth about being my father."

"Did he?"

"I'll know for certain as soon as I find Grandma's coming home quilt and take it to her. She will tell me the truth." Again her voice cracked. "I hope."

"She'd be a fool not to when you consider the millions that will be yours now."

She faced him. "Millions?"

"Half of Friedlander's estate should be yours." He laughed icily. "I never thought when I agreed to help a beautiful waif down in Asheville that she would be an heiress."

"I don't care about any money!"

"It would pay off your grandmother's debts."

"But what good will that do me now? I'm not interested in anything but my grandmother's coming home quilt. I thought you understood that!"

"I'm beginning to." He reached for his hat on the table behind him.

"Where are you going?"

"To get my bag at Mrs. Coates's boardinghouse." He scanned the room quickly. "It's going to take a while to search this whole house. I might as well live in comfort while we're doing it." His grin returned. "After all, I've gotten used to letting you take care of my expenses."

She ran her tongue across her bottom lip. "Do you think that is wise? Jakob—"

"We'll deal with your brother when I get back."

"But he is going to be so upset."

"Do you think so?"

"His father is dead."

"I'm sure he'll be a fervent, albeit less than genuine mourner." He kissed her swiftly. "Wait here, Chandelle. Promise me that you won't do anything stupid this time."

"I didn't do anything stupid last time." When his grin widened, she sighed with a smile. "All right. I was foolish not to wait for you before I came here. I promise not to do anything stupid this time."

"Good."

"Take the carriage. It will get you there and back more quickly."

He shook his head. "Bad idea. I'd better take the trolley. We don't need to draw more attention to anyone or anything connected to this house while the police are investigating in the hopes of putting some blame on someone for the accidental death of one of Philadelphia's leading citizens." He brushed his hand against her cheek again. "Trust me on this, Chandelle."

"I do trust you."

Surprise widened his eyes, but he said nothing as he walked out of the room.

She sat on the very edge of the divan. Hearing the front door open and close, she shut her eyes as grief suffocated her again. Not just for her ailing grandmother, not just for Esau, not just because her life had been irrevocably changed by this quest, but at the thought of how, as soon as they found Grandma's coming home quilt and returned to Asheville, Matt would walk out once again.

And he would not be coming back.

She had known how risky it would be to fall in love with a man who had so many dragons to slay and castles to storm. By giving him her heart, she would never be complete once he left.

What else could go wrong?

∞

SOMETHING MUST BE WRONG.

Chandelle paced along the silent corridor on the second floor. She paused by the front window to look at the street, trying to disregard the crowd still gathered by the spot where her father had been run down. Twilight was slipping into the street, because the sun had vanished across the river almost an hour ago.

Where was Matt? He should have been back hours ago. No one had come to the house except the undertaker, who had been considerate enough not to ask to speak with her. The papers that the butler Dowdle had given her were on the desk in Esau's office. She should read them, but she could not think of anything except that Matt had not returned.

Wrapping her arms around herself, she turned from the window. A scream seared her throat as she saw a dark form behind her. She was glad she had not let it escape when a sconce on the wall was lit, and she realized the form belonged to Jakob.

She whispered, "I didn't hear you come in."

"I thought it prudent to use the kitchen door instead of being bombarded by the public's prurient curiosity." He looked past her to the window. "I see you are enjoying watching the mourners file past."

"I wasn't watching." She sighed. "I don't want to see them. It reminds me that our father is dead. I wish I could have known him better."

"So you stand here, like a ship captain's wife on her widow's walk, staring out into the night to do his memory honor?" He closed the distance between them, but she did not edge away. With the window at her back, anything he did would be visible in the street.

Shock riveted her. Jakob Friedlander was a gentleman, wasn't he? He had been raised to embrace this luxurious life that she had never imagined. *But so had Matt.* That thought was a comfort, for, in spite of all his declarations otherwise, Matt could not rid himself of his past. He was gentle and kind and cared about others, even though he wished he did not.

"I was just looking out," she answered.

"For whom?" He put his hand on the window frame beside her ear. "Don't bother to answer. I know. You were looking for Matheson." He snarled an oath. "I didn't believe it was true, but you *did* welcome him under my father's roof."

"Our father." She would not let him bully her. "I asked Matt to come here to help me find my grandmother's quilt."

"Quilt?" When she began to explain, he cut her off. "I've heard enough of this. Not that it matters, sister." He still managed to hiss out the word *sister* as if it were an insult. "From what I've just learned, you needn't worry about him bothering you again."

"What do you mean?"

"Surely you are not so lost in your feigned grief—"

She pushed past him. "My grief at our father's death is sincere. More than yours, it seems."

When her arm was grasped and she was spun to see Jakob's fury, she knew she had been foolish to repeat Matt's opinions.

Each word twisted out past his pursed lips. "You know

nothing of me. How can you understand the depth of my grief at *my* father's death?"

"And you know nothing of me." She tried to pull her arm away, but his fingers tightened, grinding into her skin. When she winced, she snapped, "Release me at once."

"You do not give orders in this house. Even though you persuaded my father in his dotage that you were a long-lost daughter from some misguided affair, I recognize a fortune hunter when I see one." He pushed his face close to hers. "You will not see one penny of my father's money. All you'll see is your lover's death."

"Death?" she choked.

"I have it from a good source that Matheson is the primary suspect in my father's untimely death."

"Matt?" She drew away and grasped the knob of a door behind her, fearing her knees would collapse. "You know that is absurd!"

"Is it? There are dozens of witnesses that will testify that my father and Matheson were arguing before my father's death."

She forced herself to stand straighter. "And will they also testify that *our* father struck Matt with his walking stick and that Matt did not retaliate?"

Jakob sputtered for a moment, then said, "They will tell the truth of what they saw. Will you?"

"I saw nothing. Matt saved me from seeing anything."

"That is very convenient for both of you. I was told he would not allow you to speak to the police. Why?"

"Because he knows how distressed I am."

"Maybe." He chuckled. "Or maybe he wanted to be sure you were well rehearsed in the lies he was spinning for the authorities. He's long wanted to see the downfall of this family."

"You're insane. He left Philadelphia because he hates the rivalry between the Friedlanders and his family."

"He told you that?" Again Jakob laughed. "You innocent fool. He left because I married the girl he loved."

"Married? You're married?"

"Was. She died only a few months after we were wed.

By that time, Matheson had left Philadelphia like the beaten dog he is, vowing to repay this family and his own, which had refused to consider the match because his father had already arranged for him to marry someone else."

Chandelle pressed her hands to her icy cheeks as she stared at Jakob's triumphant smile. She had never guessed that Matt had loved a woman he could never have. She did not want to imagine the heartbreak he must have suffered when his family denied him the love filling his heart. Then to lose that love to a man he despised . . . She feared her own heart would freeze in sorrow for him. And for herself, because, if he still loved that woman, that explained why he was willing to offer Chandelle ecstasy, but not his heart.

"If he played a hand in my father's death," Jakob continued, smiling even more broadly, "it seems quite logical to assume that you were a part of it." He seized her face in his broad hand. "Did your greed get the better of you, Chandelle? I guess you couldn't wait for your share of the Friedlander fortune to shower on your paramour."

Unsure which nonsense to respond to first when her heart was crumbling, she said, "You are mistaken."

"Am I? Or are you? You may have acted out of hand, because you gave Father no time to change his will to include you. How ironic that he was on his way to call on his attorneys when he died!" He shoved her away. "Now you will get nothing but seeing your lover tried and executed. You are as great a fool as your mother. At least, she had the good taste to bed a Friedlander instead of a Matheson."

Her hand striking his face echoed through the hall. She did not look back as she ran to her room and slammed the door closed, but she could not shut out the fear that followed her.

The police must be looking for Matt, for she was certain Jakob had told them his poisonous fabrications. Maybe they already had Matt in custody. Was that why he had not come back? She hoped he was in hiding, but he could not stay hidden forever. The policemen would be watching the train station, so he could not go there.

She never should have asked herself what else could go wrong. Too late, she knew.

∞

CHANDELLE FOLDED THE SLIP of paper that had been delivered to her minutes ago and put it into her quilting bag. The telegram contained one word.

Hurry.

Trust Marnie not to waste money when a single word would let Chandelle know that her grandmother's situation had worsened.

She glanced around the bedroom. She had never had such a wondrous place to sleep, and she doubted if she ever would again. Once she left this house, Jakob would guarantee she was never allowed in again.

He was equally determined to keep her from searching for her grandmother's quilt. He had chided her before half the servants last night when he stopped her from going up to the attics. Tearing about the house in a search for something that was unlikely to exist would create a bad impression for those who would be calling to offer their sympathy. Maybe after the funeral . . .

She could not wait that long. Grandma needed her quilt now.

Matt had friends who would sneak into the house to get the quilt. That thought had chased after her as she paced her room all night.

But Matt was in so much trouble himself, and it was her fault. She had to find a way to help him as he had tried to help her. That would take more money than a dollar a day plus expenses.

Chandelle smiled grimly as she opened the door to Esau's office. Going to the desk, she drew out the top drawer. Early morning sunshine filtered through the closed drapes that showed the city that this household was in mourning. She hesitated as she reached into the drawer, then pulled out a handful of the money Jakob had collected from his political benefactors.

She had never stolen anything, for her first lessons had been filled with how Captain Friedlander had almost destroyed her family by stealing from them. But this money might buy allies to help her help Matt. She froze when footsteps came along the hallway. If she was discovered here, Jakob would send for the police and have her thrown in jail. Then no one would help Matt or her.

The footfalls passed the closed door without pausing. Chandelle stuffed the money into her bag. She shut the drawer and tiptoed to the door. Cautiously she opened it. Peeking out, she slipped through the shadows by the stairs. She hoped her frantic heartbeat did not betray her, for it pounded in her ears even more loudly than the clock on the landing.

She hurried along the street. Risking a glance back, she released her breath. None of the drapes had been pulled aside to let someone see her leave.

At the corner, she waited for the trolley. She would take it to the train station where she could hire a carriage to take her to Jesse's cigar shop on Fitzwater Street. Maybe she could convince Matt's friend to find a way to convey a message to him. Then she would make a second stop.

She looked down at the address she had written on a slip of paper. Broad Street near Jefferson. The serving girl who had given her the address had been very nervous about admitting that she knew where the Matheson family lived. Involving Matt's family in this might be the only chance to get help to prove him innocent of murdering Esau Friedlander.

She only wished she could know if he would accept that help.

CHANDELLE HESITATED AS SHE reached for the knocker on the front door of the huge Italianate mansion that claimed half a city block. Was she doing the right thing?

Finding Jesse in his cigar shop had been easy. Persuading him to help her by delivering a message to Matt had been as easy, although it had taken twenty dollars to buy his cooperation. She would have balked at the high price if she had not guessed he knew where Matt was. Her hints that he should tell her had gained her nothing but a cool smile.

A butler in immaculate gray livery opened the door. "Good morning, miss."

"I would like to speak with the Mathesons, please."

"Mrs. Matheson never receives callers earlier than two o'clock. Mr. Matheson—"

She pushed past him. She was tired of the restrictions of this strangulating society. There was no time for niceties when Matt was in danger of being convicted for a crime he had not committed.

"Miss—" The butler reached to halt her but pulled his hand back. She knew he could not overstep his bounds to use physical force to halt a lady.

Good! She would use these conventions to help her. Walking past the parlor, she was delighted to find a blue dining room beyond it. A man and a woman were sitting at the long table. Other chairs had been pushed back, but no one sat there.

The man looked up from his newspaper when the woman gasped in surprise. These must be Matt's parents, because Chandelle could see a resemblance to his dark coloring in the woman's still-black hair. The man's face, though wider than Matt's, had the identical firm lines as his mouth pulled down in a familiar frown.

"What is the meaning of this intrusion, Beers?" he demanded.

The butler answered, "Mr. Matheson, she would not be stopped. I tried to explain that you were not at home to guests at this early hour."

Chandelle edged away from the butler again. "Mr. Matheson, I am sorry to intrude, but I must speak with you and Mrs. Matheson immediately."

"Who are you?"

"Chandelle McBride."

His frown wavered. "Have we met, Miss McBride?"

"No." She hoped her smile was secure. All doubts that she was in the right place vanished when she looked past the woman to a painting over the fireplace. The young man in the painting, although he wore the clothing of a generation before, could have been Matt.

"Miss McBride?"

She pulled her gaze from the painting. It must be of the man standing before her.

Taking a deep breath, she said, "No, we have not met previously, Mr. Matheson. I hope you will forgive this presumptuous call." She squared her shoulders. "I am a friend of your son's." She almost choked on those words. She and Matt were so much more than friends, but that could be over. Even if he could be saved from misguided justice, he might be pining for the one woman he had loved.

"Dorian?" The woman pressed her hand over her full chest. "You know where he is?"

"Dorian?" Chandelle repeated.

"I thought you said you were a friend of our son, Miss McBride." Mr. Matheson's scowl was now firmly in place. "If you do not know so much as his name, you can understand our doubts about your claim."

"I had no idea his name is Dorian." She wondered if she would ever accustom herself to that name for him. Matt fit him so much better. "Until two days ago, I've known him as Matt Winchester."

"Do you know where he is?" Mrs. Matheson repeated. "We had no idea he was even in Philadelphia until we heard that he has been accused of murdering Esau Friedlander."

"He didn't do that!" Her fear burst from her in a cry. "How could you believe that he would do such a thing? You are his parents!"

"He severed any bond with this family when he left Philadelphia," Mr. Matheson said in a stern tone that echoed Matt's. "If you know where he is, Miss McBride, you should tell him to turn himself over to the authorities without delay."

"I don't know where he is." She paused to pray that she had not made things worse. "But he may be coming here."

"Here?" Mrs. Matheson came to her feet. "Here? He's coming here?"

Her husband put a calming hand on her arm, a motion so like Matt that Chandelle had to look away. "I think you should sit down, Mrs. Matheson," he said.

"But he's coming here." Her voice fractured. "He's coming back."

"Is this true, Miss McBride?" Mr. Matheson asked. "Is he really coming here?"

"Yes," she answered with all the confidence she could muster. "Will you hear him out instead of calling for the police?"

"I will hear him out." He put his hand on his weeping wife's shoulder. "Then I will call the police as necessary."

"No!" Chandelle cried. "You can't do that! I told him that you'd agreed to help him."

"I never agreed to such a thing."

"Mr. Matheson," his wife gasped. "He is our son."

"Who may have finally done what he said he would do to repay Jakob Friedlander for marrying that Cutler girl. I will not have this family shamed more."

Chandelle stared at him in astonishment. It might have been Esau Friedlander speaking. These two men cared more about their reputations than their children. Her dreams of her father had been so different. Maybe Matt's had, too, and that was why he had left. She edged toward the hall. She must leave, too, and warn him not to come here.

Mr. Matheson's shout followed her toward the front door. The butler stepped in front of it in a belligerent pose. His scowl warned he would not hesitate to use whatever means he must to halt her. There must be another way out of this house. She whirled and gasped as she discovered Mr. Matheson right behind her.

He motioned grandly to the sitting room on her left. "Miss McBride, I trust you will join Mrs. Matheson and me while we wait for our son to arrive."

She faltered, wanting to devise some excuse that would convince them to let her leave. Mr. Matheson took her arm, steering her to a chair on the side of the room farthest from the tall windows.

How could she have been so wrong? She had thought that Matt's family would be like her own in North Carolina, strong-willed and hot-tempered enough to disown each other over an insult, but pulling together when anyone outside the family tried to cause trouble. Grandma had not spoken to Cousin Pike in years, considering him a fool twice over for his moonshining. Yet she had rallied the family around him when he was arrested, making certain no one would speak poorly of him in court.

But Matt's family was not like that. Her assumptions had betrayed her and, she was afraid, him.

∞

MATT KNEW HE WAS in trouble. Two men had been shadowing him since he got off the trolley several blocks south of here. Police? He doubted that, because they would have grabbed him by now and hauled him before some judge who was in Jakob Friedlander's pocket.

He looked at the slip of paper Jesse had given him when his friend had brought him something to eat this morning. The paper smelled, as everything did in Jesse's shop and in the storage room above it, of tobacco. Right now, he wished he was still in that storage room enjoying one of Jesse's finer cigars while he tried to figure a way out of this mess.

Now these two were following him. Had Friedlander set them on his trail to find him? Not likely, because Matt had made sure no one could figure out where he was.

Chandelle has.

That was because he had made the mistake of telling her Jesse's name. Friedlander had no knowledge of his connection to Jesse's shop.

Unless he has had Chandelle followed.

Jesse had assured him that she had been alone. Before he had even talked to her, he had checked the street. No one suspicious had been about.

Matt climbed the steps to the fancy front door of the fancy house in the fancy neighborhood. Why was she having their meeting here?

The door opened, and he stared at a face he had not seen in years. His father's butler Beers! *This* was his parents' house? He had assumed that they still lived south of here.

He started to turn, then heard the footsteps right behind him. Looking over his shoulder, he saw two burly men on the lower steps. He raised his hand toward the gun under his coat, then drew it away as they mirrored his action. Who were they?

"Will you come in, Mr. Dorian?" asked the always proper Beers.

"Only if you call me Matt."

The butler flinched at his cheerful answer, but said, "As you wish, Mr. Matt."

"Just Matt is good enough."

Beers nodded and stepped back to let him enter.

The two men followed Matt inside, and he guessed his father had hired them. To make sure he didn't cause his family more trouble? They were as silent as the grave. He grimaced at the thought.

"Your coat, sir?" Beers held out his hands.

"I'll keep it. Thanks."

"Sir?" He pointed at Matt's chest. "I must insist."

"I'm sure you must." He held up both hands. "You'd better take my gun out yourself. I don't want these two to get hurt when I prove I can outshoot them."

Ignoring the grumbles from the men behind him, he waited until Beers gingerly plucked the gun from beneath his coat. He almost laughed when Beers's nose wrinkled in disgust. He did smell rather like a sewer. His coat was smeared with dirt and some things that had not yet dried.

"They are waiting in the front parlor, sir," Beers said quietly.

"Then I shouldn't keep them waiting."

He lowered his voice even more. "*She* has been waiting here against her will for almost two hours, sir."

Matt nodded, fighting the fury that could destroy any chance he had of saving Chandelle from her misguided attempt to save him. His father had no right to impose his imperious will on her.

He went to the broad doorway and looked around the room. His father was standing by the hearth while his mother and younger brother and sister were perched on chairs nearby. The perfect family portrait. Where was Chandelle? He smiled. Father probably had her stashed away in one of the shadowy corners until he discovered how his wayward son would act.

Mr. Matheson cleared his throat before saying, "If you linger there much longer, Mrs. Matheson may not be able to restrain her tears."

"I have no wish to cause her further dismay." Matt took a single step into the room. A hiccuped sob drew his gaze to his mother, who was dabbing her eyes with a lacy handkerchief. "Good afternoon, Mother."

"Dorian..." She pressed the handkerchief to her face.

Knowing it would take her some time to compose herself, he looked past her. His eyes widened. Could that pretty young woman, whose hair was as dark as his, be his baby sister? "You have certainly grown up, Adrienne. And, Carl, you must be a foot taller than you were when I last saw you."

"It's been almost eight years since—" His brother, who was almost man-high, clamped his lips closed when Father glared at him before locking gazes with Matt.

Nothing else had changed, it seemed. His father still stood in that stubborn stance, master of his home and his stores and everything else he could lay claim to. Only his elder son had rebelled, refusing to obey his decrees.

"It has been a long time," Matt said, taking pity on his siblings.

"Dorian!" moaned his mother. "It is so good to have you home." She hastily lowered her eyes after a guilty glance at her husband.

"I understand you are using the name Winchester now," his father said.

"Yes." He laughed without amusement. "I doubted if, even if you had chosen to try to find me, you would have conceived of me keeping any part of this family's name as my own."

"I doubt if, at this point, I could conceive of anything you might do."

"For once, we are in agreement." He let his shoulders ease from his stiff pose. If his father had intended to order those men to shoot him, he would not have all these witnesses cluttering up the room.

"If you have come here looking for help now—"

"I did not come here looking for your help, Father. I am surprised that you are not dancing in the streets. You said so often that you wished Esau Friedlander was dead." He ignored the gasp from his sister as he went on, "However, I am not a paragon of filial sycophancy, doing you this great favor, so you can ease your fears. I did not murder him."

"Dorian," his mother choked out. "Such language!"

"Forgive me, Mother." Again he bowed his head in her direction. "My current employer has scolded me many times for forgetting how to treat the gentler sex."

"Dorian!"

He smiled. "Forgive me again for using words that apparently disturb you, Mother. As you can see, Chandelle is right." Slowly he turned toward where she sat in the corner. His breath faltered. Even though her tawny hair was pulled back in a demure bun, his fingers recalled when it had been a silken river flowing over her and over him. His senses were filled with the memory of its fragrance and how it tickled his lip when he sampled the rapture along her neck. Strain tightened his voice as he said, "I'm surprised, Father, that you thought you could keep a golden angel hidden."

Chandelle rose as Matt held out his hand to her. She wanted to run to him and beg his forgiveness for her horrid mistake. She had promised him that she would wait for him to return, but again she had thrown herself headlong into trying to make things right. All she had done was make them worse. She longed to fold his fingers between hers. He had offered her comfort so often that way. Maybe her touch now would ease the straight lines of his face. His hint of a smile could not dim the unrelenting pain in his eyes.

"I'm sorry," she whispered, stepping past a marble-topped table.

"I know." He seated her on a chair beside where he stood. Putting his hand on it, he said more loudly, "Chandelle, I should have guessed you would not miss the opportunity to see this homecoming. Not quite the happy occasion you envisioned, is it?"

"It should have been."

Her terse answer surprised him, for something flickered in his eyes. "Don't judge all families by yours in Asheville."

"I won't make that mistake." She lowered her voice. "Again."

"Can we deal with the unsavory business at hand?" asked his father impatiently.

Matt's fingers dug into the upholstery. Chandelle was surprised he and his father were not circling each other like boxers seeking any weakness.

"I trust," Matt said, "you know that Chandelle was only trying to make things better."

"That has been clear from the beginning," his father replied.

"You should not have kept her against her will."

"Beers is being melodramatic again, I see." He pushed himself away from the hearth. "I wished Miss McBride to remain here so that she would see your idiocy for herself."

Chandelle surged to her feet. "I shall not testify against Matt. He—"

"If you will allow me to finish, Miss McBride." Mr. Matheson bowed his head toward her before looking at his son again. "I want her to realize, Dorian, that you are going to have our help whether you wish it or not."

She gasped. Everything Mr. Matheson had said, everything he had done had suggested he would turn his son over to the police without delay. She watched as he motioned for the two men behind Matt to take their leave. She wished someone would explain this odd family to her. She could not ask now. She was an outsider here. If she said or did the wrong thing—or anything!—the wounds that had festered within this family could be inflamed again, never to heal.

"It's not a matter of wishing," Matt replied evenly, again relaxing. Did Mr. Matheson realize that Matt was standing like this to conceal his true feelings? "It's a matter of needing. I understand a warrant for my arrest is forthcoming at any moment."

A reluctant smile swept across Mr. Matheson's face. "You always had good instincts for knowing when trouble was en route, Dorian."

"I prefer the name Matt."

"But," his mother whispered, "Dorian is such a proud name in this family. The first Dorian Matheson was—"

"Mrs. Matheson," her husband said, "I believe luncheon would be appropriate now."

She came to her feet, nodding. "Of course, Mr. Matheson." Crossing the room, she paused only a moment to touch Matt's sleeve.

Chandelle bit her lip as she tried to imagine such tepid displays of affection in Grandma's house. There, they had shared enthusiastic hugs and pet names and shouts of heated anger as well as trills of laughter.

"You are excused as well," continued Mr. Matheson.

She was about to protest when she realized he was speaking to his two younger children. Carl, who resembled his fine-boned mother, strode out without a comment.

With a whisper of taffeta, dark-haired Adrienne rose and followed her brother and mother out of the room. She stopped in the doorway. "I am glad you are home... Matt."

Chandelle looked at him. His face was still taut, but his hand slipped to her shoulder. Wanting to put hers over it, she hesitated. Such a show of emotion might make everything worse.

What was she thinking? Nothing could be worse. Her father, a man she barely had had a chance to know, was dead. Her beloved grandmother had lied to her and could even now have passed on without her coming home quilt. And Death might not be finished haunting her, because if it was believed that he had killed his family's rival, Matt could be the next one dying.

Matt... the man she loved. As her fingers rose to slide up along his wrist beneath his stained cuff, she rested her cheek against his hand. She could not deny the truth any longer. He had once possessed everything she could ever have imagined wanting, but he had tossed it aside to live his life as he chose. In doing so, he had become the man who had won her heart despite her efforts to keep him away.

His dark gaze softened as he turned his hand so it cupped

her cheek. Caressing her face for a moment, he drew it away and wove his fingers together behind his frock coat.

"Have you sent for the police, Father?"

Mr. Matheson shook his head. "I had considered doing that, if you were foolish enough to come here and cause trouble."

"So that is why you had those two gargantuans waiting for me?"

"I had not been sure what you'd do after all I've heard."

"But you sent them away."

"You have told me that you played no part in Esau Friedlander's death, and I believe you."

"Why? You seldom accepted my word before."

"Then you were a foolish boy." Mr. Matheson sighed as he glanced at Chandelle. "Now it appears you have become a man of some value, if you can convince Miss McBride to look past your obvious faults to fight so vigorously to defend you."

"Miss *Friedlander*, Father." He frowned at her. "Didn't you tell my father about your relationship to the Friedlanders?"

"She told me," Mr. Matheson said before Chandelle could answer, "while we were waiting for you."

"And," Chandelle said, coming to her feet, "I have been a McBride all my life until the past few days. I thought it might be simpler right now if I remained one."

"She has also filled me in on some things that I have been curious about." He walked over to Matt and grasped his arm. "It seems you have made a very good life for yourself, son. You created your own business which does not lack for patrons. I was right when I said that you had a head for such things." He paused. "I'm proud of you, son."

Matt stared at him for a long moment before saying, "Thank you, Father."

"I suspect you and Miss McBride have several things to discuss. I will have the drapes drawn in the dining room while we enjoy our luncheon. Any passersby will believe they are being cleaned at this hour." He bowed his head toward Chandelle. "Miss McBride."

"Mr. Matheson," she replied. She watched as he left the parlor, then she did what she had wanted to for so long. She flung her arms around Matt, drinking in the rich smells ingrained into his coat. Pressing her face to his shoulder, she whispered, "I'm so glad you are here."

"Me, too." He tried to tip her face toward his, but she shook her head, wanting to hold on to him until she could truly believe that she was in his arms. "Does this obstinacy mean you want me to kiss you only like this?" His lips touched her cheek gently. This time when he tilted her face, she raised it to look up into his eyes. "Or like this?"

When he kissed her other cheek, she closed her eyes. "Yes," she whispered breathlessly.

"You mean you like that better than this?" His mouth found hers easily.

Stronger than the first time he had kissed her, the longing took control of her. She became a part of it, knowing she could fight it no longer. She wanted his heated lips over hers as he stroked her, reacquainting her body with the firmness of his.

With a sigh, he released her. He looked around, and she knew he wished, as she did, that they were at Mrs. Coates's boardinghouse where they could forget that the police were searching for him.

"You know," he said, going to the doorway and closing the double oak doors, "that Friedlander is going to use you coming here to help convict you as an accomplice in Esau Friedlander's death."

"He told me that already." She hesitated, then said, "And he told me that he married the woman you love."

"I'm sure he also added that I made an idiot of myself at their betrothal party, vowing to see him pay for that."

She nodded, unable to speak. He must love that woman still, because he had not corrected her "woman you *love*."

"I did not play a part in your father's death," he said, grasping her hands. "You believe me, don't you, Chandelle?"

"Yes." She could say that much.

He grinned, and she wondered if she had become so adept at hiding her feelings from him that he had no idea how her heart was breaking. "I thought you must when you wasted no time coming to Jesse's shop to give him the message for me."

"I wasn't sure how long it would take him to deliver it."

"Jesse *will* do anything for money. He would have sold you his mother for a hundred and ten dollars."

"I didn't give him—" Fire scurried up her face when he chuckled. "I thought I gave him twenty."

"So he told me. We're going to have to work on that ciphering problem of yours after we do what we have to do."

"What's that?"

He looked at her in bafflement. "Why, get your grandmother's quilt, of course."

"But it's at the Friedlanders' house."

"So that's where we'll have to go."

"Jakob will—"

He gave her a secretive grin. "Be busy with his father's funeral. I have a few very enterprising friends who can make sure he's not there when we arrive. Some of my friends are going to surprise you. We'll find the quilt and get it to your grandmother right away." He lifted her hands to his lips, kissing one, then the other. "Then everything will be perfect."

She forced a smile. "Then everything will be perfect." *Except that you'll be gone along with my heart.*

19

CHANDELLE DISCOVERED MATT HAD not been jesting when he said his friends might surprise her. She was amazed when he asked the hired carriage to stop in front of the Friedlanders' house. She was shocked when he led the way up the steps to the door. By the time he knocked and the door opened as Dowdle ushered them in, she was utterly dumbstruck.

"Mr. Jakob—" The butler flashed an uneasy glance at Chandelle. "Mr. Friedlander is attending to matters at the store."

"For how long?" asked Matt.

"I heard him tell Anthony, the coachman, to return for him at four."

"Excellent." Taking Chandelle's hand, he said, "I assume we can reach the attics from these stairs."

"I will show you the way, Mr. Matheson."

"I go by Winchester now."

Dowdle wore a horrified expression as he reached for a lit lantern waiting on a table. "I couldn't call you that."

"Then call me Matt."

"But, sir—"

Matt took his arm and steered him toward the stairs.

"Just call me sir if that suits you, but let's hurry. I don't want someone seeing us and running to tell Friedlander we're here."

As Chandelle hurried up several flights of stairs with them, she noticed no one else seemed to be in the house. Dowdle must have given the staff tasks that would keep them far from these staircases. With all the uproar in the house in the wake of Esau's death, it would not be difficult.

Her foot caught on a riser. Matt's hand on her arm kept her from falling.

He paused, a concerned expression on his face. "Do you need us to slow down?"

"No." She took a steadying breath. "I need for my thoughts about Esau Friedlander to slow down."

He brushed her hair under her bonnet. "I know you haven't had a chance to mourn your father, Chandelle."

"He did welcome me here." She took a slow breath. "I need to get Grandma's quilt. Then I'll have time to..." She could not think about her grief at losing the father she had barely found. Later. Later, when she had time to mourn.

Matt put his arm around her shoulders as they followed Dowdle. His gentle squeeze nearly undid her resolve to hold back her tears until she had done as she had promised Grandma.

The glorious wall coverings of the lower floors vanished along with the elegant furniture. These must be the servants' quarters.

Dowdle scurried along the passage to a narrow door. He shoved a ring with two keys and the lantern into Chandelle's hands. "This is the way to the attic that Mr. Friedlander—the late Mr. Friedlander—allowed no one but himself to enter."

"Why?"

"I don't know. If—" He rushed toward the stairs. In the distance, she heard the frantic ringing of a bell. She hoped it was a caller, not Jakob returning home early. If he discovered Matt here, he would waste no time alerting the police.

Unlocking the door with the larger key, she raised the lantern high. There was no need, she discovered as she entered the attic. A single dormer, which must be invisible from the street, threw sunlight into the room. Her fear that the attic would be filled with boxes vanished when she saw a single wooden trunk set in the shadows.

Matt took the lantern as they walked across the empty floor. Sounds from the street reached up through the window, oddly distorted by the distance. Everything seemed as out of kilter as if the world had stopped spinning for a second.

"Are you going to be all right?" Matt asked when they paused in front of the trunk. He blew out the lantern and set it on the floor.

"Yes."

"Do you want me to open it?"

She shook her head. "I've come this far on my quest. I shan't stop just before its end." Putting her hands on either side of his face, she drew his mouth down to hers. She had not thought her heart could beat faster, but it did as she savored their slow, deep kiss.

"What was that for?" he asked, grinning. "Not that I'm complaining."

"For luck." *And because I want to kiss you as often as I can while you are still in my life.*

"Glad to oblige any time you want a little bit of good fortune."

"I need a lot now."

Although it was the hardest thing she had ever done, she turned from his outstretched arms and knelt by the trunk. She could not let his kisses woo her into forgetting how short the time they had left might be. It must already be nearing three o'clock. They would have to search the other attics if the quilt was not here.

She lifted the key ring and slipped the other key into the lock. It clicked so loudly, she flinched. Matt's hand on her shoulder calmed her.

The top rose with a creak. She peered in to see a military

uniform. The thick wool coat was covered with medals, and the epaulets bore the rank of major. Although she wondered when her father had been promoted because Grandma had spoken of him only as "Captain Friedlander," she did not pause to look at the uniform. She pushed it aside as she reached deeper into the trunk. Her fingers found boots and books and a packet of letters. Her hopes that they might offer some clue to her muddied past were dashed when a quick scan showed that all were postmarked "Philadelphia."

Sitting on her heels, she sighed. "Grandma's quilt isn't in here."

"Don't give up so easily." He knelt beside her. "Some of these old trunks have more than one compartment." He ran his hands along the top and chuckled as he undid a pair of hooks. It popped open.

She caught a bundle of cloth as it fell out. With a soft cry, she unfolded it to see the very patches her grandmother had described over and over. The light blue piece from Grandma's first wedding dress, the dark wool from her second husband's best coat, the wisps of fabric that had been Chandelle's mother's christening gown. Holding it to her face, she whispered, "I can't believe it. We found it."

"And something else." Matt held up another patchwork quilt. "Could this be your mother's?"

Her fingers quivered as she reached out to touch it. Never had she been so close to anything that was so completely her mother's. Seeing where the quilted top stopped and the old quilt backing went on uncovered, she whispered, "Yes, this must be my mother's." Raising tear-filled eyes, she struggled to say, "I never dreamed I could return this to her, too."

"Maybe you should keep it to give to your daughter, a gift from her grandmother as your coming home quilt is a gift from yours."

She nodded, unable to speak past her joy. Taking her mother's quilt from Matt, she spread it out over her grandmother's. Grandma would be able to tell her what each piece of her mother's quilt commemorated. She could, if she was still alive. They must get these quilts home without further delay.

Rolling them up, she paused as she saw the undeniable blue of a Union uniform shirt at the end of her mother's quilting. It had been sewed in, but not quilted.

"She must not have had time to finish quilting it before she gave it to your father," Matt murmured.

"She must have loved him very much." Maybe Esau Friedlander had not always been so hard-hearted and driven. Maybe he had shown her mother the kindness that Chandelle had seen hints of.

"Enough to give him her beloved quilt." His lips quirked. "And your grandmother's. I wonder how your grandmother reacted to that."

"I'm glad I wasn't there."

"But you were." He put his hand over her stomach. "You were here within your mother, a more cherished legacy than any quilt could be, for you were a promise of a continuation of the tradition of strong-willed, beautiful McBride women."

She rested her head on his chest. Never had the circle of her past and her future seemed so complete. "This must have been the shirt of my father's uniform. My mother included the pocket and the buttons." Raising her eyes, she curved her hand along Matt's cheek. "Do you realize what this means?"

He nodded. "That she considered him an important part of her life?"

"Yes. Odd that she didn't quilt it like the rest of the quilt."

"Maybe she didn't have time."

"She had her whole pregnancy."

He grinned. "She might have been making clothes for you."

"She still would have found time to finish this piece. Grandma drilled that into me. Finish each piece as it's added, because another might come along that's as important."

"Or . . ." He shuddered and stood.

"Or what?"

"Or it might not be ready when it's needed." When she grimaced, he added, "It's *your* tradition." He held out his hand. "You have what you need, so let's go before Friedlander gets back."

"All right." She continued rolling up the quilts. Something crackled. "What was that?"

"What was what?"

"Listen." Chandelle ran her hand along the quilts. The sound came again. Something was in the pocket of the uniform shirt. She opened it and pulled out a small piece of paper. Unfolding it, she read the few words. "They were married!" she gasped as she realized she held a marriage certificate for Lorraine McBride and Esau Friedlander. "Why didn't my father tell me that?"

"He must have assumed that you knew."

She shook her head. "I told him Grandma told me how my father had died in the war."

"He might have dismissed that as your grandmother's attempt to keep you from ever wishing to search for your father and his family." As his thumb coursed along her jaw, he whispered, "Remember, he knew your grandmother well. Although I have not met her, I suspect she did not take a Yankee captain invading her home and winning her daughter's heart lightly."

"Maybe she will forgive both of them when she has her quilt." Holding out her hand to him as he stood, she said, "Let's get our tickets now, so we can be on the first train heading south tomorrow."

"I don't think that will be possible."

Chandelle almost asked why, then realized it had not been Matt speaking. She rose slowly and continued to hold on to his hand as she stared at Jakob Friedlander. He held a pistol aimed at them.

"You have made it so very simple now." Jakob laughed. "There was some concern among the policemen I spoke with that you had no real reason to slay my father, Matheson, but this robbery might give credence to that."

Chandelle cried, "You know Matt did not kill our father. You know it was an accident."

"You're wrong," Matt said quietly. "It wasn't an accident."

She stared at him. "Not an accident? Matt, you didn't kill my father."

"No, I didn't. Your dear half brother did."

"You're lying," Friedlander snarled.

"Am I? While you were playing the poor, grieving son, I spent some time asking some questions of people who have no reason to lie for you. That included the teamsters who were on the street yesterday." He smiled, and Chandelle remembered the dirt and odors coming off his coat. Not only of tobacco, but of horses and barns. "I learned it was supposed to look like an accident until I happened to be there at an opportune time, and your dear half brother thought he could get rid of his father and me at the same time. Instead of winning his election on the vote of his late father's sympathetic cronies, he could win it as the scourge of crime."

"It was *an accident* that has proven very convenient for me." He smiled at Matt and walked closer to them. "I have heard that you visited your parents today." He looked down his nose at Chandelle. "And that you were there as well. You should know, Chandelle, that I have many friends in this city."

"They won't be your friends when they learn that you murdered our father." Gripping Matt's arm, she gasped, "Do something."

"What do you suggest?" he asked in that calm tone he used when facing disaster. "Beers took my gun at my parents' house."

Snickering, Friedlander said, "I also learned while tending to *my* father's business that you and your family have come to a reconciliation, Matheson. That suggests that your father will be hiring some very expensive lawyers to keep you from hanging. All that money he had intended to put into expanding the new store on Chestnut Street will be tied up with your defense."

"And," Matt replied evenly, "when the land where Father plans to build is put up for sale to cover some of those legal costs, Jakob Friedlander will be there, eager to buy at a bargain price."

"It is a very nice location."

Matt laughed. "I would say so. Right across from your main store. You could control that end of Chestnut Street."

"And put Matheson and Sons out of business."

"You could if you weren't going to pay for your own father's murder. I guess you'll have to leave overseeing the family business to your sister."

"My sister?" he snarled. "She's the whelp of a whore! My mother was barely buried when her mother seduced Father when he was still mourning for the only woman he had ever loved."

Chandelle bristled, but Matt whispered, "Don't. Whatever you say will infuriate him more. Don't let him see that paper you found. Let me—"

"What are you conspiring about now, Matheson?" Friedlander shifted nervously from one foot to the other, his fingers uneasy on the gun. "Don't expect any help from my sister." His lips twisted. "She won't be much help to you once she's dead."

Matt's smile vanished. "You don't need to kill her." He took one of the quilts from Chandelle. "All she's ever wanted is this stupid quilt to bury her grandmother in. Let her go and do that."

"You know that is impossible." He laughed again. "So I beat you again, Matheson. I took one woman you loved from you." He raised the gun toward Chandelle. "Now I'll take the other one. Only this time you won't be able to run away with your tail between your legs."

"I didn't run away before. I left because I wanted to prove to myself that I could make a life for myself, not be a parasite like you, Friedlander."

"But you hated that I married Linda Cutler."

"Yes, because I knew, despite her infatuation with you, that you would make her miserable." He shoved Chandelle back, edging between her and Friedlander's gun. "I did accept the job that Chandelle offered because I thought I could repay you for Linda's suffering, but, by the time I got to Philadelphia, I had discovered how little it all mattered.'' He chuckled, pushing Chandelle back another step. ''How little *you* mattered, Friedlander. I have another life now, one that I enjoy. You're still a lickspittle.''

''But I won her heart from you!''

''It may gall you, Friedlander, but she and I had realized that we had no future before you swept her off her feet. So you see, you never took her from me.''

He shifted so the gun was aimed again at Chandelle. ''Then I shall have to enjoy taking this one from you even more. It will be doubly sweet when you are blamed for her murder as well as my father's.''

''Let her go. Send her to North Carolina. She'll stay there if she promises.'' He glanced at her, and she was shocked to see his eye close in a lazy wink. He knew that she had not once been able to keep her promise to stay and wait. ''She's incidental. Let her go. It's me you're after.''

Friedlander paused to consider it.

Chandelle gripped Matt's sleeve. Why had he chosen *now* to be a hero? So many times she could have used his help, and he had let her handle the problem herself. She could not let him sacrifice himself for her. With a cry, she jumped forward.

''No!'' Matt grabbed her arm. He whirled her back, stepping between her and the gun.

''Why did you stop me?'' she cried.

''I'm not going to let you get yourself killed.''

''You didn't seem to worry about that when we were almost robbed on the train.''

''I helped you.''

She stared at him, forgetting even her brother and his gun. ''You helped me?''

''I clubbed the thief on the back of the head. That's why he fell when you did your razzle-dazzle-one-two-three.'' One side of his mouth tipped reluctantly. ''I guess I couldn't resist the chance to play your hero even then, Chandelle.''

Repeating his words without sound, she wanted to be in his arms, protected as she had been since he came into her life. She yelped when Friedlander shoved between them. Matt raised his fist, but froze when the gun pointed at her again.

"Friedlander, let her go," Matt said quietly. "Send her to Asheville. She'll keep quiet if she can return in time to see her grandmother one more time."

"Matt—"

"Be silent! Friedlander, you know it's true. No one will heed her when it's discovered that she has every reason to defame your family for destroying hers."

No, Matt could not do this! Not even her grandmother's coming home quilt was worth this. She watched as Friedlander turned toward Matt.

Thad's voice burst from her memory. *The razzle-dazzle-1-2-3 is easy. Grab him quick. Don't give him a chance to think. Pull and duck. He'll go flying.*

Yanking Grandma's quilt from Matt's arm, she flung it at Friedlander. He cursed as it struck his arm. He shook it off and aimed the gun at Matt. She seized Jakob's wrist.

He knocked her against the wall and laughed when she slid to the floor, her head aching with the blow. "You are truly stupid, little sister."

The soft sound of the hammer being drawn sliced through the agony in her skull. She leaped to her feet and grasped his arm. This time, she did not hesitate. She set her feet and tugged. When she leaned forward, she fell to the floor. The violent crash of gunfire echoed through the attic.

Hearing a cry of pain, she struggled to raise her head. "No!" she shrieked. "Matt!"

A hand appeared in front of her face. Matt's hand. She caught it and let him draw her up to her knees. Squatting beside her, he held the pistol. If Matt had the gun—She saw her brother writhing on the floor, clutching his leg.

"For once, under pressure, you calculated correctly," Matt said with a chuckle. "Razzle-dazzle-one-two-three, not the razzle-dazzle-one-three-six or some other combination."

Hearing gasps behind her, she looked to see Dowdle and other servants crowding through the door. She came to her feet and picked up the two quilts. No one spoke as she crossed the attic.

"Dowdle, please send someone for the police."

"Yes, Miss Mc—"

"Miss Friedlander," she corrected softly.

He smiled as he turned to pass her orders to one of the young boys by the door.

"Will you have someone tend to Mr. Friedlander?" Matt asked as he handed the butler the pistol. When Chandelle gasped, he smiled at her. "I think it would be best if your half brother awaits the police here."

Friedlander roared a curse and tried to stand. He collapsed with another string of oaths.

Dowdle squared his shoulders. "I would be glad to, sir."

"Miss McBride—" Matt smiled at Chandelle. "Miss Friedlander and I will speak to the police downstairs."

"Of course, sir."

Matt guided Chandelle through the crowd of curious servants, who stepped aside, wide-eyed. As they started down the stairs, she was glad for his arm around her waist.

"Don't worry about Dowdle double-crossing us," he said as he opened the door to her father's office. "Once I spoke with him about my suspicions, he was determined to halt your brother from killing again. Dowdle is a good man, and his loyalty belonged completely to your father." He went to the window as wheels rattled toward the house. Looking out, he said, "Now Dowdle and all of this will be yours."

"I don't care about that. I must take this quilt to Grandma."

The front door opened, and people rushed up the stairs.

Matt ignored them. Putting his hands over the quilts she held, he said, "You really did it, Chandelle."

"With your help."

"We make a good team." His smile dissolved into a serious expression. "When we started on this, I had no idea that you were planning on helping me come home, too. Not that I'm wholly home yet, because there are more bridges to cross, but, for the first time in many years, I believe I can come home. I think I'm beginning to understand what these quilts mean to you. Really understand."

"I'm glad."

"We'll leave tomorrow on the train south." He picked up one end of her mother's coming home quilt and smiled. "You might as well pack all three of your quilts in your trunk."

"All three?"

"Didn't you say that a McBride woman pauses in sewing her coming home quilt while she is making her wedding dress?"

"Yes..." Her eyes widened. "You want to marry me?"

"I thought that's what people in love do." He drew her into his arms. "Say you love me, Chandelle, as much as I love you."

"I tried to tell you that before." She swept her fingers up through his hair. "At the boardinghouse."

"I know." His lips brushed her forehead before he gave her a wicked grin. "I would say that hearing you say that scared the pants off me if I'd had any pants on at the time."

"Scared?" she whispered, too amazed to smile.

All humor left his face as his hands glided along her arms and around her waist. "That you would have a change of heart, too, and fall out of love with me."

"Never."

"Then tell me, Chandelle." His voice became a husky whisper. "Tell me that you love me as much as I love you."

"I love you." Leaning her head on his chest, she smiled. "I think I have loved you from the very beginning."

"That was pretty stupid of you."

Her head jerked up. "Why?"

"I was doing everything I could to be as unlikable as possible."

"And doing it well."

He grimaced. "You didn't have to agree so quickly."

"I always agree when it's the right thing to do."

"Then will you agree to marry me?"

She touched the blue patch on her mother's quilt, but he tipped her face toward him.

She saw his honest entreaty as he whispered, "Say you will marry me, Chandelle, and I will never leave you as your grandmother and your mother were left." Even his mustache could not shadow his smile. "I won't need to go hunting for adventure or a great battle to fight. I will have enough battles to fight with you." He took the quilts and tossed them onto a chair. Dropping to one knee, he asked, "Will you marry me, Chandelle, and make my life the best adventure I can envision?"

A knock at the door was followed by Dowdle peering in. His eyes widened to see Matt on his knee before her, but he said in a prim voice, "I'm sorry to intrude, Miss Friedlander, but the police wish to speak with you and Mr.—with both of you immediately. They need you to answer some questions."

"We'll be right there," Matt answered. "Right after you answer my question, Chandelle. Will you marry me?"

She knelt beside him and whispered, "Yes," as she welcomed his lips.

Epilogue

MATT TOOK A SNIFF and set the cup on the table. He had prided himself on being able to swallow almost anything, but the liquor up here on this mountain could curdle a man's gut. Tonight, he was taking no chances on being ill.

He looked across the yard to the front porch of the small house. As if there were no people between them, he caught Chandelle's gaze and held it. He walked toward her across the well-worn yard.

Earlier today, he had admired how exquisite she looked in her simple white wedding gown as she walked down the church aisle toward him. Her gown had no frills or ruffles, just a layer of lace and another of satin that followed her enticing curves. She had gently turned down his mother's offer to bring a dress from the Paris collection offered at Matheson and Sons. So gently that Matt suspected his mother now believed it had been her idea for Chandelle to wear a retailored version of her grandmother's wedding gown.

Tonight, he would be able to savor Chandelle out of that charming gown. Tonight the kiss they had shared at the altar would only be a prelude for the pleasures yet to come.

But, for now, he stared into her eyes. Those fiery, quicksilver eyes that had haunted him since she walked into his office and offered him a job that had brought rewards he never would have imagined were waiting for him.

Who would have guessed this job would turn out like this? His head was still stuffed with the figures the attorneys for Matheson & Sons and Friedlander's stores had tried to fill it with yesterday. Maybe it would have been better if his father had disowned him, because the complications of falling in love with Chandelle seemed simple in comparison to the arrangements that must be made to make sure the two rival department stores lived happily ever after, too.

Instead of disowning him, his father, who tried to be gruff but treasured his family as much as Chandelle treasured hers, had set aside a part of his business as his son's, if Matt ever decided he wanted it. Matt still was not sure about that. Later, after their honeymoon, Chandelle and he would decide what they wanted to do in the years ahead in addition to loving one another with all their hearts.

He had taken enough money, however, to pay off the debts on this farm perched on the mountainside. The banker in Asheville had been thrilled to receive the draft drawn on the accounts of Matheson and Sons of Philadelphia. As soon as the wedding ceremony was complete, the banker had waylaid Matt's father. He guessed they were off talking business somewhere while his mother tried to look at ease among these openhearted, vivacious people who were so unlike the closed society that had nearly smothered him in Philadelphia. The last time he had seen his sister and brother, they had been tagging along with Thad and several dozen of Chandelle's cousins in some sort of game.

Chandelle . . .

He smiled as he looked from her to her grandmother, who was sitting in a rocking chair, her coming home quilt draped across her lap. Chandelle could now laugh that the last telegram she had received in Philadelphia had been sent from her grandmother, who had recovered enough to write the impatient, terse message.

"Quilting even today, Mrs. McBride?" he asked.

When she glanced up at her granddaughter beside her, Matt's smile broadened. He had feared that the labyrinth of lies that Elitta McBride had created to protect her infant granddaughter in the midst of the war and the years that followed would drive Chandelle away from her beloved grandmother. His consternation had been for naught. Chandelle had listened to her grandmother's explanation of her dread that the baby would be reviled or taken from her if the truth was known, and then she had forgiven her grandmother as they wept together. Their love stitched them together as completely as the pieces of fabric in their coming home quilts, and that love would never come undone.

"I have a lot of pieces to add in," Mrs. McBride said. "Been saving them all these years, so I have to make up for lost time." She chuckled, and in her eyes was the twinkle she had bequeathed to Chandelle. "Take my granddaughter over to where Pike is tuning up his fiddle. She needs to dance."

"I believe that is an order, Chandelle." He held out his hand.

"I believe it is," she replied in that soft voice that turned his blood to fire.

She placed her hand on his. He touched the glittering ring that he had put on her finger and smiled at her as he led her to where her large family was gathering to dance. Shouts welcomed them.

With another laugh, Matt spun her into his arms. The guests cheered as the dancing began. All other sounds vanished when he bent to whisper in her ear, "From the moment I saw you, I knew you were trouble."

"Me?"

"Yes, you."

She smiled as the music surrounded them. "Cousin Pike doesn't play waltzes often. He usually prefers to call square dances."

"Remind me to thank him for taking the trouble. It seems as if your family is good at trouble."

Grimacing at his weak jest, she said, "You deserve any

trouble he or I have given you. After all, you said you'd do anything for money."

"I wasn't including falling in love. That I was glad to do for free."

She took his hand and led him away from the others. As they stood under a tree, its shadow hiding them from the others, her eyes glowed with the passion he yearned to sample again and again. Slipping his other arm around her waist, he pinned her against the tree so her soft body was molded against his.

Her voice was as light as the music as she whispered, "I wasn't planning to fall in love either when I went looking for my grandmother's coming home quilt." Her lips grazed his with a promise of what awaited them through the rest of their lives together. She raised his hand to press it between her breasts. "But now we both know the truth."

"What is that?" he asked as he drew her closer.

In the moment before his lips found hers, she answered, "That my heart was coming home to yours."

Author's Note

I HOPE YOU ENJOYED reading *The Coming Home Quilt* as much as I enjoyed writing it. My next quilting romance will be available in January 2000 and is titled *Woven Dreams*. Its quilt may offer the clue to find a murderer even as it helps two people who live to help others learn to trust their hearts.

Readers are welcome to contact me at:
Joanna Hampton
VFRW
PO Box 350
Wayne, PA 19087-0350
or by email at: jaferg@erols.com

My website is:
http://www.romcom.com/ferguson

A Quilting Romance

Patterns of Love
by Christine Holden

When Lord Grayling Dunston appears on Baines Marshall's doorstep asking for her only quilt, she sends him on his way. But Baines discovers that Mary's Fortune is no ordinary quilt—its pattern reveals the map to a treasure Gray desperately needs to pay off his debts. When the quilt suddenly disappears from her home the two embark on a journey that deepens their attraction and changes their lives...

❑ 0-515-12481-8/$5.99

Prices slightly higher in Canada

Payable in U.S. funds only. No cash/COD accepted Postage & handling: U S /CAN $2.75 for one book, $1 00 for each additional, not to exceed $6 75; Int'l $5 00 for one book, $1 00 each additional We accept Visa, Amex, MC ($10 00 min.), checks ($15.00 fee for returned checks) and money orders. Call 800-788-6262 or 201-933-9292, fax 201-896-8569; refer to ad # 823 (5/99)

| Penguin Putnam Inc.
P.O. Box 12289, Dept. B
Newark, NJ 07101-5289
Please allow 4-6 weeks for delivery
Foreign and Canadian delivery 6-8 weeks | Bill my: ❑ Visa ❑ MasterCard ❑ Amex _____(expires)
Card# _____
Signature _____ |

Bill to:
Name _____
Address _____ City _____
State/ZIP _____ Daytime Phone # _____

Ship to:
Name _____ Book Total $ _____
Address _____ Applicable Sales Tax $ _____
City _____ Postage & Handling $ _____
State/ZIP _____ Total Amount Due $ _____

This offer subject to change without notice.